EDEN

Biblical Fiction of the World's First Family

BRENNAN MCPHERSON

EDEN

Biblical Fiction of the World's First Family

Copyright © 2020 by Brennan S. McPherson

ISBN: 978-1-7324436-6-2 (softcover)

Published by McPherson Publishing

Sparta, WI, USA

Cover design by Josh Meyer Photography and Design

Edited by Natalie Hanemann, nataliehanemann.com

Author's Note

This novel is a work of fiction based solely on the Genesis account of Adam and Eve's lives from Genesis 1–4. In writing these pages, I did not consult extra-biblical sources, such as the Book of Enoch, because they are widely mistrusted by every major Christian denomination as poor sources of historical truth.

The Bible, however, is true and trustworthy. I believe it is all we can rely on for an accurate account of these ancient peoples' stories. Ironically, rather than restrict the imagination, sole reliance on the biblical text frees us to imagine what might have been—so long as we do not confuse our imagination with history.

Everything that is stated explicitly in Scripture happens in this book. However, because of how sparse the original narrative is, I was forced to make many imaginative inferences from the text itself.

We all have strong assumptions about the beginning of the world, and I have found that no two visions of Eden seem to be exactly the same. This is why I believe you will enjoy reading this book more if you attempt to approach it with an open mind.

If you encounter something that runs contrary to what you thought happened in the biblical account, remember that at the end of this book is a 13-page study that walks through the original account and explains the creative decisions made in writing this fictional adaptation. If you are sensitive to details that run contrary to your expectations, reading that study before reading the book will improve your enjoyment of the novel.

Because the worldwide flood destroyed all archaeological evidence of what these peoples' technologies, homes, food habits, rituals, and lifestyles were like, we are left with a blank canvas and the text of Genesis. But the prevailing theme of Genesis is man's pervasive fallenness contrasted with God's incredible mercy. So, each book in this series is less about the historical minutia, and more about exploring that core theme in the lives of these important figures in Genesis.

If you are looking for a light read, you may want to look elsewhere. The stories in Genesis are shocking and intense. They reveal, in great detail, good and evil, mercy and violence, faithfulness and idolatry, and holiness and sin. Therefore, each book in this series is intense and contains themes and events some readers might find disturbing.

In addition to differing visions of Genesis, there are also several common misconceptions about Genesis. For instance, some suggest that it had never rained on Earth before the Flood. This idea is erroneous, ecologically impossible, and found nowhere in Scripture. It originated from a misinterpretation of one short Bible verse that mentions a mist rising and watering the ground in Eden. But this verse was referencing what seems to be day 2 or 3 of creation, because it also mentions that no plants had yet sprung up. I cover this in more detail in the textual analysis of Genesis 1-4 at the end of the book. However, if you still think this means it never rained before the Flood, consider that a rain cloud *is* a mist that rises and waters the ground.

In addition, many claim that the world was perfect before Adam and Eve sinned, but this is never stated in the Bible. After each day of creation, God said that what he created was "good." The serpent, a being created by God, blatantly lied *before* Adam and Eve sinned. The forbidden tree itself is not the Tree of Good and Evil, but the Tree of the *Knowledge* of Good and Evil. The implications of these details are massive. Drawing conclusions from a false base can only lead to subsequent false conclusions.

Some of you reading this will remain unconvinced. To those, I ask that you give me the benefit of the doubt that I crafted this story with great care and attention to the text of the Bible, and that different interpretations of Genesis—so long as they do not contradict Scripture—are valid potentials. If you believe I have contradicted Scripture, message me through my website so that I can consider whether an adjustment to the book is in order.

That being said, I want to state again that you should read the study at the end of this book very carefully before messaging me about perceived Scriptural errors.

Eden contains many imaginative additions to help you feel the weight of these ancient peoples' lives. My intent in writing this book was not to replace Scripture, or to add to it, but to entertain you, reinvigorate your enjoyment of the book of Genesis, and help you see the truths Genesis communicates from a fresh perspective. I pray the book accomplishes those goals.

One last note, I do not capitalize deity pronouns ("he" in reference to God) because most Scripture translations don't (such as the KJV, NIV, ESV, and NLT).

...

If you are interested in getting a free devotional sent to your inbox every Saturday morning, sign up for my email list and download two free e-books at my website here:
https://brennanmcpherson.com/newsletter/

PART I

The Beginning

Chapter 1

The moon hid behind a curtain of grey clouds. Adam stood in the shadows behind his home staring at the bonfire outside their small village until his eyes burned. But he wasn't so much staring at the fire as he was the figure standing beside it and waiting.

For weeks, Enoch—the newly appointed prophet chosen by God—had hounded Adam to come and share the stories he'd withheld from his children. To lay bare the secrets of his soul, so that the young man could record a history of the world for future generations.

Adam had been the one to invent their system of writing. For posterity sake, he was drawn to the idea of such a massive undertaking. And he couldn't deny that he was attracted to the idea of confessing his sins to someone chosen by God to leave the hills they called home and never return.

But that wasn't why Adam was standing outside his home shivering.

What lit a spark in him to sit beside that fire was the knowledge that Enoch was the only man in the last six centuries to hear the voice of Adam's father, the Almighty Creator God.

Adam had ruined everything. And since Eve's passing last

year, he had lived alone feeling the weight of a life filled with regrets.

There beside the fire stood the only person who could talk to Father. And once Enoch left, Adam may never get the chance to speak with the Almighty again.

Yet if Enoch were to fulfill Adam's request, Adam would first need to fulfill Enoch's.

Enoch tossed more logs onto the bonfire, sending sparks skittering upward. Adam's eyes followed those swirling shards of light until one by one they blinked away, leaving only the stars glowing like so many silver eyes behind them.

Adam suppressed his fear, pulled his outer tunic closer, and walked into the ring of light.

At the sound of his footsteps, Enoch turned and met his gaze.

Adam nodded and sat on a flat stone close enough to feel the heat. Enoch didn't look surprised to see him. As Enoch sat beside Adam on a fallen log, it seemed he had even expected him.

"Do you feel prepared to leave?" Adam said.

Enoch tipped his head. "More or less."

Adam opened his palms to the heat. Enoch looked at Adam's hands, and his eyes widened. Adam looked at his fingers and realized that in the orange firelight, his blisters looked painful indeed. "The older I get, the worse they look at harvest."

"Do they feel the same?"

Adam shrugged and smirked. "More or less."

Enoch stared into the flames.

Adam yawned and stretched, then turned his back to the flames to even out the heat.

"You want something from me." Enoch picked up a stick and broke it into smaller pieces.

"And you want something from me."

"Sounds fitting."

"So, what shall we do?" Adam said.

Several breaths passed between them. An owl hooted in the distance. Cold and clear.

"If you tell me everything, and leave out nothing, I will grant you any reasonable request you can think of." Enoch continued staring at the flames.

"Speak to the Almighty on my behalf."

"Done," he said. "So long as you don't try to hide anything. I need everything. Every mistake, every joy, every detail that matters. I have gathered all that I could from the others. I never realized until doing so just how much you've withheld from us."

"You want me to tell of how I broke the world," Adam said.

"Well, yes. But all of us have sinned, Adam. What right do any of us have to criticize you for your mistakes?"

Adam showed Enoch his blisters again. "Why wouldn't you? Right or wrong?"

Enoch nodded and chewed his bottom lip.

"Have you recorded their stories on tablets already?"

Enoch shook his head. "The Almighty has gifted me with a memory nearly as powerful as yours. It is all in here." He tapped his temple. "Soon to be here." He tapped the stone Adam sat on. "But I will need to travel far. To carry that many heavy tablets would be unwise."

Adam nodded, relieved because that meant there would be a limit to how easily the others in the village would come to understand whatever secrets he shared with Enoch. "If I tell you my story, you must not tell it to anyone here while I'm still alive."

The wind shifted, blowing a bit of smoke into their faces. "I will do what you ask."

Adam pulled his tunic over his nose until the wind shifted again. "I must admit . . . this past week, I've been wondering . . . maybe if I tell everything—confess for the first time the full weight of my mistakes—someone might find a way to finally be released from the curse of death that my sin purchased. After all, we *are* still searching for the fulfillment of my Father's promise in Eden, and . . . who knows how much longer I will be alive."

"Is that what you want me to speak to the Almighty about?" Enoch said.

"No." Adam rested his elbows on his knees. "What I want to say to the Almighty is personal. But it matters more to me than anything." After a moment, he added, "You still agree?"

"Of course. I am the prophet of the Almighty. I do not bandy my words lightly. But if you are to share everything with me, you must begin right away. I leave soon."

"Where would you like me to begin?"

"Where else? At your beginning."

"*My* beginning?" Adam said.

"Yes, if you can remember that far."

Adam scoffed. "If only I could forget. But that will take many hours."

Enoch nodded. "Would you prefer to begin in the morning?"

Adam shook his head. "If I am going to confess my sins, I'd rather begin before other ears rise to hear them."

"This isn't just about your sins," Enoch said. "This is to chronicle the significant events of the history of the world. I need everything."

"You will get it. Now, enough niggling. Let me begin."

So Adam, first of men, lifted his arm as if to grasp the hand of some distant memory and pull it through the veil, into thick existence.

And he began, "In my beginning was not darkness . . .

Chapter 2

In my beginning was not darkness, but Light.

As I opened my eyes for the first time, I saw dust motes swirling around five bright points. I reached for them and realized the dust was not blowing past me but instead settling across the complex shapes in my arms.

Distracted, I twisted my wrist, seeing muscle, tendon, bone, and a partial layer of skin. Clenching my fingers one by one, I saw the movement in my joints.

Fascinated, I watched as a swathe of dust poured over me like a sheet of silk and morphed into smooth, brown flesh. I ran my fingers across my new skin, and when the sound of shifting sand settled, noticed what sounded like gentle Music riding on the breath that flowed into me.

I inhaled.

Exhaled.

Inhaled again.

"Adam," I said, for I had heard that name—my name—in the Music.

I realized that my Father was singing over me, and in his singing, he had given me life and form, and had named me Adam.

7

He smiled at me, with those dark brown eyes, and let soft melodies fall from his tongue as I lay on my back.

He lifted me from the mud and burned the remaining dust from my skin with the heat of his presence. But he did not hurt me as a natural flame might. Instead, he filled and cleansed me. And the joy of him filled me with an insatiable desire to experience everything around me, to understand the world he had sung into existence.

I've never since felt so whole as I did with him in Eden. Because inside me was nothing that did not belong. Only him, and the breath he gave, and the Music he sang, and the smells of Eden, and the touch of his Light, and the taste of his name on my lips as I spoke for the second time. "Father." I smiled and laughed.

He stood magnificent, warm, compassionate. The image of the invisible condensed in a life foreknown before the foundations of the world were formed.

I felt his pride over me and laughed again, only now with tears.

My first moments were not like those of a newborn child come from a womb. Instead, they were of a child gone into the womb. Swaddled in the Light of God. Cocooned in his satisfaction.

I was Adam. Man fully formed. Reflection of perfection.

In joy, I fell to my hands and knees and bowed my forehead to the ground. Tears flowed to the soil I'd been formed from. How great! How wonderful this being was who had made me for himself, and who so unendingly satisfied me. Nothing I've experienced in my long years could ever make me forget it. That sense of purpose. Of everything being *right*.

Ah, yes. I see wonder on your face, Enoch, at how tears could be present in a world yet unbroken by sin.

Have you never wondered why the kiss of a lover can bring tears to our eyes? It is because some goods are so great that they must be given vent. For not all tears spring from sorrow. And not all aches are unwanted.

Yet still, my Father lifted me and wiped my cheeks. Then he led me across hills and valleys, puddles and rivers. He pointed at plants and skittering animals and insects, and it seemed as though I could hear the echo of his melodies in their movements.

For we were the product of his imagination. Brought into being by his very Words.

Sound. That is what we were. And within that sound? Words, melody, rhythm, tone, complexity, meaning, love, beginnings, endings, everything that is or will be, flowing from the tongue of my Father.

A symphony rumbling the universe.

As he showed me each new creature, words bubbled up from my memory of the Music and attached themselves to the animals' forms. I gave them voice, and my Father thanked me for naming the creatures.

I smiled, grateful to please him.

My eyes followed the flight of a bird into the blue expanse above and, for the first time, I noticed the sun cushioned by clouds. The moon, too, sat at the edge of the horizon, pale white and pure in its light.

I smiled at the sight of them. When I saw that the expression only pleased Father more, I let go of his hand to dance again. The world spun with color. I smelled powdery flowers and mushrooms crushed underfoot. I heard the chortle of streams over rock beds, the rush of air as I twirled, and our laughter joining myriad melodies crashing together and growing until I fell to my seat and closed my eyes.

Sensations rushed in and out too quickly to identify. In their wake remained a buzzing satisfaction.

His feet flattened grass as he stepped near and sat. I opened my eyes and crawled on hands and knees to the nearest stream. I looked through the crystalline liquid that flowed over the smooth rocks beneath it. The flowing liquid reflected the Light in bright shimmers.

But I saw something else that stole my attention. A dark face. Smooth, strong, and beautiful.

I reached for it and realized the hand that belonged to the face in the water mirrored my movements.

Father said, "That is you."

I felt my face, and the image in the water did the same.

My mind spun. How strange to consider my own self. For nothing else I had seen in all my time was anything like me, except for . . .

I turned back to Father. He frowned, and for the first time, I felt a question rise inside me. My hands shook, and I struggled to swallow. I was not worried, only curious and overwhelmed by so many powerful experiences at once.

He pressed my arm and said, "This world I have formed is too large for you. You are not supposed to be alone, and so I will make for you a helper."

I looked back at the reflection and wondered if the helper would look like me.

"The helper will be Good," he said.

Good. I tried to smile. *Good* was familiar. *Good* was in the Music. And it was ripe with meaning that I could not quite take hold of, like a memory with its innards faded away. "Tell me," I said, "what is Good? What makes it so . . ." I searched for words but failed to find them. "Good?" I chuckled, but Father remained sober.

"Listen well, my son. You may eat of every tree of the garden, but you may not eat of the Tree of the Knowledge of Good and Evil, for in the day that you eat of it, you will surely die."

He pointed toward a seemingly insignificant tree on a grassy knoll in the center of a lake, as if the water guarded it.

Die. I tried not to frown. *Die* was familiar. *Die* was in the Music too. In fact, it was everywhere. I knew that it was linked to endings, and that if I died, that would mean everything would change.

"Sleep now," he said and brushed my eyes closed. I wanted

to remain with him. To be reassured that nothing would ever change. But my body obeyed its Maker, and the Light receded, replaced by dreams of a new creature that would change everything. For good, and for evil.

Though I did not yet understand either in full, just as I did not understand *her*.

Chapter 3

As my Maker had commanded me to sleep, so he commanded me to wake. I opened my eyes to a swath of thin clouds like wisps of sheer cloth, and the glow of his Light hovering over me. The sun was half-set and the day cooler. But I could hardly keep my eyes open with him bending so close. I covered my face with my forearm as his footsteps retreated and his brightness dimmed.

With a yawn, I rubbed my eyes and rose to a seated position, noticing I laid in a quiet grove. I remembered that he said he would make a helper for me and placed my hand to my side. My bones were no longer symmetrical. Something had been taken from my flank, though the flesh remained unbroken.

Surely my Father would tell me what had happened while I slept. I looked around, but found the only other creature with me was . . .

I didn't know what, exactly. Only that she was new, and she was like me, only different. Her skin was dark like coal, and the richness of the hue drew my eyes. Her figure resembled mine, yet her shape differed. Where my body was hard, hers was soft. And sleek and strong. A strange, new vision of complex beauty.

I struggled to a stand, still shaky. We stared at each other.

Her long, smooth hair fluttered in the breeze. Her dark eyes regarded me with a piercing intelligence that none of the animals held. I felt, in that moment, that she understood my very thoughts.

She lifted her slender hand and pointed behind me. "Why did he leave us?"

I followed her finger to an opening between the trees leading out of the grove.

"I don't know," I said and dared two paces closer. "What do you remember?"

"I woke to the Light, and he commanded you to wake. Then he left."

One more step, and I could reach out to touch her. Her voice warmed me in a way wholly different from the Light. Hers was a dizzy, buzzing heat. I stretched out my arm and traced my finger down her torso. A shiver shook my shoulders.

She shifted closer, breath pulsing fast like the rhythm in my wrists. She felt it too. The fascination. The wild, young excitement. Pure and powerful, like the rush of a river overflowing its banks.

Helper, he had called her. But as I drank in her form, other sounds clustered to form a name that attached itself as a banner across her arm.

I opened my mouth and pronounced it slowly. "Completion."

"What?" she said, her voice a whisper, breath gently brushing my neck.

Completion only carried a portion of rightness. More words took shape until they overlapped to form a greater concept.

"Woman," I said.

She tipped her head, as if to ask if I was referring to her.

Yes. She who was formed out of me, *to* me.

I set my hands on her shoulders. She started to pull away, but I gently urged her to stay, and she examined me. With a nod, she straightened and pressed her chest against mine.

I tilted my head, our noses touching.

She closed her eyes and kissed me.

Yes, she was that way from the beginning. As though the rib God formed her from contained the greater part of all my resolve.

I saw, in that moment, that she was more than the sum I had given. For the weight of her pull felt impossibly heavy. The warmth of the sun faded at her touch. The memory of the Light dimmed behind the gleam of her eyes.

We held each other, happy.

Complete.

For a moment.

Until the Light returned.

We let go and faced him as his feet brushed the grass and left little imprints that slowly disappeared.

She stepped toward Father and said, "Where did you go?"

"There," he said and pointed. "To give you time to meet."

My mind began to clear in his cleansing Light, and I realized those moments with her had been a gift from him. I couldn't hold back a smile. "Out of all the creatures you have shown me," I said, "I found no creature like this. At last, this is bone of my bones, and flesh of my flesh. We are the same, and yet so beautifully different. In her softness, she upholds me. And in my strength, I long to hold her gently."

"Have you yet named her?"

I nodded. "She shall be called Woman, because she was taken out of Man."

Our Creator tipped his head, a smirk at the corner of his mouth. "But is that a proper name?"

She looked at me, hands on her hips, head high. That confident, almost haughty, look of hers. "Yes, is it?"

I cleared my throat and shifted on my heels, which sank softly into the moist ground. "How about . . ." I stared at her again, letting the sounds return and cluster. "E-v-e . . .?"

She raised her brows. "Eve?" Then squinted as if tasting the word and finding it pleasant enough. She shrugged. "And you are Adam?"

Adam. Man. Yes, that was my name. And Eve, for she would be the mother of all.

I smiled again at my Creator. "You've taken a portion of my beauty and formed it into a work of *surpassing* beauty, intelligence, and worth. A precious living creature, the likes of which I have never seen."

Father nodded, his Light catching rainbows in the mist that began to fall. "Precious, she is. More precious than the world. Treat her as such."

I nodded and looked at her. Overwhelmed. The Light offered a peaceful stillness and fulfillment. But she gave a tilted excitement, a strange thrill that struck at my throat and quickened my breath.

The differences between flesh and spirit stark even before the world was broken.

He urged me forward, but I paused. A sense of awe deepening in my chest. It was all too wonderful to contain.

Father laughed, and she stepped forward, a hint of humor sparkling in her eyes as well. A laugh bubbled up from us both like water from a spring. She took hold of my shoulders as I had hers, and we pressed together as if we'd never become two.

We stood there, bathed in my Father's Light, urged on by the Music to dance left, now right, now spinning together, the world a whirl of splendor. She warmed me—small, yet strong enough to hold me upright. Her beating heart setting the rhythm of mine rushing.

I smiled and asked Father, "Is this what it feels like to hold the world in your arms?"

"Better," he said. "Much better."

But as he turned away, his smile faded.

"Wait," I said. "You are leaving again?"

He paused, back to us. "I will always come if you call me. But now you must *choose* me."

"Choose you?" I said. "I choose you forever. Stay!"

"Yes," Eve said. "Stay!"

He turned, and the sorrow in his face seemed to dim the

Light. "My son . . ." He crossed to me, and I let Eve go and threw my arms around my Maker as his Light enveloped my naked body.

Emotion flushed my face as I held on to this being so ultimate, yet so intimate. He loved me. I knew he loved me. And because of that, I loved him.

Eve approached and laced her arm under Father's. She rested her head against his shoulder, and I glanced at her and saw her smiling.

"There are times," he continued, voice muffled against my shoulder. "When I must become more distant."

"Why?"

"Because that is the way of the world." He let go and held me at arms' length. "Love is a dance. To come together, you must part. There is a rhythm to your life. A rhythm to all life. Just as in six days I created the world, and on the seventh I will rest, so you must rest every seventh day. Each morning the sun takes its course, and night follows. A cycle repeating until I tell it to stop."

"Don't tell it to stop," I said. "I want this to go on forever."

He smiled and whispered, "Me too," then nodded. "You won't forget anything that I tell you, for I have gifted you both with more powerful memories than any who will come after you. Still, you must keep my words at the front of your minds."

"I will," I said.

"So will I," Eve said.

I wish I had known, in that moment, the weight of his warning.

Sometimes I wonder if everything could have been different. If *I* could have been different.

Though I know that this, too, he has used, and will continue to use, for his glory.

Still . . . most days I wish he hadn't.

But it's not his fault.

No. It was never his fault.

Chapter 4

Long after Father's footsteps faded behind the sounds of the garden growing, Eve said, "What will we do now?"

I could hardly take my eyes off the lingering sparkle of Light where he'd stood. "He has given us Choice."

"Choice . . . " She echoed.

A sense of duty spread my ribs like the hands of my Father. The woman, like me, was body, soul, and spirit. She too held responsibility for this gift of life.

I pressed my hand to my chest, where I could still feel the breath my Father had breathed into me swirling beneath my flesh. What did that mean for me?

"I would choose to see the rest of this garden," Eve said. "Is there much more to it?"

"Of course," I said.

Her lips spread into a wide smile, and I admired the brightness of her teeth between those soft, dark lips. After a moment, her smile softened. "What?"

"I was just thinking."

"About?"

I spread my arms. "I think I am supposed to give you everything Father gave me."

"What did he give you?"

I smiled. "Let me show you."

I slipped my hand into hers and pulled her, hurrying out of the grove, down rows of fruit trees. Monkeys swung from branches, yelling as we passed beneath them. Birds chirped and flew through little gaps between trees. Ferns and bushes rustled in the wind, and Eve pointed at each new creature and said, "What is that?"

A small herd of gray elephants shuffled with surprising grace through the trees. She stopped and stared, eyes wide at the prickly hair on their long ears that waved back and forth. "And those?"

"Elephants," I said and smiled as she looked at me with wonder again.

I brought her close, and the elephants turned toward us and extended their trunks to touch our faces.

Eve scrunched up her nose and, as one blew a blast of air through her hair, spluttered and laughed. The elephants turned back to grazing, and Eve said, "How do you know so much?"

My chest rose in pride. "Father tasked me with naming every beast."

She leaned closer and placed her hands on my chest. "I wish I could have done that!" She reached and ran her nails gently through my hair.

I nodded. "Perhaps in the future, Father will bring new creatures into the world, and you will be able to name them."

She laughed again. "I would love that." We stared at each other.

"Can I kiss you again?" I said.

She shrugged, a suppressed smile glimmering in her eyes. "Can you?"

I pulled her close and kissed her with all the passion that rose in my chest. I spun her gently through the air, and nearly stumbled and fell. We let go of each other, and she hopped backward and spun away with a laugh.

"Watch this," she said and loped toward the nearest tree,

whooping like one of the monkeys we saw earlier. Grabbing hold of the low branches, she swung herself up, sending squirrels leaping away.

I laughed so hard my side ached, then swung myself up a parallel branch.

She breathed hard and pulled back the strands of her hair caught on twigs.

Apples of varying ripeness grew between patches of leaves sprouting from the branches. I grabbed a red apple streaked with yellow, twisted my wrist, and broke it from its source. "Our Father has given all this fruit to us to eat."

Eve grabbed a darker apple and broke it away.

I pressed the skin of the fruit against my teeth. The crisp, sweet taste of fresh apple burst across my tongue. My mouth tingled and ached with the intensity of the flavor.

She did the same and hummed her approval.

We finished our apples and tossed the cores, already browning, in the air. I jumped to the earth as Eve swung herself down carefully.

"Come on," I said. "There's so much more!"

We ran faster now, the grasses soft beneath our feet.

A flock of colorful birds alighted on the path before us, and I raised my hands and yelled as we ran through them, sending them fluttering and chirping.

Eve tossed her head back and laughed. "Again!"

As soon as the birds settled back, pecking the ground, we sent them flying away.

Then again.

And again.

Like little children drowning in delight, because that is what we were.

Oh, Enoch, if I could only return to those days of naked innocence, when everything was new. I haven't laughed that hard in decades. Even now, I remember the tears running down my face.

Eve was wiping her face and moaning, overwhelmed with joy.

"This place is too wonderful," she said. "I love everything!"

"Me too," I said, bending forward and resting my hands on my knees, taking deep, hard breaths to settle the pulse that thumped in my chest and throat.

She smiled at me, her expression calming. "But . . ."

I straightened. "But?"

"But when I look at you . . . everything else seems dull."

Words failed me. My breath stopped at her tender admission of deep, real affection. I decided then that whatever it took, I would please Eve. I would satisfy her and be to her what Father was to me. I would make her laugh. I would warm her with my arms and fulfill her with my company. My heart would rise to those words.

And fall broken in as many pieces as there are stars in the sky.

But I knew nothing of brokenness yet. I knew only Father, and Eve, and the world he'd given us.

"I feel the same," I said, voice just loud enough to be heard above the gentle breeze that rustled the brush.

She straightened. "I'm thirsty. Where is water?"

I cleared my throat and waved her toward me. "This way."

We walked at a leisurely pace through narrow paths that slowly widened to a broad road paved with a carpet of creeping thyme. The tiny leaves sent a fragrant wind as we crushed them underfoot. The dense copse thinned until the trees were more like freckles on hills like great green faces.

In the midst of a little valley on the far side of some hills lay the river Pishon. One of the river's tributaries filled a small lake just outside the center of the Garden. We made for that lake and were passed by a herd of antelope leaping around a pair of giraffes.

As we crested the hill, Eve gasped.

I did, too, though I had already seen it. For the sight was breathtaking.

Buffalo stood ankle-deep in the water, tails swishing at the flies that swarmed them. Hippos yawned, their jaws all that could be seen above the surface that continued like a great mirror reflecting the clouds and colors above. Tigers, birds, massive reptiles, and countless other animals all bathed and drank of the water here, and no harm came to any of them.

We reached the edge of the water and Eve cupped water and began to drink it from her own hand. A young wolf came by and began to lick my leg. I smiled at it and ruffled the fur on its head. It yawned and wagged its tail.

A hawk swooped over the lake, and a fish skipped across the surface of the water, its shimmering body slapping the lake and sending an echo off the hills.

Eve looked up at the sound and said, "What is that?"

I followed the line of her finger and noticed the tree Father had shown me growing on a grassy knoll in the middle of the lake, as if guarded by the water. "The tree?"

"Yes. Why does it grow there?"

I shrugged, remembering what Father had said with a shiver. "Because it is not for us."

She raised one brow at me, and the intensity of her gaze bore down on me until I dipped to scoop more water to drink. "But you said Father gave us all the trees to eat of."

"All but for that one," I said, flicking the excess water from my hands.

She stared at the tree a bit longer. Then she began trudging deeper into the water.

I grabbed her shoulder. "What are you doing?"

"I just want to see the tree up close." She glanced at it again. "From here, it seems as though more fruit grows on that tree than on any other."

Indeed, it seemed the tree was so heavily laden with brightly colored fruit of irregular shapes and hues that the branches would break.

"I bet it tastes wonderful," she said.

But I held her back, and she furrowed her brow at me. "Eve. We must not eat of it."

"I just want to look at it," she said.

I pulled her back even harder. "Nor touch it, lest we die."

Her hair lifted in the breeze. "Die?"

"Yes, die. End." I swept my hand to indicate everything around us. "Lose all that we know in this blessed land."

Her hand slipped over my hand, which still held her shoulder. Her eyes questioning. Not fearful, but curious. "Would you go away too?"

"I . . . yes. I don't know. Maybe."

She pursed her lips and looked down at our reflection in the water. I could tell she was momentarily distracted, just as I had been when I first discovered my own image. But she didn't seem as surprised as I had been.

I think it was because she knew my face and assumed hers was like it, but I had seen nothing but wild beasts.

"Well," she said at length. "I am hungry. Join me?"

I nodded, "Of course."

And we turned away.

I had no idea, at the time, why I felt such relief at her relenting. Neither did I have any clue that I had just made a grave mistake.

You see, Enoch, I had not deliberately lied. In my mind, I had meant that she should not touch it for fear of the death that might come if she was enticed to eat the fruit of the Tree of the Knowledge of Good and Evil. But she understood me differently. And the space between my intentions and her understanding was the beginnings of a shattered world.

Chapter 5

We followed the river back to the fruit tree forest, picking vegetables from sprawling bushes on the way. We found prickly cucumbers, red and brown-streaked tomatoes, and more blackberries than we could carry, tasting everything before moving on.

The blackberries stained our fingers and faces, and we laughed at each other as we carried cucumbers and tomatoes to the river to wash the dirt from them.

I knelt and held them beneath the rushing current, the pure, clean water bringing shivers to my body.

Eve pointed at little raised bumps that appeared all over my skin and said, "How silly!"

I pressed my arms against my sides to conserve my warmth, but the water was like ice.

I lifted the clean vegetables from the water and arranged them on the grass. Eve picked up a cucumber and took her first bite. Her eyes widened. "This is a new flavor."

I nodded. "Sweet but not like apples."

She shook her head. "The taste is cleaner, like water. Here —" She held it out for me, and I took another bite.

The cold, refreshing flavor brought on another chill, this

time of delight. "Wonderful!" I pointed at the water. "It is different when it has been chilled."

Eve laughed. "Like your skin." She continued eating as I considered how I might gather larger portions of vegetables and submerge them in the water for longer periods of time.

I noticed the vegetables hung from little vines and went to the cucumber plant again and lifted one of them. The cucumber swung in the air, secure at the end of its vine.

An idea struck me. I tore off myriad vines approximately the length of my arm, all of which grew cucumbers at their ends. I arranged these side by side on the grass and held them in one fist, lowering them gently into the water and keeping their vines on the shore.

The water tugged, but did not swipe them away.

I lifted them out again and crossed the vines over each other once, twice.

Eve watched me with interest.

I tried to put the cucumbers back in the water and leave the vines on the grass, but the water began to tug them apart.

"Wait," she said and set her hands to the severed plants. She coiled them around each other, then looped them together in a simple knot.

She gently tugged them apart, but the knot held. We smiled and placed the cucumbers back in the water, making sure to weave the knotted vines around a small tree that had begun to grow by the shore. Its trunk merely the width of two fingers.

The cucumbers floated and bobbed in the water, but the current didn't carry them away, for they were caught both on each other and on the small tree.

Eve handed me the rest of the cucumber she'd been eating, and I ate as well.

Looking at the center of the vegetable, I noticed some of the pale seeds, arranged in such beautiful symmetry. I dug them out and held them in my palm.

What were they for? And why did they grow in such a pattern?

I had not seen Father for some time, but before I could stand to look for him, Eve bid me to lay next to her and rest in the shade of a nearby tree.

I did, and she kissed me, and we held each other until we fell asleep.

. . .

When I woke, the heavens were black and lit by silver stars. In the eastern sky, a wash of shimmering colors waved like transparent silks in the wind.

I stood and spun. The moon was high, its perfect body circular, distant, and bright. I stepped on a twig and it cracked.

Eve shifted to her side and breathed out long and slow. I thought to wake her, but as I dipped, her expression was so beautiful and peaceful that I decided against it.

I looked back at the river, whose shimmering form now glittered in the starlight. I crossed to where we'd hung the cucumbers.

They were gone, apparently washed downriver while we slept.

I frowned. Would the flavor have been better had they remained all along?

I cupped and drank water, then reached toward the heavens as if to feel those little points of light.

"Adam?"

Eve's voice seemed distant and small. I looked back and saw her searching for me. She couldn't see where I stood nearly twenty paces away.

"Yes," I said, voice low.

She turned, eyes straining in the dark. "Where are you?"

"Here," I said. "Looking at the stars in the sky."

She looked up, mouth wide. "Is that them?"

I nodded, then remembered she couldn't see me. "Yes."

"Why is everything so dark?"

"The sun is gone," I said.

"Will it return?"

"Father said it would."

"What should we do?"

"Sleep, I think." I opened my palms and looked at them. The cucumber seeds were gone. "Eve?"

She crawled on hands and knees toward me. "Would you come closer? I can hardly see you."

"Where are the seeds?"

She considered this. "I don't know."

The sky was beginning to slowly change from black to deep blue, and the stars dimmed as day returned. "Go back to where you were laying and look for them."

"Why don't you?" she said.

"I'm going to look by the river. I think I might have dropped them there."

She crawled back to our little spot beneath the tree and felt around for them as I did the same by the riverbank.

"We'll never find them," she called and sat with her back to the tree. "They're too small. We should just gather new seeds from the cucumbers we have left."

"They are gone. Floated downriver."

She cleared her throat. "Then we shall return to the plants later. Come, be with me."

"Just give me a moment." I had wanted to ask Father how the seeds worked, and I wondered if the brightening sky was proof of Father's return to Eden.

I wanted to be ready when he came.

I swept my fingers slowly through the sand at the edge of the river and carefully tested the little sprigs of grass.

"Oh!" Eve said.

I felt something small and smooth and tried to pick it up, but realized it was a beetle instead.

"Adam?"

I spun back and wiped my hand on the grass.

Eve stood with her hands cupped before her. Nose to nose with a gray serpent hanging from the tree we'd slept under.

I jogged back in the dim glow of morning now growing to a deep shade of pink. The serpent's body coiled around the lowest, thickest limb. Its six-clawed feet clung to the branches. The beast's eyes seemed to stare at both Eve and me at once.

Eve nodded. "Thank you."

The serpent's tongue tested the air and tickled Eve's nose. She laughed and stepped back, and I peered into her cupped hands to see what appeared to be a pile of dried cucumber seeds.

"Did it give you those, Eve?" I said.

The serpent swiveled its nose toward me, then slid slowly up into the tree and disappeared.

Eve smiled. "The seeds fell on my head as I was searching. When I looked up, I saw that serpent hanging over me."

I held out my hand, and she poured them into my palm. I pushed the seeds with my index finger, considered their rough forms, and plucked one from her hair. "These are dry. And there are more here than I gathered yesterday."

Eve shrugged. "Perhaps it knew what you intended and gathered some."

"Perhaps." I stared back up into the branches. But I had encountered no animals so cunning as to know my desires and to offer me something to satiate them. Not in all my time in Eden had I found a beast who looked at me with such knowing as that one had.

In fact, I did not remember ever seeing the serpent.

Of course, you must understand, Enoch, I felt no fear. Only the sense that something was missing. Like a dream whose details disappear when you wake.

I had no idea I had encountered evil incarnate, for I did not yet have any personal experience of evil, and all such danger eluded me.

I wish I had told Eve in that moment to stay away from it. To never talk to it again. But part of me wonders if anything would have ended differently. Would we not have made a similar mistake eventually? Or, if not us, one of our children?

No, I am not trying to avoid my responsibility. The weight is mine to bear, and mine alone. For my Father gave it to me.

To bear up under the weight of our brokenness is the grief due every man. For time stretches only forward, and there is never any way to turn back and clean our footprints from the sands of time.

As I held the seeds and considered their meaning, quiet footsteps approached, and the Light grew between trees, branches, leaves, and bushes.

"Oh," Eve said and hopped toward the sound of our Father's footsteps.

Father stepped out from behind several pomegranate trees, and Eve threw herself into his arms. He laughed and spun her, then smiled at me as I jogged up and wrapped my arm around his shoulders. "Have you enjoyed my garden?"

"Indeed," Eve said. "Everything is so wonderful. Adam showed me many of the trees, and we ate fruit and saw monkeys and elephants, and hippos in the water, and—"

"We danced and ran and chased birds," I said.

"Oh, that was my favorite part. And then . . ."

She looked toward me as if inviting me to contribute more to the conversation—though there was no reason for it, other than love, for we both remembered everything in perfect detail —a blessing, at first, and now in my old age, a curse.

"Then we gathered cucumbers," I said, unable to hold back a wide smile, "and tomatoes, and we washed them in the river. Eve discovered how to tie the cucumber vines together around a small tree so they did not float away."

"Except, we fell asleep, and when we woke, they were gone."

Father chuckled. "The knot loosened because of the river tugging at it."

"Will you show me how to tie a better knot?" Eve said.

"And other things?" I added, hopeful.

"Of course. Ask, and I will teach."

Eve smiled and tipped her head to indicate me. "Adam would like to ask you about the seeds that he found."

"That *we* found," I corrected as I lifted my right fist, which held the seeds. I slowly unfurled my fingers. The dry seeds rested in a little mound on my palm, and I pinched one with my thumb and forefinger to hold it in the light.

Father took it from me and examined it closely. "Where did you get these?"

"Cucumbers," I said.

"We were looking for cucumber seeds we had gathered last night, but they had disappeared, so the gray serpent gave us these," Eve said.

At the mention of the serpent, a small shiver rippled through my bones.

"Oh?" Father examined us both. "And what did you want to know about them?"

"I want to know why they grow in such a way, and what they are for."

Father nodded. "These seeds are what you will use to grow more cucumber plants. Look inside." He broke the seed in half and turned it so that we could peer at it. Eve and I scrunched together, our bodies huddled against Father's. "A single seed, when planted in the right soil, tended, and watered, will become a full plant that will bear fruit. This is one of your tasks. To tend my garden and grow its beauty and order."

I nodded. "Will we work together today?"

Father dropped the seed and wiped his hands. "Not today."

"You're not leaving us again, are you?" Eve said.

He smiled and ran his fingers through Eve's hair. "No, my daughter. Today is a day of rest." He swept his arm to indicate all the life around us. "I created everything you see in six days. The earth and the stars and the moon and the sun. The plants and the trees and the birds and the fish. The creeping things and animals and you and your man. But on this, the seventh day, I have chosen to rest from all the work I have done. And you, likewise, will rest with me every seventh day. From now until . . ."

Until the world was changed.

I know now that was what he meant, yet he did not say it. Perhaps because he did not want to spoil our joy with the sorrow that would be ours all too soon.

But he told us nothing about the gray serpent. Part of me knew implicitly that we should avoid the beast and wished that Eve had not mentioned it. For the Light in Father's face had flickered at the mention of its name. And I sensed a dark shadow growing longer behind me.

"So, what *will* we do today?" Eve said.

Father smiled. "I will make us a meal, and we will eat together."

We followed Father, who walked at a leisurely pace through the garden and gathered ripe corn off tall green stalks. After, he harvested sugar cane, nuts, berries, and peaches. We arranged our food in small piles, and he told us to gather little branches, grass, sticks, and one flat, very thin rock.

After doing this, we saw he had gathered still other materials. A small boulder sat beside our pile of tinder, and he struck it with another hard stone until the boulder split, leaving one half like a bowl.

He turned to arranging the tinder and pulled out two other types of stones. He shaved a bit of a soft stone off onto the pile of tinder, then struck it with a sharp stone, sending sparks flying. One of the sparks caught on the tinder, and Father softly blew the flames to life.

I stared at the dancing flames, mesmerized and awed. He motioned for us to add to it, and Eve and I added sticks and twigs until the fire grew strong and sure.

Father set the stone bowl between his legs and began to shuck corn. With the sharp rock he had started the fire with, he cut the kernels from the stalks and let them fall in the bowl. With another round stone, he mashed them.

He broke the canes and squeezed the juice over the mush.

He added berries and smashed nuts, stirring it together with his hands.

Now the fire had red-hot coals, and he set the thin rock atop them.

We sat and watched as he grabbed little wads of the mush and laid them on the flat rock. The mush sizzled and thickened and cooked. When it was finished, he used sticks to carefully shift the stone off the fire.

We waited for it to cool, chatting about the previous day. Father laughed with us, and we felt the joy of his presence like a deeper sense of rest than sleep could ever offer.

Finally, Father took the little corn patties and gave them to us. Then he took one up for himself, and we ate. The patties were wonderful, crumbly, sweet, and satisfying. Any pieces that dropped, we picked up and ate.

Then we drank from a nearby stream, and lay together on the grass.

Father taught us songs, and we sang and clapped our hands and danced in the meadow.

He was a good Father. I have thought of those days countless times since, and in all these years, his kindness and openness have been a balm for my weary soul. On days when he seemed uncaring and far away, it was a gift to remember him near and gentle.

His voice sounded like you might imagine. He was like us, and we were like him. We knew he had the power to create or destroy everything we saw, but still he made us breakfast, and held our hands, and stomped his feet as he taught us to dance. For he had pulled on the human visage to be with us—to walk in the garden, to let us hear his footsteps and voice—so that we would see his personhood and know we were fashioned after him, not the other way around.

I am sorry for my tears, Enoch. I only miss him.

His gentle touch . . . the sound of his voice.

His personality, his laughter, his wisdom.

His nearness and his embrace—so human, so fatherly, yet so powerful and otherly.

No one—nothing—is like him.

. . .

The three of us napped by the river. I awoke after a thick droplet of liquid struck my face.

I sat up and glanced at Eve and Father, whose peaceful expressions still held the joy of sleep.

Another droplet struck the grass next to me. I lifted my hand and touched it. Brought the wetness to my nose and sniffed.

Water.

Several more droplets came, and I looked up and saw the sky was filled with billowing, dark clouds.

"Father?" I touched Father's shoulder.

He inhaled and rubbed his face. "Yes, my child?"

"What is that?" I pointed.

Eve groaned and turned away, guarding her face with her arm.

Father stood and motioned me away. I followed and we sat with our feet in the river.

He smiled at me. "Remember when you awoke in the Garden yesterday?" His voice was quiet so he would not disturb Eve.

I nodded.

"There was a mist that wetted the plants and rose into the sky."

As he said it, the memory returned.

"That was some of the first water the soil of Eden tasted. Would you like to know where it comes from and how it works?"

Droplets of water fell faster. I nodded.

"That cloud up there is the same as the mist you saw that watered the ground. The air you breathe holds tiny bits of water. As the sun heats the rivers and lakes, more water rises into the air." He spread his fingers to illustrate the water flying up. "But the air can only hold so much before the water grows too heavy and must fall back to the earth."

The droplets now fell in thin sheets that began to soak our

hair. I laughed as the cold droplets made me shiver. Eve grumbled behind us as she tried to continue sleeping amidst the rain.

"This is a delicate balance, and the workings of the universe hinge on its specific design, which I planned and knew before the foundations of the world were formed."

At every turn, his knowledge and mastery of all things awed me.

He grinned, splashed his feet in the river, and soaked me more. I gasped as the cold water struck my torso. Then splashed him back, and he laughed and stood.

"Shall we swim?" he said, with a twinkle in his eye.

"Swim?" Eve groaned. "What about sleep?"

I pointed at his tunic and said, "Your tunic."

He shrugged as the rain intensified to thick waves that sparkled in the sunlight peeking beneath the clouds. He pulled his tunic off and sprinted and jumped into the river.

Eve rose and watched us, swiping wet hair from her eyes.

"Come," I said to her. And ran after Father.

I plunged under the current, the cold nearly wrenching a gasp from my chest. My feet swept through the water, searching for purchase. Father's hands found my arms and lifted my head out of the water.

I gasped and spluttered, and we laughed as Eve splashed in next to us.

"Kick your legs and swipe your arms back and forth, like this," Father said.

I tried to do as he said, but the current swept me away. He pulled me to where the river was not too deep and let me practice over and over again.

Where I struggled at swimming, Eve excelled.

Soon, she was splashing from one side to the other. But I had little confidence in making it to the middle and back.

After, we rested by the river while Father left to gather fruit for us.

When he returned, he had just one fruit for each of us. The

fruit was strange, unlike any I'd yet seen. I took hold of it and said, "What is this?"

"Fruit from the Tree of Life," he said. "Eat and your weariness will disappear. It bears fruit every month for us to eat and be sustained."

We ate, and though it was sweet, it wasn't as sweet as the apples. Yet it satisfied something deep inside us and became our favorite food in the garden. Father ate from it, as well, and Eve examined him as he chewed.

"Do you get weary too?"

Father smiled. "Why do you think I slept with you today?"

"But you are stronger than any other," Eve said.

"You crafted the universe," I said. "How could you grow weary merely playing with us?"

"I chose to become human so that we would be together, and so that I could be your father in practice as in spirit. I gifted rest to all creatures. But I specifically designed humanity to need and love rest because in weariness we find a force that draws us together." He stood and faced the forest of fruit trees, expression darkening into a slight frown. "Soon, you will cherish rest more than anything else. You will long for true, lasting peace."

"Why can we not have peace forever? This day has been wonderful. I will always enjoy this."

"This is our day of rest. Even before—" He stopped himself and swallowed hard as his eyes suddenly shot to the ground, and he dug his toes into the sand. He took a deep breath. "There are seasons. Some will be harder than others. So long as you obey me, and keep your heart set on love for me and for each other, you will walk in the Light and have perfect peace. Tomorrow, we will work very hard."

He refused to speak the truth prematurely, that he knew we would betray him. Instead, he merely affirmed the truth that obedience in love would give us peace.

As he mentioned the Light, I realized it still hovered about him, seemingly setting his skin aglow. But you must understand, Enoch, the Light was not an "it" but a "him." The Spirit of

God himself, manifested in the force and substance of light. He was there, with our Father and his progenitive Word, at the beginning of all things.

"What is work?" I said.

"An activity I have planned for you. Tomorrow, I will show you much."

Chapter 6

As always, he was true to his word. The next day, he showed us new ways to care for his garden. He taught us to prune, and which plants needed it. He taught us how to use the fibrous stalks of certain plants to weave into baskets to aid us in our gathering work.

We sat cross-legged with piles of reeds beside us and wove until the day grew hot. Then he brought us to a spring that fed the Pishon, and he began to dig in the soil and turn up orange earth.

He poured water into the soil and mixed it together with his hands. Working the thick slop until it was smooth and malleable.

"This," he said as he slapped a wad of the stuff onto the ground and began to shape it, "is clay." He pressed it flat and urged the sides up into a small bowl. "You can use it to shape little bowls and plates for holding your food. Let it dry in the sun, or bake it on a fire to harden it."

He took a smooth stone from the spring and began to rub the clay bowl, smoothening its texture. "You may also burnish the clay to make it less porous, so it does not absorb moisture." He motioned toward the little collection of clay that he had made while he continued burnishing his bowl. "Go ahead, try forming a bowl yourselves."

Eve and I grabbed wads of clay, slapped them on the ground like he had, and tried to flatten the material, but hers cracked, and mine became no more than a tiny cup.

"Grab some water and mix it, Eve," Father said as he gathered twigs and sticks to build a fire.

I tried to help her, but she motioned me away. "I want to figure it out myself."

"Very well," I said and took my cup to Father, who had already started a small flame in a bed of kindling and now gently blew it higher.

I fed the fire with the little sticks he'd gathered while he broke larger branches and brought other pieces of wood. As before, I sat mesmerized by the flames while he fed the fire that turned the sticks and twigs to glowing coals.

Again and again Eve went back to the little clay pit and dumped water in and kneaded the soil into usable slop. I didn't look at her work because I wanted to honor her desire to work alone, lest I be tempted to help her. In truth, I was impressed by her tenacity. Her willingness to keep working in the midst of failure.

Father and I sat and chatted about different types of earth, and how some held bits of metal that could be extracted by heat. He described how to make a simple furnace, along with more complicated ideas for venting it properly so that the heat could be greatly increased.

Finally, as the coals in our open fire became hot enough, and the flames less wild and inconsistent, Father set both my cup and his bowl on the embers to bake.

Eve approached. But when I looked up, I did not see a bowl in her hands, but rather a beautifully crafted pitcher, with a spout for pouring and a handle for holding it comfortably.

"W-what?" I spluttered. There were even crosshatched designs around the mouth of the pitcher, to beautify it.

Father tossed back his head and laughed. He slapped my

shoulder softly and said, "My dear Adam. You don't know your wife yet!"

Eve smiled, her white teeth and dark skin gleaming in the firelight, drawing my eyes from the flames to an even greater allure. She sat next to me, and I wrapped my arm around her and urged her close. She scooted to my side, and I could nearly have laughed, I was so proud to be hers.

"You must teach me," I said.

She tossed back her hair, showing her long neck as she glanced at me with a smirk. "Maybe tomorrow."

. . .

Each day, Father taught us more. As he did, he worked alongside us. Always he modeled the work he asked from us. And so we grew to love him even more than we thought possible.

His heart was warm, his arms quick to embrace, and his mouth always ready to praise the good we did.

For some time, we were content to be with him. To learn all he taught us and put it into practice.

But every seventh day, he rested. And so you see our habit of keeping that seven-day cycle comes not from my mind, but rather from the behavior of God himself in human form.

Many cycles of work and rest passed. He taught us to make tools. We built clay furnaces and began to form little slabs of metal that could be worked into crude tools.

After crafting a metal hoe, we began to dig more readily into the soil and to plant new small vegetable gardens. We planted rows of corn and wheat and other grains. And we dug little trenches to irrigate the land.

The sense of excitement rushed us headlong. With the fruit of the Tree of Life, our weariness was stayed, and with the guidance and endless knowledge of Father, we were given all that we needed to thrive and progress in our work of caring for his garden. We grew wise in caring for the plants and crafting tools and building furniture from wood and woven materials.

But Eve was always the most innovative. She was the first to build a chair and an elevated bed that would keep us from the wet dew in the morning.

We were taught about animals and the way they interacted with plants. We kept the grazers from our new gardens so they would not consume our new rows of grains. We watched the bees and ants as they crawled across the flowers and pollinated, bringing heavy fruit to the stalks.

When our grains grew, we were awed anew by the immense diversity that Father had woven through his creation. Every head of corn seemed to differ in color, size, shape, and flavor.

He taught us how to cultivate and select different varieties, and how to make certain they did not intermingle. He also taught us to revert plants to other varieties over multiple generations, for the benefits of one type could outweigh another with fluctuations in climate or soil type.

He taught us how to keep sheep, goats, cows, camels, and on and on and on.

At the time, it never struck us, the rapid pace of his teaching, the constancy of his presence. We could imagine no other life. Could not even fathom that there was any reason other than love that pushed him to teach us.

But I am now more convinced than ever that he was preparing us for what was to come. Ensuring we had the knowledge and the tools to weather life on our own.

But not even his training could prepare us for the horror of total isolation.

Chapter 7

I saw the gray serpent again after our fifth day of rest with Father.

He left to grab more fruit from the Tree of Life. Eve and I began smashing rocks in search of gemstones. We had grown to love their luster and wanted Father to teach us the techniques to beautify and polish their forms.

I was busy hitting several rocks on the edge of a boulder when Eve wandered off. She had a habit of doing that, so at first I did not wonder where she went.

Then I smashed one of the rocks and a chunk of stone fell away revealing the glitter of onyx deep inside.

"Eve!" I said and peeked around the boulder to see if she was near.

She crouched amidst a separate pile of rocks with a round stone in her arms, nearly nose to nose with that gray serpent.

I stopped, rubbed the dust from my hands, and approached them.

"You are certain?" she said.

The serpent looked her in the eyes and licked her nose.

"Well, then, thank you for sharing." She stood and noticed

me, then said with a smile, "I found some emeralds. Come, let us break them open and see."

I looked at the stone in her hands. "Emeralds? How do you know?" The rock looked no more remarkable than the others we had been working through all morning.

"The serpent told me." She pointed, but the serpent was gone.

"I didn't hear it say anything," I said.

"That's the strange thing. It never speaks, but I still hear its words."

"Is it the same serpent who gave you cucumber seeds?"

She nodded, enthusiastic. "He was the one to give me the idea to craft a pitcher with a handle. And the elevated bed, and those swimming techniques and—"

My eyes widened. "I thought those were your ideas."

She shrugged. "I have learned to listen to the serpent when it speaks. It is a clever one. Still, it only gives hints. I have had to figure out how to make it all work. So, really, I am the clever one, am I not?" She grinned mischievously and pressed her shoulder into my chest.

I chuckled and wrapped her in my arms. "Of course. What does a beast have on my love? Even one so clever as that serpent."

She lifted the rock and smiled at it expectantly. "Shall we take a look?"

We took her stone to the boulder and broke it open to find the largest emerald we had yet seen. It measured the size of both my fists pressed together.

I wish I could say the shiver that ran through my bones at the sight of it was the realization of the serpent's true intent. Instead, it was excitement at the thought of finding the serpent and asking it to reveal the secret things of the world. What Father would not answer when I asked him.

For there were questions Father remained silent on, and even a small few that he commanded me to not ask about again, like when I asked him again what Good and Evil were.

I would not seek the answers to those mysteries, of course. Only those that Father meant to reveal yet had not gotten around to.

I took other smaller stones and began chipping away at the excess still attached to the gem. As we worked to free the emerald from its encasing, Father returned with fruit for all three of us from the Tree of Life. His was already partially eaten, and when he saw the emerald, he said, "That is a wonderful jewel."

"Indeed," Eve said, and I remember feeling the strangest urge to quiet her. "The gray serpent told us to try opening this rock, and we are very glad we listened."

"The serpent speaks much to you," he said.

Eve smiled and tipped her head. "He's become my little friend."

Father turned to me. "Does it speak with you too?"

I shook my head.

"Interesting." His long stare sent another shiver down my back.

I forced in several bites of the fruit Father brought. My mind not on the taste, but on whether I would be able to find the serpent later that day, and what it would do when I spoke to it. Would it speak only to Eve? I never remembered hearing its voice.

If it wouldn't speak to me, none of my questions would find answers. What would—

Father's arm slid around me, and I felt the tension melt from my shoulders. I looked up at his expression. Welcoming, but serious. Like a Father who knows his son is caught in things far beyond him.

"You know that I love you," he said.

"I know," I said. "And I love you."

"I know." But his mouth curved downward. "Stay awake. Stay aware. Remain with her."

I looked at Eve, who was chipping away at the remnants of the stone around the emerald.

"All right," I said.

He smiled, then, but there was something unhappy about it, as if his eyes had forgotten to listen. "Have you tended to your new gardens yet, today?"

I groaned in realization. "Not since the day before yesterday, when we rested." I broke from him and knelt beside Eve.

Her dark eyes glittered at me, and her teeth peeked from behind her lips. "I've almost got it."

I leaned forward and kissed her on the forehead. She smiled and wiped her skin, then focused once more on freeing the jewel. Forehead creased. Lips pressed together.

"When you're done," I said, "let's tend the new gardens."

She nodded. Stone ground on stone as she chipped it off. Bits of grit struck my skin.

"There," she said and lifted it. Pure green gleamed as she twirled it in her hands. She took a deep breath and blew it out hard. "Finished, for now."

I stood and offered her my hand. She took it and leaned into me. "Ready?"

"Ready!"

We started down the path toward the gardens, my eyes canvassing the treetops for gleaming, gray skin.

"I'll come too," Father said.

"Oh," I said and reverted my eyes to the path before us. "Very well."

The walk was pleasant, but warm. Even in the shade, sweat glistened across our arms despite the breeze that wound its way through the narrow paths.

Always, Father's footsteps remained just behind ours.

We reached the little gardens that had begun to grow and unwound a bit of the fencing we'd erected to keep out the grazing beasts. Eve and I entered and crouched, pulling little flowers and grasses that had begun to grow in the dark, loamy soil between vegetables.

Most of the first garden seemed well-watered but for the southern corner. A large beast, perhaps one of the elephants that made their home nearby, had upset the irrigation by stepping on the ditches we'd dug.

I took up the hoe again and deepened the ditches where the water failed to flow. Soon, moisture flooded the little pathways and began to seep into the soil next to our young vegetables' roots.

In this area, there was enough sunlight to feed young plants, yet for part of the day, the fruit trees offered a dappled covering for the plants who disliked direct, heavy sun.

Still, a few of the plants that hadn't gotten enough water had dry, brown leaves shriveled by the heat. We pulled those off to make way for fresh, new growth, and to ensure the water and nutrients fed only what would bear good fruit.

After, we moved to the second new garden in another opening farther down the way. Our work there was similar.

At no time did Father help us. This was no real surprise, for he had slowly let us bear more and more responsibility. And he had fathered us and put us in his garden to tend it.

Still, even before having our eyes opened to evil, I realized his words and behavior were a warning for me to be wary of the serpent. Only, I could not imagine why.

Because if Father had formed the serpent, why should I be wary of it? I was not wary of anything in the garden. None of the beasts posed us danger. They were all kind to us. And none of the plants could harm us, either.

Except . . .

My eyes widened as I stared through the thicket and visualized the Tree of the Knowledge of Good and Evil sprouting from that little island amidst the lake, branches spread toward the sky.

He had told us to be wary of that tree. It was bad for us, and if a bad tree existed, that meant Father had created it. Didn't it?

I could not decide. Curiosity bubbled out of me in shallow breaths. I chewed my knuckle as I considered odd possibilities that I had never considered before.

Could it be that Father had not created everything in this

world? What if there were other creatures who made things? Who knew the secret things we knew nothing of?

Eve and I made things, in our own crude way. What if the craft of making things could be refined to such an art that new creatures and beings could be formed?

I glanced through the trees again, but saw no gray form watching me.

Could it be that the Tree of the Knowledge of Good and Evil was the one thing created by the gray serpent, and not by Father?

After all, Father was very good. And everything he did and made was good. So, how could he make something not good?

Unless the tree actually *was* good. But then, why could we not eat of it? He had told us to stay away from it.

I turned and saw Father watching me. That same serious look on his face.

He shook his head and turned away, and I felt the urge to go to him, throw my arms around him, and assure him that I loved him and would always follow him.

I regret to this day that I turned away and sat in the dust instead.

What a fool I was, Enoch. What a raging, sorrowful fool.

. . .

Father left us. At the time, I felt it a gift. An opportunity to find the serpent and discover the truth of the matter.

Now, I realize it for what it was. Father giving the opportunity for my heart to bear what fruit it had begun to tend.

You must understand that at that time, I still had not disobeyed. I had no sin in me. No corrupt nature pushing me to indulge in evil. I merely had innocent curiosity.

But that curiosity had been fed by the presence of evil, which seemed to me foreign and unrecognizable. And Eve's relationship to the serpent was as innocent as you could imagine.

That was why, when I approached Eve and said, "Let us search for the gray serpent again," she rubbed the dirt from her knees and examined me.

"That sounds wonderful. But what about the fruit trees? We have not tended them yet."

"Do you not think the serpent will be resting in one of the trees? We can tend to those that need our help as we search for it."

She nodded and smiled. "Sure. But why are you interested in the serpent? Did the emerald change your mind?"

I turned away. "I want to ask it questions."

She hopped into my view and laughed, trying to steal my attention. "What sorts of questions?"

I smiled despite myself. "Questions of the secret things Father has yet to tell us."

Her smile broke, and her eyes dimmed as she thought through the meaning of that. "Not the forbidden questions?"

"No, not those. Merely those Father has yet to answer."

"Like what?"

I shrugged. "I have not decided yet."

One of her eyebrows raised. "But you know you want to ask of the secret things."

"Do you not, as well?"

She tilted her head. "The serpent has given me knowledge in the past, so I suppose it makes sense that we could ask more of it."

"Do you know where it makes its den?"

Eve shook her head and examined our surroundings. "No. But I have tended to see it often near the pomegranates and the pineapple brush. Perhaps we could begin looking there."

I laced my fingers through hers and kissed her thick, beautiful lips. "Lead the way."

. . .

The pomegranates housed colorful birds and a family of

little monkeys, but no gray serpent. A sloth crawled between the pineapple brush with a baby clinging to its back, and we stepped over it as we made our way to the stone-fruit orchard.

We climbed through peach trees and shook plums loose. We rattled brush with sticks and called for the gray serpent.

Nothing.

Eve squeezed my hand and leaned into my shoulder. "I think it is time to return."

"To what?"

"Our work."

"We've worked enough. We can learn something of the ways of the world as afternoon crawls on."

She looked up at me, wanting to argue but holding back.

"Come," I said. "Let us follow the bend of the river."

She looked back the direction we came, expression unsure.

"I am going, if you are not," I said. "But earlier, Father told me we should stay together. Would you disregard his advice?"

Her gaze shot back to mine. Brows edged downward. "He said that?"

I nodded.

She crouched and thought hard. "If I come with you, we will work later tonight."

"Very well," I said and offered her my hand.

She stared at it and folded her arms.

When she did not take my hand, I turned and walked on, and she stood and followed at a distance.

The pathway flowed left, then right over rolling hills covered with fruit-bearing trees of all kinds until the roaring rush of water crept through the rustle of leaves. As the orchards ended, we found our path aligned with the side of the Pishon. The clear water toppled over uneven stones that tossed up white rapids. Fish leapt, gaping mouths arcing through the air while other larger fish lurked like shadows in the reeds.

I stopped and felt my breath seize as I glimpsed something out across the water.

"What?" Eve said.

Colorful snakes slithered across the surface. "Water snakes."

She smirked and shook her head. "They don't look like the gray serpent at all."

"No, I know," I said. But for a moment, the shimmer of their scales had fooled me.

As we arrived at the last little hill, a tributary split from the Pishon, the one that fed the little lake where the forbidden tree stood atop a little grassy knoll.

I led Eve to the edge of the fresh water, where myriad animals gathered to drink and wash. Otters floated on their backs past giraffes whose long tongues lapped the water. I stepped beside one's towering spotted legs and patted its fur.

It glanced back at me, then drank more, neck bent, legs sprawled to let it reach.

Eve walked to the edge and submerged her feet. The waves slapped her ankles as she smiled at the animals.

I stepped beside her, the cool liquid balancing the heat of the sun on my skin. I took a deep breath and let it out slow, listening to the steady rush of the lake on the shore, the distant splashing of the beasts wetting themselves, and the flutter of pelican wings overhead. My eyes followed the slow wave of the forbidden tree in the distance.

I nearly suggested we turn back. Father's prohibition, along with the chasm separating us from the tree, rendered the idea of swimming to the small island ludicrous.

I lifted my thumb to point back toward the orchard just as a cold, slithering form dragged smooth scales across my ankle. I jumped back and looked down to find the gray serpent shooting into the water.

With clawed feet paddling and slender body shifting side to side to propel it forward at a deceptively quick pace, the serpent swiveled its head back and looked at us with one silver eye. Its tongue flashed through the air as it dipped flush with the water and made its way toward the grassy knoll.

Without a thought, I splashed after. When the water became too deep, I dove, body gliding effortlessly through crystalline water. I bobbed to the surface and began propelling myself with arms and legs, tipping my face to the side to breathe.

After a moment, I heard a second splash.

I made my way slowly, and by the time I crawled onto the grassy knoll, my limbs and chest burned with exhaustion. Eve stood ahead of me, her dark form shaking as the wind dried the water from her skin.

The serpent hung from a low branch, staring at us just as it had when it gifted us with those dried cucumber seeds.

I struggled to a stand and Eve swallowed hard.

"It is touching the tree," she said.

"Yes," I said.

"It has not died," she said, confusion and worry rippling across her features.

"Father prohibited us, not the serpent. The creature will be fine."

She sighed. "I was worried it might have made a fatal mistake."

"I love that about you."

"What?"

"Your protectiveness."

"I care for it," she said.

"Like I care for you."

She smiled and pulled her wet, wild hair behind her ears.

"Come, taste and see," I heard. A thin, distant voice.

I looked from the serpent to Eve. "Did you hear that?"

She nodded, brows furrowed, mouth twisted in a frown. "But why would it tell us to taste what has been forbidden?"

I shrugged. "Perhaps it does not know that we have been forbidden to eat it. Come, let us speak with it, to find what it wants."

I pulled her up the hill till we were nearly within reach, but she resisted me.

"Serpent," I said, and it looked at me. "What do you speak of?"

"I don't want to speak to you," it said, its mouth unmoving. Eyes reflecting everything like perfect, round mirrors.

I frowned. "But I want to talk to you."

It turned from me and nuzzled Eve's cheek.

She frowned and said, "Good morning, serpent."

Its tongue flickered like flashing flames.

Her eyes widened, and her cheek twitched.

"What?" I said. "Is it speaking to you? I can't hear it."

She nodded and cleared her throat. "It asked if God truly said, 'You can't eat from any tree in the garden.' He never said such a thing, did he?"

"Of course not. Father himself has given us much fruit to eat in his presence."

The muscles in her face relaxed, and she gently pushed the serpent back. "You heard him. We may eat the fruit of the trees in the garden. But about the fruit of this tree here, in the middle, God said, 'You must not eat it, or touch it, or you will die.'"

Its tongue flashed again, and had it not been a serpent, I would have said it was smiling.

Eve twisted away and stopped her ears with her hands. Her breaths came in shallow pulses, and she walked down the knoll to the edge of the water to sit.

The serpent glanced at me but stayed on its perch as I went and laid a hand across her back.

"No," she said. "I will not speak with it anymore. I do not like how its words make me feel."

"What did it say?"

"Ask it yourself."

I stood and stared at it.

Its tongue flashed at me. Silver eyes peering from the sides of its slender, triangular head.

I ascended the hill and said, "Serpent. What did you say to Eve?"

"I don't want to speak to you."

"Answer me," I said.

But its only response was to slither farther up the branches.

I returned to Eve and said, "It still will not speak to me."

She huffed out a breath and looked across the water while hugging her legs and resting her chin on her knees.

"You must tell me what it said to you."

"It said, 'No! You will not die.'" She lay back on the grass, squinting in the light peering through the clouds above. "Which is it? Will we die, or won't we?"

"We must ask it what it means," I said.

"Why?"

"Because I do not know the answer. But it wants to speak with you. It knew how to dry cucumber seeds. It knew we wanted them, while no other beast seems to understand our language. It knew techniques for crafting we had not even imagined. It knew——"

"I know——" She raised her hand to quiet me as she pushed herself up on her elbows. Face set as she stared out across the water. Thoughts churned behind her eyes. "I remember. But if the serpent is true, how can Father also be true?"

I shrugged. "That is why we must speak with it. We must understand what is happening, for we have encountered nothing like this in all our time here. This is our responsibility. To care for this garden."

She looked back at the tree.

I offered her my hand and helped her stand.

We walked back and stood under the wide branches.

"Serpent," Eve called with her hands cupped around her mouth. "What do you mean that we will not die?"

Something heavy crashed through the leaves and fell through the branches. Eve cried out and reached to catch it, likely thinking the serpent itself was falling. Instead, a massive, ripe fruit landed in her hands and she stared at it, mouth gaping as she glanced back at me. Fear and fascination alternating across her features.

"I am . . .," she said.

I nodded. "Alive. Yes."

Slowly, her frown turned to a smile.

Even as my frown deepened.

I did not realize in that moment that I was feeling the approaching footsteps of evil. But the swirling confusion paralyzed me. I felt the desire to turn back, but had I not wanted to speak with the serpent about the fruit?

The serpent's head swooped down from the branches and let out a slow hiss that sounded like laughter. Then, we both heard its voice. "You see? I speak the truth. And I will speak more now. God knows that when you eat of this fruit, your eyes will be opened, and you will be like God, knowing good and evil."

Eve showed me the fruit. Hesitantly, I ran my hands across its leathery texture. It was warm, as if it had been sitting in the sun. Shades of purple ran across its uneven form, and though it looked strange, the smell of its skin was like the aroma of many flowers at once.

"This is a very large fruit," she said. "So large that I would guess that if we ate it, we would not hunger the rest of this day."

I thought a moment. Father himself had called it the Tree of the Knowledge of Good and Evil, so I did not doubt that eating the fruit would give us wisdom that we had not yet had the privilege of receiving.

Why then had he warned us?

Eve stared at the fruit as if it were a gateway into every secret.

For comfort, I laid my hand over hers. "Eve? Perhaps . . ."

She pressed herself against me, and I could feel the sweat gleaming across her skin. Could see the rapid thumping of the pulse in her neck. She looked up at me, and I could tell by the look in her eyes that she had already decided what she would do. "If I eat of it, and something happens to me. Would you . . .?"

I slid my arms around her waist. Conflicting thoughts raged through my mind and twisted my emotions into a muddled mess. Yet the only words that reached my mouth were, "You are my love. My only . . ." Tears grew in my eyes.

She kissed me on the cheek, and we held each other and sighed to relieve the pressure in our chests. I felt so strange and could see in her eyes that she felt the same. She trembled beneath my fingers.

She raised the fruit slowly.

My eyesight dimmed, and I remembered what the serpent first said to us as we approached. *"Taste and see."* The serpent had invited us to eat the fruit. It had led us out here on purpose. It knew what we had been looking for.

Except, Eve had not been looking for it; I had. But that hardly mattered in the moment.

Because it had fooled her into thinking the fruit was good to eat, and muddled my brain enough that I had done nothing to stop it.

We both wanted to be like God. Why wouldn't we? He was our Father. We wanted to ascend and see new wisdom with eyes unclouded, as every child does.

And I knew what I had spoken to her was the truth. She was my love. My passion. The very best part of me, taken, and formed by the hands of our Father himself.

My helper.

I did not want to live without her. In that moment I felt convinced that I could not live separated from her, just as I could not live separated from Father.

She pressed the fruit against her teeth and punctured the skin, sending dark red juice dripping. She chewed long and slow. Grimacing as the flavor spread. She swallowed and shivered, then handed me the fruit. "Eat."

I grabbed the fruit and brought it to my mouth. But now, amidst the scent of flowers wafted an old rotten smell, as if the fruit's insides had decayed and now churned with poison.

I looked from the fruit to Eve, who shuddered like a bush during a storm. She was still alive. She had not died as we thought might happen.

I shook my head. Had I really just hesitated to make certain I would not die? What was wrong with me? How could I now leave Eve to her fate out of fear of sickness or death?

I brought the fruit to my mouth and bit down hard and fast, before any other thoughts could take hold of me.

The flavor of coppery blood filled my mouth. A euphoric rush sped my breathing, followed by a dark, oily flavor that stopped my throat and darkened my vision. With difficulty, I chewed and forced the bite down.

It slid long and slow, and my stomach threatened to regurgitate everything. I covered my mouth and coughed, letting the rest of the fruit fall from my hand and roll to the lake, where it slowly bled red into the clear water in thin rivulets.

Nausea rose like a tide, and I moaned and spit the remaining juice to relieve myself, if only for a moment. My skin felt cold as winter soil. I was certain countless unseen eyes stared at my uncovered flesh like vultures wanting to peck at a carcass. I wrapped my arms around myself and glanced at Eve, who now held herself and rocked, eyes dashing back and forth.

What was happening? For the first time, I felt self-conscious. As if my feet could not be planted in the right spot, and my body never poised in a manner pleasing to the eyes. I had never before cared about being right, because I only knew wholesomeness. Never felt the need to prove myself because I had never felt unacceptable. Never felt the voracious lust to be good, because I had only known that I *was* as I had been *made*.

Now, for the first time, I felt that it would be good for me to be *unmade*.

For every blemish in my skin, every mannerism, every action and word, and every thought had been tipped sideways.

Distant Music came to us on a sudden wind. Its melody familiar and warm.

My eyes widened and I said, "Eve, do you hear that?"

She quieted and, after a moment, began to weep. She buried her face in her hands and returned to rocking.

"It is the Music I heard at the beginning of everything," I said.

"Yes," she said, her voice thick and shaking. "I know it."

But now we can no longer dance to it, I thought. For I knew that if I set my feet to it, I would be like a drunkard profaning the beauty of the sacred. The beating pulse in my veins had been replaced with the stumbling rhythm of a different Music altogether. No longer sacred but irreverent and carnal.

What had happened to us? We were still alive, but we had been changed. The very thought of Father made me want to run.

I was a naked, foolish, evil man. I had pushed Eve to come to this cursed place, and now we had eaten the cursed fruit. I had listened to Eve. And she had listened to—

The serpent!

I twisted toward the tree and searched for any sign of the beast but saw only branches and leaves heavily laden with fruit that slowly waved in the lake breeze.

A hippo moaned in the distance, and I crouched and looked for somewhere to hide.

"We were wrong," I said.

"Don't speak to me."

The bitter bite in her voice twisted me toward her. The way she glared at me. I knew not what it was in that moment, for I had never encountered it. But I know now that it was hatred. For the first time since I had woken to the Light of my Maker, I was encountering the hatred of another creature.

How cruel that my fear of separation from her had pushed me to the very sin that now separated us. The ache of the sudden void between us threatened to crush my soul. I reached for her, but she slapped my hand away and growled, "Don't touch me!"

I stood, dumbfounded.

Her eyes took in my figure from top to bottom, and the growing grimace on her face sent heat to my neck. I rushed to the tree and grabbed hold of the branch the gray serpent had sat upon, shaking it as if to break it while sending more fruit thudding to the earth. "Serpent! Come out to face me!"

The echo of my anger ricocheted off the hills and came back once and again. The sound of the desperation in my own voice drained the warmth from my face.

I stopped and looked back at Eve, who now glared at the water as if she would descend beneath it, never to surface again. I let go of the branch and looked at my hands, which shook. I felt what she felt. For we had lost our innocence and now ached for what had been taken. Into that void poured only bitter regret that fueled a fury as deep and hot as a forest fire. My fingers clenched into fists.

I looked at Eve once more and felt the compulsion to strike her. I was trying to give her what she longed for, yet she had rejected me. Was it not her fault that I had eaten the fruit? If she had not, I would not have. If she had not listened to the serpent and told me what it said, I would not have been changed.

She made her choice. How could she hate me for her own mistakes?

"Eve," I said. Fury carving my voice into a growl. "Look at me."

"Shut your mouth," she said.

That sent a wash of red over my vision. What happened next, I remember like a terrible dream.

I rushed over and grabbed her by the hair. She cried out and thrust her elbow into my abdomen, drawing a grunt from me, but I held on and spoke through gritted teeth, "Don't you dare talk to me like that."

Eve's face twitched. "Let. Go."

My eyes narrowed, and I drew hard at the air through flared nostrils. I wish I could say that I had the self-control to do as she said. But I was facing powerful emotions I had never before encountered. I was confused, searching for a way to make sense of what had happened.

I thrust her away.

She fell and toppled down the knoll to the edge of the water, where she glared up at me. Only now, amidst the hatred, came tears. She swiped at them and turned so that I would not see her cry.

My mind was spinning beneath the tumultuous storm of contrary emotions. I ached for her pain, yet when I thought of how she'd disrespected me, I still wanted to strike her. I knew what I was feeling was perverse and should never be, but it did not matter. Evil had taken root inside me, and its potency was overwhelming. I could feel it pulsing like a living thing, a clot of darkness in the base of my throat.

How could I hope to fight it? You must understand, Enoch. I am not making excuses. I realize that my sin is my own. I chose slavery for me and for all who would come after. Still, if I had truly believed that there would be no turning back, I would never have made my choice.

Yet even if Father had told me the dangers in great detail, I would have found a way to disbelieve him.

Everyone strives to blame another for sin, but sin is inside us. Sin is the purposeful twisting of our hearts to anything other than our original Father. Everything that happened from then on was my fault. I know that now.

At the time, I had no idea.

Chapter 8

We stayed on that grassy knoll until our skin completely dried. But again, on a rush of wind, I heard the distant Music of our Father, and a shiver shook my shoulders. I crossed to Eve on hands and knees to keep low to the ground and avoid being seen. "Eve," I whispered.

"What do you want?" Her voice was thick with emotion. The hatred was gone, replaced by a flood of tears that matted her hair to her cheeks.

This time, I did not make the mistake of reaching out to her. "We must find a way of hiding our nakedness."

Her arms were already covering her breasts, and her legs were pulled up underneath her. She looked down at herself. Back across the water.

I stood and waded into the water, and she did the same. When the water covered my torso, I dove forward and swam back.

I could hear her strong strokes beside me. Again, as before, she passed me. We reached the other side, and I splashed out, realizing only then that all the animals were gone. Everything in the garden had gone silent. Even the breeze had calmed, except for that sudden wind every now and then, which carried quiet melodies to our ears.

I led her back to the orchard of fruit trees, searching for somewhere to hide. But even the closest portions of the forest seemed bare and exposed.

I leaned against a date palm as Eve stood looking at the treetops for any sign of the birds. Then my eyes caught the smooth leaves of a cluster of fig trees. "Eve," I said.

She rubbed her arms to warm herself and did not respond.

"Can you think of a way to tie those leaves together?"

She crossed to the leaves and tore a few away, examining them backward and forward. After a long moment, she nodded and strode away, holding them over her naked form.

I gathered a bunch of leaves for myself and jogged after.

I followed the sound of her footsteps, but as the wind came again, it brought the Music louder and threatened to drown out the sound of her in the garden.

I burst into a sprint and held my breath.

After rounding a corner, I found her crouching among the river reeds. She was pulling stalks and stripping them into long, thin lines. She sat cross-legged in the dust and poked holes in the fig leaves with her little finger. I tried not to cower at the sense that something was coming to meet us.

She glanced up, saw me staring at her beautiful, naked figure, and covered herself again. "Stop looking at me like that."

I cleared my throat and crossed my arms, trying to calm the heat that rose to my face. "You are my wife."

She raised her chin proudly and said, "You are *my* husband. And you will listen to me. Or I will give you none of myself."

I sat and drew with my fingers in the dust to suppress an angry reply.

She began to thread the reed fibers through the leaves, then tied them together to make a sort of belt. She packed several of these reed fibers with leaves and knotted them around her own torso. She nodded, satisfied, then motioned for the leaves I had brought.

I handed them to her, and she did the same.

I needed her help to knot the belt, for her fingers were thin and nimble where mine were thick and strong. As she finished, bent double to see her work, she steadied herself with her palms on my hips and rose to meet my gaze.

I raised my hands to her shoulders, a soft, silent apology. The feel of her dark skin warmed my chest. She brought her arms over her chest and tentatively leaned into me. I held her, and together, we shuddered.

Then, on another rush of sudden wind, came our Father's Music. And with it, the sound of footsteps—distant, but clear.

My breath stopped, and my pulse sped as my vision dimmed. Eve's head rose, and we both looked down the road through the orchard.

"Come," I said. "We must find somewhere to hide."

She nodded, and we ran to lay in the underbrush.

His bare feet slowly crushed fallen leaves and cracked a twig. He stopped. Turned once as if sensing something near. His Light, for the first time, was gone. Or maybe it was so dim we could not sense it.

I held an arm around Eve, pressing her harder against the ground, until she squirmed. But neither of us dared to breathe or speak.

But our Father knew, and he called to us, "Where are you?"

I pressed my forehead to the earth from which he had formed me. Wishing that I could disappear back into it and never face the disappointment I knew we would see in his eyes.

"Adam?" came his voice again.

Something was moving near us in the brush. A slow, slithering hiss. I saw the glint of silver scales and stood. Eve grabbed at my wrist as I rose as if to stop me, but I pulled away.

The bush we hid in had scratched my skin and drew little drops of blood, but it stood roughly waist-high, so half of me stayed exposed.

Father stared at me. Eyes wet with compassion and sorrow.

I looked down, unable to meet his gaze for more than a

moment. That's when I saw the triangular head of the serpent gazing up at me from beneath the covering of the bush.

Eve finally rose beside me and clung to my arm.

"I heard the sound of you in the garden," I said, "and I was afraid, because I was naked. So I hid myself."

Father sighed, and I noticed for the first time he was clothed in a white robe rather than the earthy, brown tunics he normally wore. "Who told you that you were naked?"

I stepped out from the bush and kicked a stone through the dust toward the serpent, who slithered out as well. Eve followed, nearly falling as she tried to keep hold of my arm.

"I, uh . . ." I searched for some way to explain how I knew that I was naked.

"Have you eaten of the tree of which I commanded you not to eat?" he said.

I looked up and tried to shrug away Eve, who kept pulling on me. I felt I would perish beneath his slow, intense gaze and struggled to find a way to explain why I had made such a terrible mistake. After what seemed an infinite silence, I grasped at the only thing that might take his eyes from me. "The woman, whom you gave to be with me . . . she gave me fruit, and I ate."

Eve gasped and looked up at me with narrowed eyes. The serpent's tongue flickered out, and we both looked down at it. She pointed and said, "The serpent deceived me, and I ate!"

Father stepped forward, and the Light suddenly burst into full intensity like a transparent flame at the center of a great fire. "Serpent!"

The serpent twisted and writhed in the Light, clawed feet clenching, bones cracking. It hissed and groaned as if in great pain.

"Because you have done this," Father said, "cursed are you above all livestock and above all beasts of the field; on your belly you shall go, and dust you shall eat all the days of your life. I will put enmity between you and the woman, and between your offspring and her offspring; he shall bruise your head, and you shall bruise his heel."

The serpent spun away, as if released, and slithered off, hissing through the brush.

Then Father turned toward Eve, who finally let go of me, and now cowered with her arms over her face. "I will surely multiply your pain in childbearing; in pain you shall bring forth children. Your desire shall be contrary to your husband, but he shall rule over you."

Then, he pointed at me, and I thought that my heart would burst asunder, for it beat so quickly and violently. I felt such an intense desire to sprint away that my legs crumbled beneath me. "You! Because you have listened to the voice of your wife, and have eaten of the tree of which I commanded you, 'You shall not eat of it,' cursed is the ground because of you; in pain you shall eat of it all the days of your life; thorns and thistles it shall bring forth for you."

Now the ground in front of me split, and thin, green shoots shot up, covered in sharp points that grew and multiplied.

"And you shall eat the plants of the field," he said.

I looked at the beautiful orchard we stood in, and the earth began to tremble. The space between us and the trees all around lengthened as the soil expanded. My mind spun at the sudden sense of displacement. The space between me and Eve also expanded. As did the space between us and Father, who held out his hands as if silently commanding the earth to change before our very eyes.

Then his finger pointed at me again, and I felt that the righteous anger of my Father was directed double to me over Eve. "By the sweat of your face you shall eat bread, till you return to the ground, for out of it you were taken."

I breathed hard, barely strong enough to keep myself from planting my face in the dirt under the weight of the Light and his terrifying gaze. I had never before feared him. I had only experienced his love, acceptance, tenderness, and wise teaching.

Now all of that was gone. Replaced with distance and disappointment.

"For you are dust," my Father said, "and to dust you shall return."

My tears watered the earth and blurred my sight as I moaned.

The Light dimmed, and footsteps neared. My Father's soft hand lifted my chin.

I sat, knees splayed to either side. The fig leaf loin-cloth hardly kept together, seeming now so pathetic.

In Father's eyes, I saw only love, compassion, and grief as deep as the black between stars. "I will make you both a better covering."

Chapter 9

Father led us to a flock of sheep on a hillside just beyond the orchard. He knelt before a flawless male and held a stone knife to its neck. I glanced at Eve to see if she knew what he was doing, then grimaced as he dragged the blade through the beast's throat.

It twisted and tried to escape, but our Father held him close. Fear grew in its eyes as it realized what was being done to it. Blood flowed down its wool and stained our Father's white tunic. Tears grew in our Father's eyes, and he buried his face in its shoulder.

When the last of the life had left the animal, our Father began the slow, terrible work of skinning it. Eve and I could hardly watch. The sun moved on from its zenith toward the edge of the sky by the time Father finished my covering. I tried it on, and he made adjustments so it fit me well.

Then he began work on Eve's covering.

By the time he finished, the blood had dried and caked on his clothing, and his hands were stained and glistened in the failing sunlight.

Eve and I stood arm in arm to keep each other upright. Staring at our Father as he faced away from us toward the orchard. He spoke, then, as if to himself. His voice gentle, yet its resonance grew and grew until it shook the earth. "Behold, the man has become like one of us in knowing good and evil."

My head dipped in shame, for I knew the statement a bitter irony. This was what I had wanted, wasn't it? To be like God in knowing good and evil. Yet it was nothing like I imagined. And I hated myself for it.

"Now," our Father continued, "lest he reach out his hand and take also of the tree of life and eat, and live forever—"

He raised his hand and winced, as if the conclusion was too terrible to consider.

I remember the precise expression on Eve's face lit by the dark glow of that final sunset on Eden. Completely motionless. A figurine of perfect beauty. She became to me, in that instant, an object of worship. A distant, beautiful symbol of everything I wanted yet could not have.

For I had broken myself. Had broken the world. Had broken what we'd had in Eden. Yet I could not admit I had broken her. I longed for her to remain as she had been—perfect, unblemished. As though I had been the one to sin, and she had merely shown the grace to join me.

Then she glanced at me, and that dark shadow of hatred hovered over her features once more. Shame stuck like a millstone in my throat. I stared at our feet and let go of her arm, readying myself for what tattered life remained ahead. For I felt certain that I could not regain my Father's closeness. Yet if that were true, I had nothing left but her. And she hated me.

What could I possibly do but pour all of myself into discovering how to earn back her love?

Father turned and set his hands on our shoulders. We looked up at him. Tears streamed down his face and bid the same from our eyes. "My children," he said, "I love you. But you can no longer live in this temple as priests. For you have turned yourselves into broken cisterns."

"But why?" Eve said, voice warbling. "Why can we not remain with you just like this?"

Father's eyes dimmed, and he looked into the distance beyond us, as if witnessing the great multitude of sacrifices that would come after. "The beasts I slayed to cover your nakedness are a temporary atonement. The blood of innocent animals could never wash away your evil, only cover it for a moment. Human life is all that can atone for human sin. That is why, Eve."

"No," she said and threw her arms around our Father. Father held her and rubbed her back. They wept together. I stared at the blood crusted on his white garments.

Then turned away.

"I promise that I have already made a way," our Father said. "Through your lineage, a man will come. And he will make atonement for everything."

I turned back to them and saw the longing in Eve's expression.

I bowed low to the ground, and Eve joined me.

"May he come quickly," she said.

"Adam," our Father said and lifted us both to our feet.

"Yes?"

"Remember me."

"Remember you?" I said. "How could I not? You are my . . ." Words failed me. Who exactly was he to me, now? I did not know. Only that I longed for him. For his acceptance. For life to be as it once was. For peace with the God-man I called Father.

"I will lead you out."

Over a long, dirt road, he led us far away from the orchards, to the outer edge of Eden. Then, after we made it some way into the wilderness only sparsely populated with green growth and wildlife, he turned and waved his hand toward Eden.

The earth groaned and rolled, and great cliffs rose around the land we had come to call home. A small entrance formed at the east end, directly in front of us. And a bright creature descended from heaven wielding a flashing flame that twisted back and forth as if searching for something to devour.

A guard to keep us from the Tree of Life and the garden temple of our Father.

Father did not look at us again. His shoulders shook with quiet sobs.

Eve and I turned away, and I reached for her hand, and she let me take it.

Step by step, we walked away.

"Adam!"

I turned back, heart racing with the final remnants of hope that he might change his mind and make a way for everything to return to how it had been.

"If you return to this place next year with a fitting sacrifice like the ones you saw today," he said, "I will meet you outside the garden."

Tears fell hot from my face. I nodded.

Finally, we turned and entered the unimaginable dangers of the wilderness with nothing but the skins our Father had crafted for us.

PART II

Outside Eden

Chapter 10

The fire that Enoch and Adam sat around had died without Enoch noticing. So enraptured had he been in Adam's tale that he associated the deep chill with the dark words spoken.

Now Adam fell silent, as if lost in deep contemplation.

Enoch took the opportunity to rise and gather more fire-wood, along with tinder. But it was hard to see in the dark, and he had to pat the ground for the flint he'd dropped earlier. It lay beside the wood Adam sat on.

He piled his tinder in the center of the dead fire and sparked it to life before layering twigs and sticks and logs in slow intervals.

As the heat grew, Adam shook himself from his revelry and warmed his hands. "Thank you," he said. "I hadn't realized how cold the air was."

Enoch watched him a good while. Not daring so soon to ask him to continue.

But his curiosity was mounting, and Adam had left so much untold.

"So," Enoch said.

Adam tipped his head toward him, expectant.

"How did you do it?" Enoch said.

"Do what?" Adam said.

"Win her love back?"

Adam's face twitched into a frown. "Who said I did?"

"But—"

Adam scowled and waved Enoch's words away. "She stayed with me because there was no one else. She would have died if she had gone off on her own. She knew that. She was no fool."

"Yet before she passed," Enoch said, "I saw the smile on her face as she laced her fingers through yours at the first harvest feast."

"That's the human condition. Good and evil hopelessly interwoven." He laced his fingers together and acted as if he were trying to pull them apart to no avail. He shrugged and scoffed, as if that illustrated his point well enough.

A long moment stretched between them, broken only by the crackle of the flames.

Enoch felt a surge of anger for the first time since sitting with Adam. "That's it? That's your story? You broke the world and now there's no hope? What about the Almighty's promise? The shades between love and hate? I may be young, but I'm not so foolish as to have walked through this life with a covering over my eyes. You're holding back."

"I'm telling the truth."

"You're being cowardly and dishonest."

Adam chuckled and leaned forward, resting his elbows on his knees. "I wish I had your youthful pride and vigor."

That seemed to Enoch a belittling dismissal. He pointed at Adam and felt the fire grow in his bones. "You said you would share your whole story."

Adam raised his hand as if to calm him. "Patience. I need to say my piece before continuing. Because in the end, you'll see. And you'll agree with me."

"What if I don't?"

The expression on Adam's face broke, and he seemed for a moment like a lost child glimpsing his home in the distance. "I would love to know it."

"If you tell the whole story as you said you would, I will not withhold my thoughts." Enoch looked at the silver moon in the sky and was reminded of the gray serpent. Where had it gone after Father pronounced its judgment? Was it up in the sky, looking down at them now? Or had it followed Adam and Eve into the wilderness?

When Adam first began speaking of the garden, his words had flowed like a rushing river, pent up for countless years. Enoch dared not stop it, once it began again. The myriad questions multiplying in him would only get in the way. "So," Enoch said. "What happened next?"

Adam nodded and took a deep breath. "No rest for a weary old man, eh?"

Enoch shook his head. "I don't think either of us would be able to sleep now."

Another chuckle. "I suppose you're right." He stood with a groan and turned his face to the shadows as if to remember his first night outside the garden. "We wandered until . . ."

Chapter 11

We wandered until our feet ached and the moon hung high in the black sky strewn with stars. The air was colder than I remembered it being before. As though the trees of Eden had stood like bulwarks against the onslaught of the bitter wind that now made us huddle in the cleft of boulders, where we stopped halfway through the night to hold each other. I didn't speak, and neither did she. Words only brought attention to the fact that I had no idea how to help us.

What did we need? Why had we walked so far in the dark? My mind felt hazy, thoughts unclear. My body still shook from the remnant of fear we felt in the approach of Father's footsteps in Eden. And we had no food to stymie the weakness that set in after.

As we lay back and nestled our bodies deeper into the crevice, she rested her head on my shoulder, and I closed my eyes and focused on the feel of her hair against my skin. I wrapped my arms around her and kissed her head, but she pulled away and turned from me.

"I was only trying to warm myself," she said.

I turned from her as well. It pained me to my core that she did not want me to touch her.

Was I so repulsive to her? Emotion rose hot to my face, even as my extremities shivered.

After a while, I felt her back press to mine, and I turned and she suffered me to wrap my arm around her. I wept silently into her hair until, finally, exhaustion overwhelmed me.

. . .

The morning came harsh and bright. My eyes and back ached in equal measure. I rolled to my stomach and rose on hands and knees, breathing deep to steady myself. I was weak with exhaustion, and my stomach was so empty I wondered if a pit had been delved inside, for I had never before experienced hunger so intense.

Eve was still asleep. The skin tunic that covered her naked-ness stood out as a bitter reminder of all that my dreams had made hazy.

I sat and shook my head as emotion swelled in my throat. "No," I whispered. "Father, it can't be true. Don't leave us out here."

But the sound of the wind against the dust and stones was the only response. We had broken our covenant and lost access to the beauty and safety of the garden. And now we would starve to death.

This was a barren, young country devoid of Father's bless-ing. Though the heat grew as the sun rose, harsh wind blew dirt in little swirls that stung the skin, because few grasses had yet spread their roots to hold the soil down.

I tried to swallow, but my tongue stuck to the roof of my mouth. I brought my fingers to my lips, which were dry and flaking. Confused, I pulled at the flakes, but doing so drew sharp pain and beads of warm blood. I sucked on my injured lip and climbed one of the boulders we'd slept beside to get a better view.

The boulder was large and round, and I nearly slid off, digging my nails in to find purchase. As I reached the top and assessed our surroundings, any hope left dropped through the pit in my abdomen.

There was nothing. No fruit trees. No wild beasts or birds. No rivers. Nothing but skeletal shrubs and hunched trees with sparse, dry leaves.

"Adam?" Eve said below me.

As I peered into the distance with squinted eyes, I thought I saw a small pool of water near a clutch of trees. I didn't see any fruit, but . . .

"Adam! Where are you?"

Eve held herself up on her elbow, looking left and right. Her voice had gained an edge of panic.

"I'm here," I said.

She jumped, then brought a hand to her chest. "You frightened me. What are you doing up there?" Anger flashed across her face.

"I think I found some water. Perhaps there, we might also find food." I slid down the boulder and nearly fell as my heels struck the earth. I offered her my arm, and she took hold of it and stood.

"What if there isn't any food?"

"Then we won't eat," I said. "I cannot make food grow from the soil. That is the work of—" I stopped myself, realizing it was no longer Father's work, but mine, and mine alone. "At least, I cannot do it overnight. Did you sleep?"

"Hardly." She yawned and stretched her arms into the sky. "My stomach hurt too much."

I echoed her yawn, then wiped my face to think of anything but how impossible it seemed that we would be able to survive long enough for what little food I might find and plant to grow. "Are you thirsty?"

She scowled. "How could I not be?"

"Then let us see if we can drink from the pool that I spotted in the distance."

"I want food," she said.

I walked around the boulder and started down the hill in the direction of that little cluster of trees where I thought I'd seen water.

"Wait," she said.

I ignored her on purpose. Satisfied to find some small way to treat her with the coldness I'd received from her the night before.

"Even if you find seeds to plant," Eve said, "we won't live long enough to tend them."

"How do you know?" I said, my hard steps sliding a bit in the gravel. "You don't know how long we can live without food."

"If it hurts this bad, we can't possibly continue for long."

"Stop being so weak."

She tried to grab my arm to slow me down, but I tore myself from her grasp and marched on faster, nearly stumbling on a loose stone that threatened to cut the skin of my foot.

She jogged to keep pace. "Slow down."

"No."

She cleared her throat, obviously irritated. "Why are you being so—"

I spun around. "Like you were last night?" Fury rose, and my vision dimmed as she stepped back, surprised.

Her voice quieted, and she pushed her unwieldy hair behind dark ears. "I let you hold me."

I scoffed. "You think that's enough?"

"What do you want from me?"

"I want—" *You to love me like you did.* The words stuck in my throat. I felt like a fool. Yet I could not deny the emotion that rose like a violent wave inside. I held my breath and gritted my teeth to push back the stinging in my eyes.

She bit her cheek and looked up at me with the first sign of compassion. I bit my tongue to ignore the rising humiliation at how my heart leapt for the care in her eyes. She reached out to touch me, but I turned away and pointed.

"Over there. We're not far now." I breathed deep as the emotion slowly disintegrated. I could not bear to let her see how much I needed her touch, because she had seemed perfectly fine avoiding mine. "Let's make it there before talking more of what we should do."

"Adam," she said.

But I was moving already, and she must have thought it best not to talk to me again, for she remained quiet until we reached the clutch of trees.

I stepped between the trees and stared down at a brackish little mud puddle.

She groaned and covered her head with her forearms before walking in a circle. "We're going to die."

The trees looked like they had never heard of the word fruit. And there was nothing around us but a scorpion that skittered into a hole beneath some rocks.

I crouched and peered into the hole.

"Don't tell me you're considering eating that," she said.

"Do you have any better ideas?"

She pointed at the trees.

I raised my brow. "Eat a tree?"

"No—" For a moment, that familiar look of loathing flashed across her face. "The leaves, you fool. I would try that long before one of those crawling . . ." She shivered.

I stood and tore three dry leaves and shoved them in my mouth. Yet no matter how much I chewed, they seemed only to break into smaller, inedible shards. After several failed attempts at swallowing, I gagged and spit the remainder onto the dirt. "Never again."

She ran her fingers across several greener leaves.

"Go ahead," I said.

She shook her head and looked again at the brackish pool.

I dipped once more and peered into the hole beneath those rocks. I pushed my hand in and scraped around to find the scorpion. Little legs scrambled away from my fingers. I pulled on one, felt a slight pinch, and let go. Then I took a deep breath and shoved my hand in hard and found the body of the thing. Just as I was about to pull it out, I felt a sharp sting and fell back with a cry, curling my hand in to protect it.

The scorpion dropped down just outside its hiding place, then ran away and disappeared.

I stared at the little red speck on the top of my right hand where the thing had stung me. Pain throbbed all around it. Eve was watching me from where she crouched beside the pool.

"What happened?" she said.

"It hurt me." I groaned as the pain intensified and throbbed slowly up my wrist in tandem with my pulse.

"Are you all right?" Concern clouded her expression.

I stood. "Yes." I cleared my throat and examined the little red sting again. It was not swelling. And it was such a small wound. But it hurt terribly.

"I tried the water," she said and flicked the leftover droplets from her hands. "It has sand in it, but it tastes clean enough."

I nodded and joined her, cupping water in my uninjured hand and trying to ignore the spreading waves of sharp pain climbing my forearm. After several sips, my mouth at least was wetted, though it did little to combat my thirst. I spit the grit that stuck between my teeth and then stood. "We need to keep moving."

"Where? And for what purpose? There's nothing out here," she said.

"You don't know that."

"We're cursed, Adam. Father is killing us as he said he would."

"He never said he would kill us. Only that we would die."

"What's the difference?" She crouched and hugged her knees, face twitching with emotion.

I blinked hard, trying to clear my vision. The world seemed to be tipping. "He told us to come back to the garden next year. That means he expects us to live at least that long."

"I don't want to live any longer feeling like this," she said. "I'd rather die."

The pain reached my shoulder, and my fingers began tingling. I looked at the sting on my hand, which still looked small and unassuming. I clenched my fingers, but they felt thick and slow. Warmth drained from my face, but I tried to ignore it. "Don't speak like that."

"I'll speak how I want. I feel so hollow and thin. As if all the substance of life has been poured out like the blood of that lamb Father . . ." She felt her clothing once more and winced, realizing the skin of the lamb she spoke of was now covering her body.

"You just need food and water. And rest. Once you have those, you'll feel better."

"You're lying," she said. "We'll never feel like we did in the garden. We ruined the world, Adam. And now we'll die for it."

She was right. And no amount of protesting would change that. "Well," I said, "I won't die waiting around thinking about how terrible everything is. Come."

I started to walk away, but Eve remained sitting, hugging her knees. "Go if you want. I'm staying."

But my legs felt untrustworthy. I looked at them and couldn't quite make out where they met the ground. I blinked hard and opened my eyes doubly wide, shaking my head to stop the sensation that everything was bending.

My steps slowed, and I waved my arms to try to maintain balance.

"Adam?" Eve said. "What are you doing?"

I cleared my throat as nausea rose in my belly like a tide. "Ohh," I said and winced as pain, tingling, and numbness engulfed my right arm and spread across my neck and side. It seemed to render my arm so heavy that I tilted to the side and fell.

"Adam!" Eve scuffled over to me.

Now that I was laying, the nausea overwhelmed me, and I retched foam, for there was nothing in my stomach.

Eve held my shoulders and angled my head so I could spit the vomit out and breathe. Her fingers were cold as ice, and I could hear the panic in her voice as she tried to talk to me, though her words seemed distant and muffled. "Open your eyes. Are you alright? What happened?"

"Sorry," I said, and my voice boomed through my head like thunder. "The sting."

She grabbed my hand and examined it. Found the little wound from the scorpion.

My body trembled, and sweat began to wet my skin.

"It is so small. What is happening?"

"I feel . . . cold."

"Adam, are you dying?"

I shook my head. "It will pass." But I had little faith it would, for the pain was everywhere. My sight was dim and distant, and the world spun around me.

I lay there for hours, and so far as I could tell, Eve tended to me as she could, bringing bits of water from the brackish pool, and warming my cold, sweating body.

What a fool. To be incapacitated by an insect sting. Yet in all my time in Eden, nothing had caused me pain like this.

Had this been part of the changes the world had undergone as a result of my sin? Was this, too, my fault?

The sun dimmed behind clouds as a storm rolled in. Thunder rumbled and exhaustion overwhelmed me, even overcoming the intense pain from the sting, until sleep swept me into the relief of oblivion.

. . .

I woke to cold droplets of rain striking my skin. Eve lay next to me, eyes open, staring at me. Pain throbbed throughout my arm, but it was dull now, by comparison.

"What happened?" I said, for my mind was hazy.

"I thought you were dead."

I winced as I tested my hand, which was the only part of my body still slightly numb. "You've been talking too much about death." The words came thick and slow. What was wrong with my mouth?

She pushed herself into a seated position. "I've been waiting for both of us to fall dead since the moment the fruit dropped into my hands."

"You don't even know what death means."

She offered me another hateful glance. "I know more than you think." She hugged her knees and rested her chin on them. "Death means everything stops."

"Why did you think I died, then?"

"Because you stopped breathing many times. And your face was so swollen."

I realized then how thick my lips and cheeks felt and wondered if my difficulty getting words out was due to it. That, too, must have been from the scorpion sting.

I shook my head in disbelief as more droplets fell, and the sound of them striking the leaves built a steady, mounting rhythm so beautiful that I felt the lifelessness around me doubly deep. For in the rain I heard the echoes of the Music, which had brought life and form to the world. I thought of how badly the dried leaves needed the moisture to wick up their roots. With enough water came growth and life. And if growth never came, we ourselves would die.

I cupped my hands before my face as the rain intensified and soaked our garments. The water pooled in my palms, and I sipped it awkwardly past thick, unwieldy lips. "Eve," I said, "drink while you can."

She shook her head and continued resting her chin on her knees.

I watched her as I continued to drink. She hardly even blinked as the storm above intensified into a tempest. Never did she open her mouth for a taste of the water, though I knew thirst had sapped her bones of strength as much as it had mine.

Lightning flashed, and thunder rattled the trees. Gusts of wind tossed the branches back and forth, and all we did was sit there and shiver as the temperature dropped.

I scooted close to her to huddle again for warmth, but she shoved me away. I stared at her, but she didn't even look at me.

It was as if she cared only about those waving, fruitless branches. As though I no longer existed at all.

I wish I could say I understood her actions. But I thought she had lost her mind. I could not imagine how death could seem wise when the rain was offering us another day of life. God was obviously providing this for us, yet she refused it with bitter resolve. And though I could see her trembling in the cold, she had refused my warmth, along with every attempt I gave at comfort.

I understood nothing of the madness of exhaustion, hunger, and dehydration, nor how it could strike me differently than it did her. Maybe, if I had, the hatred that welled up inside me would have waned. But I think not, for in hindsight, I believe I too was on the brink of madness. That was why I blamed her for everything.

"Eve," I said.

She ignored me.

I pushed her arm. "Eve!"

She flung her arm wide and struck me in the side of the head with her forearm.

The blow brought a flash of light to my eyes.

"Don't touch me!" she yelled. "Can't you see I don't want you?"

I stood, shaking with fury, clenching my hands and only barely holding myself back from lashing out at her. "What's wrong with you? Drink! Let us warm ourselves!"

"What's the point?"

"To survive."

"Why? What for?"

My voice rose to a near screech as emotion constricted my throat. "Me!" I beat my chest with my hands and fought the warble that threatened my voice. "We survive for each other. For the hope of being together with our Father again."

She examined me. Her eyes cold and calculating. "How long will it last? Think about it, Adam."

"You're not dead yet, and Father has offered us water to

quench our thirst. Drink, you fool. Or do you want to kill yourself?"

She shrugged. "What if I do?"

I grabbed her shoulders and shook her hard. "Throw your life away and you'll kill me too. This isn't only about you."

"No." She curled her lips into a bitter scowl. "It's about you."

My fingers loosened as her words chilled my skin.

She pulled away, and I stood and turned, considering her cold perception.

"That's why I refused you," she said. "Because since the moment we ate the fruit, you've rejected me."

"What are you talking about?" Now I truly was curious. All I had known since the moment we were ejected from the garden was her rejection of me.

"In the garden, after we sinned, I tried to hold onto you for comfort, but you offered none in return. My first reaction was to go to you. Your first reaction was to blame me. From the moment everything changed, you hurt me, and pushed me away, and treated me with scorn."

"But—" I bit my tongue as more accusations rose and threatened to spill out of my mouth. But would that not only prove her words true?

As I thought back to our final moments in the garden, I realized her accusation held a disturbing veracity. Only I had not meant it in such a way. I cleared my throat. "And?"

"And why should I live for someone who hates me?"

Pain impaled my chest. I coughed to relieve my throat of the pressure building there.

She looked up at me. "Go."

"I'm not going to leave. You're everything to me."

"I don't believe you."

"I . . ." How could I explain myself? I felt as though the greater tempest was the one raging inside me. I had no tools to deal with it. No way to sift through the thoughts that flew like a hurricane, too quick to take hold of.

"I've made my choice," Eve said. "Leave me to my choice and I'll leave you to yours. Is that not fair?"

"I'm not just going to let you die."

She smirked. "Then find a reason for me to change my mind."

Chapter 12

As the rain raged, Eve knelt like a statue beside that brackish pool.

"Eve," I said, but she ignored me.

I stood shivering as the cold rain soaked me through. Trying to think of any way to convince her to not give up.

What could I do except fulfill her demand to find food and to restore our hope?

I turned east knowing there was no hope left for us west toward Eden, because that way was barred by a wheel of flame.

As I walked in a straight line, I found a few long stalks of sparse grass that tasted sweet when chewed, but none brought any true sustenance. I wandered for half the day until the dark rain dissipated, and light peeked through the clouds.

A lone vulture flew high overhead in slow half circles. In the distance, a small pack of roving dogs scanned the countryside. When they saw me, they edged in my direction.

My encounter with the scorpion made me feel uneasy about animals. I found a tree and wrenched at a limb until it tore away. I took off the excess twigs and leaves, then tested its usefulness as a striking stick. It would work well enough. The wood was fresh and green, and the moisture made it heavy.

When I looked up from my new rod, I noticed the dogs sliding to a stop several paces from me. "Go!" I yelled and swung my stick at them, forcing them back. They hopped back, evidently deciding I wasn't worth the trouble, and jogged away.

When I passed over a hill that blocked them from view, I considered the possibility that they might find Eve. But the thought was too late, for they were faster than me, and if I didn't find food, whether the dogs were violent or not, we would not survive.

I pressed on, hoping to find fallen seeds or at least some edible greens. How difficult could it be to find sustenance outside Eden? Father had made the world and filled the garden with such overwhelming life and diversity, that to find nothing directly outside of that paradise seemed perverse.

Was he testing me? To see if I would remain faithful? If I would continue to fight to fulfill my duty to Eve, the woman he gave me to love and live with?

Or perhaps Eve was right, and we were doomed, and the words of Father were a hopeless prod to fools destined for oblivion.

"No," I said and wiped the sweat spilling into my eyes. The sun overhead was warm, though still dappled with clouds. The heat stood in juxtaposition to the chill we'd felt in the storm. I felt the skin of my knuckles, which had cracked. Dried blood settled in the lines, and I ran my finger over them.

As the sun set, I fell to my knees, exhausted. I'd found nothing in the entire expanse traversed—only patches of grass, fruitless shrubs, and sharp cactuses that could not be eaten.

Perhaps the mountains in the distance would give us some form of sustenance. I could see sparse green growth across them, but they were so distant that they had hardly moved closer during my whole day of travel. And now, in the darkness, they were no more than looming shadows on the horizon, like a dark moon in the sky, hopelessly remote.

A low rumble began in the distance, and lightning flashed again and again, but the wind was so dry that I had no hope it would bring me rain. It had been long since I drank, and I was so thirsty that my tongue stuck to the roof of my mouth. I fell to my knees and dug with my stick to find moisture trapped in the soil, but there was hardly anything more than damp dirt, for the soil was sandy, and not enough moisture had yet soaked the ground.

I worked myself to my feet again and walked in the direction of the lightning, hoping that soon enough, another storm would come with enough water to quench my thirst.

Locusts bounded between patches of grass. I tried to avoid stepping on them, and noticed for the first time a lizard skittering across the soil. I tried to chase it, but it disappeared with a flash of scales.

A rush of cool wind tossed my hair, and I spread my arms and breathed deep, trying to sense rain on its way, though the air remained dry.

I squinted into the distance and held my breath to listen.

The rumble was quickly building. And the encroaching darkness made it difficult to see. But there, ahead of me, a massive column rushed along the ground straight toward me. I struggled to my feet, pulse pounding as I turned and began to run away from it. I had no idea what was coming, but I knew it was large and unlike anything I had faced.

Another blast of wind hit me harder, pushing me along. I stretched my legs, urging myself into a sprint.

Little bits of sand struck my skin. Then, finally, a cloud of sand engulfed me and choked my breath. I stumbled and fell as I endured what felt like a thousand insect stings. I cried out, but sand flew into my mouth.

I tossed myself flat on my belly, covering my eyes and mouth with my hands and spitting out the grit. There was no shelter, and I could not hope to find my way in the absolute dark of the cloud of sand and dust. I pulled the clothing over my head and waited as the storm howled.

My body shook with fear. The storm continued until I wondered whether it would ever break. I felt as though I was slowly suffocating. With every breath, more sand settled in my lungs. I coughed so much that my chest burned like someone had set it on fire.

A sharp crack of lightning split the dust storm, making me jump. "Father!" I yelled, for I did not know what else to do. But the storm howled louder than my words.

I called out again, hoping he would show me mercy. But no footsteps approached, and the storm did not abate.

Was Eve going to be engulfed in this storm as well? I remembered the glassy gleam of her eyes. That dead, vacant expression. If she had refused the water that drenched her hair and passed by her lips, how would she survive a storm such as this?

Panic filled my limbs until they felt as heavy as the mountains in the distance. "Help her," I screamed. "Help!"

Thunder cracked again, and I winced as a nearby tree toppled.

Sand built up around me at an alarming rate. Every so often, I shifted to unearth myself. With the tunic over my head, face parallel to the ground, and hands covering my eyes and mouth, I could just barely breathe through the cracks in my fingers.

The sandstorm lasted nearly as long as the rain, and unleashed twice the fury. Its lightning flashed, and its thunder rattled rock and bone. Until, as quickly as it came, it passed.

I looked around. The surroundings were unrecognizable. Many of the shrubs and little grasses had been buried. But I could see the tree struck by lightning in the distance on a little hill. I turned away from it and considered whether to continue.

The stars were out. Night had fallen thick and dark, but the moon outlined everything in bright silver lines. I could not imagine that many food-bearing plants had survived such a storm. The air was cool, now. And it would only get cooler as night continued.

During the storm, the ache in my stomach had all but been forgotten. Now it gaped like an open wound. I clutched at the skin of my belly and felt the world spin. My eyes kept threatening to close on me, and my balance seemed unreliable.

Ahead, I could see nothing but bitter desert. No life. No food. Nothing.

I licked my cracked lips with a tongue made of leather. If I continued, soon enough my eyes would close, and I would collapse.

I turned back toward that broken tree on the hilltop. I wanted to lie down as much as I wanted water and food, and only one of those could I yet guarantee.

I stumbled toward the tree.

When at last I threw myself into its shelter, I fell asleep and dreamed a dream that would change everything.

Chapter 13

I knew I was asleep, yet when Father's hand alighted on my shoulder, it felt so real that I wondered if all the pain had just been a nightmare.

"Awake, my son."

I opened my eyes and saw Father looking down at me with all the gentleness he'd shown in the garden. Yet the Light was gone. And I was not in the garden, but rather a lifeless desert. The moon was nowhere, and the stars looked different. I felt I could reach up and touch them, even though I knew them to be infinitely remote.

Father sat with his back to the broken tree I had been sleeping beside.

"You need to go back to her."

I could imagine Eve awake where I'd left her, cold and alone. I nodded. "I couldn't find any food."

"I know," he said.

"What will I do?"

He frowned. "I will provide you with food, just as I covered you. But after, you must work to support yourselves."

I nodded.

"Do you trust me?"

I stared at the dust and drew circles with my index finger. "Yes."

"But not completely," he said.

"I don't understand . . ." I cleared my throat to free it of tension. "Everything is so different now, and I don't know what will happen."

"Do you plan to return to me?"

"Of course."

He reached his arm around me. "Then what is there to wonder about? Do you remember how to count the days of the year?"

"Of course."

"Then look forward to the Day of Atonement, when all will be changed. And next year, I will be there, at the entrance of Eden, waiting."

"Is that all?"

He nodded. "That is all you need worry about. Do you doubt me?"

Tears stung my eyes. "No."

"Then trust me. I will make all things new. All you need do is wait for my promises to bear fruit."

I nodded. Now that he was with me, my doubt melted like snow in the desert. "I will."

"It will not be easy to wait, nor to return."

I took a deep breath and looked into those eyes, so dark, warm, and present. "It is easy when you are with me."

He smiled. But the smile faltered. "You aren't with me anymore, son. Now, it is time for you to wake."

. . .

My eyes burst open, and I was alone. The broken tree beside me was gone, replaced by a green plant I recognized well: a fig tree bursting with ripe figs.

I stood and stared at it, wondering if I could be imagining this as I had the dream I'd just woken from.

But no, this was real. Father had visited me. *"I will provide you with food, just as I covered you,"* he'd said and made a fig tree grow beside me.

A fig tree. Whose leaves we sewed together in an attempt to cover ourselves in Eden.

I frowned at this gift, this gentle rebuke mixed with unmerited kindness. How painfully sweet Father's presence had been. I closed my eyes and tried to take hold of him. To imagine him close.

When he was near, anxieties fell like dead leaves. Now that he was gone, the world seemed burdened with fear like forbidden fruit.

"But after, you must work hard to support yourselves." How? If I ate those figs, what pains would roll out in front of me in the days that might remain ahead?

I could end everything. Put an end to all the unknowns by simply not eating this fruit. In a way, I would be fulfilling the will of Father, would I not? He had refused to give us the fruit of the Tree of Life, lest we lived forever in this broken state. That seemed to indicate death would be a gift.

And yet he'd offered me food to continue.

Which should I choose?

I now understood why Eve had been ready to throw away her life. The thought of living in exhaustion, fear, and anxiety forever seemed unbearable. How could I not have seen it before?

Yet equally terrible was the infinity of death. A gaping hole; yawning, abyssal, unknowable. How had she not seen *that?*

I took a deep breath and looked the direction I knew would take me back to Eve. "I chose that breath. So I will choose these figs."

I broke off several figs and tore them open. I bit into the sweet flesh and moaned as the nourishment filled my empty stomach.

I ate my fill and gathered as many as I could in my arms before hurrying back in Eve's direction. I wanted to see my companion. My love. Now that my stomach was full, I smiled for the first time in days. I could hardly wait to tell her of Father's visit, and the gift he'd given us.

Chapter 14

As I returned to the copse of trees in full daylight, it seemed smaller and more barren than before. The brackish pool was filled with sand, and the short trees provided only slivers of shade.

I rounded the copse three times, thinking I'd find Eve leaning against one of the trees, but she was not there.

I returned to where the brackish pool had been and found a gathering of her footprints. I dropped the fruit and began to follow the prints as they ambled around the copse. She must have moved after the sandstorm passed.

Finally, a set split from the rest and traveled south into the grass. I looked up and gathered my bearings. The trail went straight until the patch of grass, so I decided to continue that direction.

I hadn't made it far when I found her collapsed beside a cactus. Face in the dirt, body motionless.

"Eve," I called, and burst into a run. "Eve!"

I slid to my knees beside her and shook her.

She moaned, but she wasn't moving. I rolled her to her back and lifted her head in the crook of my arm. Her eyes fluttered, but all I saw were the whites. Her face was dusty, lips cracked and crusted with blood.

I pressed my palm to her cheek and said, "Eve, it's me. I came back. I found you."

She made a noise that sounded like a mixture of disbelief and laughter.

"Look at me."

She winced and tried to turn away.

I held her in place and pulled her eyelids back with my thumb.

Dazed, she took in my face. Then her eyes slowly drifted shut.

"Eve!"

No response.

My pulse pounded in my ears. I set her gently on the ground and sprinted back to the copse for the fruit. As I reached the remains of the brackish pool, a couple black birds hopped between the trees, eyeing the figs. I screamed and ran at them, flailing my arms, and they flew off, cawing.

I gathered the fruit in my arms once more and ran back as fast as my wobbling legs would allow.

I scraped my knees in the dust as I knelt, lifted her head in the crook of my arm, and brought a fig to her lips.

She didn't respond.

I pulled back her lips and pressed the fruit to her teeth. "Eat," I said, as heat rose in my cheeks. "Eat!"

Her eyes fluttered open. She nodded and bit down softly. Then her body went slack.

I pulled the fruit from her mouth, concerned that she would choke. I tore open the fig and chewed it into mush before spitting it out in my hand and urging a bit into her mouth.

She coughed it up, so I lifted her higher. As I urged in more of the mush, she swallowed by reflex, and I kept nursing the food into her until she'd eaten two figs.

I held her cold body and rocked, humming melodies I remembered from the Music in the garden and swiping tears from my chapped cheeks. Her breaths were shallow. The thrum of her pulse fast and weak. *Almighty*, I prayed, hoping he could hear my thoughts. *Save her. I cannot do this alone. You gave us to each other. Don't let us fail. Not after you gave us food to continue.*

The sun slipped into hiding before she awoke. When her eyes opened and she saw me holding her, she closed them again and nuzzled into my shoulder. I kissed her hair and whispered words of comfort.

I pulled back to make certain she was finally alert, and she nodded at me, though her words came slow and quiet. "You came back."

"I found you collapsed."

"After you left," she said, "I called for you. But you would not come."

That disturbed me. "I could not hear you. Otherwise I would have."

"I tried to follow you."

I shook my head. "You went the wrong direction."

She looked around. "My thoughts were hazy. I became fearful and began to hear you calling my name. I tried to go to you, but you laughed at me. No matter where I turned, I could not reach you."

I pressed her into me again and groaned. "No, no, no. That is not true. You were dreaming."

"I was awake, I think."

"Then you were dreaming awake. Look. I have found you, and I have brought food." I motioned at the remaining figs.

"You," she paused and scrunched up her face. "You fed me?"

I nodded.

"Then it wasn't a dream."

"Not that. I came back for you. Here—" I handed her another fig. "You need it."

She ate slowly, with difficulty. But it seemed to return her strength, and to clear her mind. We sat staring at the brush slowly waving in the dark as she finished the rest of the fruit.

I slipped my hand over hers, and we laced our fingers together. She rested against me, no longer distant and cold. But she turned to me with raised brows.

"Why did you leave me?"

I tipped my head. "Do you not remember?"

"No."

"Truly?"

She shook her head.

I took a deep breath and wrapped my arms around her. "I am sorry."

"For what?"

"For leaving."

She was silent.

"You told me you wanted to die," I whispered. "That the only way you would choose to live is if I found a reason for you to change your mind. I went to find food because water didn't convince you, and I wondered if hunger was distorting your thoughts. It seems that was more true than I realized."

She nodded. "So, that was no dream either."

I shook my head.

She kissed my cheek and pulled herself from my grasp to stand and brush herself off. "Then I am sorry too."

I stood beside her and kissed her on the lips tenderly, and my voice was a whisper. "It is nothing."

She smiled and ran her slender fingers through my hair.

"Come," I said, "let me bring you to the fig tree. It is far, but we must go there anyway, for it is the only food I found in this wasteland."

"How could a single fig tree sustain us?"

I shrugged. "How should I know? But I will show it to you, anyway. Come." I offered her my hand, and she took it.

We walked slowly, and for much of the way, I had to support her, for she was still weak. She stumbled twice, but I never let her scrape her knees.

Night settled like a heavy cloak with silver holes in it. I stared up at the expanse, realizing I could use the shapes of the silver clusters high above as a way of telling direction.

"It's not nothing," Eve mumbled beside me.

"What?"

"What I said to you."

She was still thinking of her madness beside the brackish pool. I shrugged. "You were not thinking clearly."

"I wanted to die."

That chilled my breath. After I found her collapsed on the ground, I'd believed it all due to some terrible madness.

"After you left, the fear rolled over me like a boulder, and I realized I'd made a terrible mistake. But it pained me that you had left with little argument."

"I didn't know what else to do."

"I thought you didn't love me."

An ache grew in my chest. "I love you more than my own life."

She looked at me, eyes piercingly clear yet uncertain. After a long moment, she nodded, but her eyes did not change.

"Come," I said, for I hoped that with time, the distrust between us would wane. "We are not far now."

When we reached the fig tree, it was no longer growing by itself. A small orchard of fruit trees had sprung up around it, and a little spring of water bubbled from the ground and flowed west in a narrow, clear stream.

"Here it is," I said. Then rubbed my eyes to make certain I was seeing clearly.

"I thought you said it was just one fig tree."

I scratched my head. "It was. Or at least I thought it was. For the first time, I doubt my memory."

We crouched beside the stream and drank our fill. Then washed the dust from our skin and sat cross-legged amid the trees.

"How did you find it?" she said.

I considered whether she would believe me. But she was

staring at me. I laughed, feeling heat rise to my face. "Well . . . I had a dream."

"You slept?"

I nodded. "After the rain and the sand storm, night came, and I collapsed. In my dream, I think Father visited me." Tears threatened to return to my eyes, and my voice fell as soft as a gentle breeze. "If I could only tell you how it felt to see him again."

Eve's eyes went cold. "He did not come to me." But her words rose in pitch at the end, as if she were asking a question.

I averted my eyes and pushed the dust with my palms, for I had no answer. "He told me to wake, and when I woke, I found that I was sitting against a fig tree."

She raised one brow. "You fell asleep beside it without realizing?"

I shook my head. "I fell asleep beside a large fruitless tree that had been struck by lightning and burst asunder. The dream was no mere dream. I believe Father gave us this garden so that we might survive and find our way back to him when the seasons change."

She looked around us at the myriad fruit and nut trees. "No matter where it came from, I am grateful."

I nodded. "We will make the most of it. Let us tend this orchard and grow a garden to match that of Eden."

She looked down at that little burbling stream. "I think we will never again see anything like Eden."

I shrugged. "Then we will do what we can to honor the memory of it."

She pursed her lips. "Some things are better left forgotten."

Chapter 15

We began working the small garden immediately, though work was difficult until we crafted more tools. I found a brittle black rock that could easily be chipped. I struck it with stones until it took the rough form of an axe head. I secured the head into a rough rod that I cut with the axe head from the straight limb of a tree nearby.

This took the better part of a day, but it allowed me to more easily cut wood from the fruitless trees nearby, and to craft fires to warm us when the chill grew too intense. And it certainly did in the coming weeks.

After the axe, I built other tools to care for the garden. Large, scoop-shaped sticks for digging in the soil. Thin poles for poking holes and planting seeds. And a small shelter to shade us from the sun and provide a barrier against wind and rain.

In the ensuing weeks, we planted new rows of fruit trees and vegetables, though we could only plant some, for many still flowered and had not yet borne fruit. We stuck sticks in the earth to mark where the seeds went, and scratched horizontal lines into the wood to differentiate whether fruit trees or vegetables would grow there.

Finally, Eve dug to find clay as I formed little channels to divert water to the seeds. By the end of the day, Eve piled a mound of clay into a hole in the ground. We dug a culvert so the stream wetted the clay to be worked. Then we mixed it and formed little slabs that we stacked to build a furnace that dried in the sun.

We used all that Father taught us in forming the furnace. We built a chamber at one side with a paddle attached to a stick shooting upright that we could spin to blow air into the furnace in order to increase the heat. Only thus could we hope to melt crude ores and build better tools.

Yet we were far from that. For life in the wilderness was more difficult than expected. Though we had a small orchard, our bellies ached, and the weariness of tending to our duties mounted high. We had little time for rest or for trying new things, and the skin of our hands and feet grew rough and hard.

Likewise, we spent little time enjoying each other's company. By the time we finished our duties, we had little energy left to do anything but stare at the stars. We abandoned our Sabbath celebration, and Eve began to mark time by scratching vertical lines on the trees around us. Our minds were on surviving until the day we would return to Father, and we bent every moment of every day toward that end.

We did not realize that food and shelter were not enough for the human spirit to survive.

At night, six weeks from leaving Eden, we huddled in our open shelter and held our breath as wolves howled and paws scuffed around us. As one stepped onto our elevated shelter, I leapt from my spot with a wooden rod and struck it. The beast yelped and spun away, and the other wolves fled in confusion as I chased them around the orchard, roaring like a bear.

After they fled, I stalked through the trees, peering with wide eyes into the black to make certain they wouldn't return. Owls swept through the gray sky above. The only sounds were those of the wind and the plants we tended.

When I returned, my foot made the shelter creak.

Eve shot up. "Adam?"

"Yes."

"You frightened me. I thought you were—"

"They are gone. I made certain."

"Why didn't you come sooner?" Her tone came sharp and hard.

"I was making certain none returned."

She grumbled something too low to hear.

I laid next to her, but she would not suffer me to touch her.

"What?" I said.

But she did not respond.

"You are mad at me," I said.

"You left me alone in here."

I shot up on one elbow, forgetting that she could not see me in the dark. "I protected you."

"You should have stayed."

I scoffed. "I suppose I *could* have, though it would have been foolish."

"And leaving your wife defenseless wasn't?"

"No, it wasn't."

"Right," she said, and turned away.

I sighed, scooted from her, and laid alone.

The wind bit my skin, and the animal skins Father crafted for us seemed uselessly thin. Every time I nearly fell asleep, the chill struck me awake.

A third of the night passed in weary misery. My mind raced in circles. Again and again I imagined every step of the attack. Each time, I became more irritated at her reaction.

I felt her shivering through the little platform we'd built. We were both aching with cold, sleepless in the middle of the night, yet she refused to warm herself because it would necessitate touching me. And I refused to warm myself because it would show her I needed her.

How strange our thoughts and moods become in the sleepless hours of night. I was awake enough to think, yet exhausted enough that thoughts rushed unbidden, and terrible emotions came with them, until I felt I couldn't breathe.

Then her hand bridged the distance between us. Warm, soft on my side.

I blinked, woken from my thoughts like a man from an evil dream.

I felt a rush of emotion, though I pushed it away and held my breath. She tugged gently on my tunic, as if to urge me close.

Instead, to my shame, I pulled away. Her bitterness had wounded me. I realized her openness was the opportunity I had wanted—the chance to make her feel like me.

After a quiet moment, she began to weep.

Several breaths passed before I realized my mistake and turned toward her, placing my hand on her shoulder.

"Don't touch me." She thrust me away.

"I am sorry," I said, but she shot to her feet and walked off.

I knew that to chase her would be a mistake. So, instead, I laid back and hoped she would return.

I spent the rest of the night alone.

Chapter 16

I had wounded my wife. I see now that she had been damaged beyond repair. And yet, like a fool, I kept expecting her to return to who she was in Eden.

But after the pain of losing our intimacy with Father, her playful spirit closed like a door stopped with stones. I did not realize the complexities of heartache. I knew only that her warmth and excitement were gone and thought it proof she no longer loved me.

That was why, when she offered me bitterness, I lashed out and tore at her heart like a cornered animal. Because to me, it was just another reminder that, for us, there would be no going back.

The day after the wolves attacked, we tended the garden as strangers. We cooked our own food and shared nothing. That next night we slept alone, shivering in the cold. We built our own baskets and tools.

For a while, it was livable. We coexisted without striking sparks in each other's eyes.

Yet that is not love. Neither is it life. For loneliness is the deepest pain the human heart can endure.

Weeks later, out of desperation, I began offering to help her with her tasks. When I cooked food, I gave her some. In the morning, I left water in a bowl beside her so she could rinse the dust from her face.

Slowly, she began to open back up to me. We began to talk throughout the day. These conversations went well, and eventually I asked if she wanted to lay together at night, for warmth and comfort. After some thought, she agreed, and we found greater comfort than either of us wanted to admit.

Yet it was not for love that I did this, but rather for hatred of complete isolation, because the length of her resentment had offended me, and I did not understand her.

Still, I began to see more clearly that Father had been right. It was not good for me to be alone. And had he not made her from my own rib, I would have died of loneliness long ago.

Slowly, the warmth between us returned, though it never reached the heights of what we had in Eden.

One day I found her sitting in our ramshackle shelter in the middle of the day, staring at the waving grasses and wild grains that sprung up. The bamboo that we'd built our shelter out of, which had sprung up miraculously beside the creek just as all the other plants in our little garden had, now hung over the shelter and tossed shade across her legs.

I stopped pruning the fruit trees and sat beside her, waving away gnats and wiping sweat from my face.

She did not move.

I slid my hand over hers and squeezed.

She breathed in once, then let it out.

"What is on your mind?" I said.

She bent forward and her black hair fell over her eyes. "I want to be happy."

I swallowed hard and looked at the grasses and the shadows that waved over my bare feet in the dirt. "Me too."

"Because I am not," she said.

I swallowed again, and took my hand from hers.

She looked at me long and slow. "Do you not feel the same? Do you not wish that all of this would end?"

I shrugged. Part of me did. But to admit it felt dangerous, for I saw the shadow of the madness that nearly took her from me returning. "I want to live."

"So do I. Do not take me for a fool. But this—" She motioned with her hand.

"What do you want? We have a garden. We have work to do. We have each other . . ." I gritted my teeth as my anger mounted. No, I thought, this was not what I wanted. The friction of my fury against her would only light her desires on fire.

Her hand warmed my shoulder. I looked at her, fighting to push back my frustration.

"I've been thinking a lot lately about what Father said," she said. "In the garden."

"What?"

"When he spoke to the serpent, he warned it of my offspring."

"The serpent is gone."

"Is it?"

I looked at her with squinted eyes.

"Sometimes," she said, "when I wake in the middle of the night, I think I see it staring at me over the edge of our shelter. Often in my dreams, I hear its hissing laughter."

I had dreamed of the serpent, as well, but never thought it meant anything.

"'Taste and see,' it says. And I run, and it pursues me through dark lanes between shadowy trees."

A shiver ran down my shoulders, for I, too, had dreamed such a dream. I nodded. "You think having a child will put an end to everything."

"I think it is our destiny, our purpose now that everything has changed," she said.

"But what of the Almighty's words in the dream he gave me?"

She shrugged. "This is the first I have heard of any words he spoke to you. Besides to tell you to wake up."

My eyes widened. I brushed the dirt from my knees. "He

said it was enough to wait and to return to him. That we are to look to the Day of Atonement."

A clever gleam grew in her eyes. "Day of Atonement? What is that? And why did you not tell me of this before?"

"You heard him speak of it as we left Eden."

"He did not call it that, then."

"He spoke of it as the day when everything would be changed. What can that be except the day we return with a sacrifice?"

She tipped her head. "Sounds like the day our child sets us free."

I sighed and rubbed my face. "We've barely survived, Eve. We need to learn to live before trying to keep a child alive."

"What if we are so unhappy because we've only been living for ourselves?"

"It would be foolish to attempt raising a child now," I said.

"What better time could there be? I cannot think of anything we might wait for."

"For life to be easier," I said.

"It will never be easier."

I stood and turned from her. "You are blinded by your desires. What if it just makes life more difficult? What if it doesn't make you happier but more miserable?"

She tossed up her hands. "What difference does it make?"

I cleared my throat. "What if I could make you happy?"

Her expression twisted. "What?"

"What if I could be enough?"

"Adam . . ."

"I will serve you better."

"That's not—"

"I will treat you with only tenderness. I will never speak another harsh word. I will—"

She stood and clutched my arm. "Stop."

I stared into her eyes.

"You're not enough."

I rubbed my face hard and resisted the urge to walk away and hide. "I was enough in the garden."

"No," she said. "You weren't."

You were enough for me, I wanted to say. But I didn't. I said nothing.

She tipped her head in understanding and said, "In the garden, we did not suffer. We knew nothing of evil. To compare our lives now with our lives then is just . . . unfair."

"It is Father, isn't it? He is gone now, and—"

"Don't speak to me of Father," she said. And for the first time, I saw the spark of anger in her eyes.

"Why won't you let me try to do better?"

"I'm not asking you to," she said.

"Just give me time."

"I want a child."

I kicked the dirt.

She sighed and pushed her hair back. Then crossed to me and slid her fingers between mine. She leaned forward and kissed me softly on the lips. "Please."

I looked into her eyes, brushed my palm across her dark cheek, and ran my fingers through her hair. I wanted her. Wanted the tenderness, comfort, and intimacy she offered. Yet was she not aware of this? Was she not trying to use me in this moment?

I did not realize that her anger at the Almighty came from her inability to understand why we could no longer be with him. I thought instead that her unhappiness only came from her lack of love for me.

I pulled back. Not wanting to admit that her intimate touch was all I needed to feel wanted, accepted, needed.

For she obviously did not need me thus.

And the thought of having a child to care for amidst all the work that daily piled ahead of us—my heart warned me it was a dangerous road. Once we turned down it, there would be no returning.

Yet she was right. Life alone like this was not sustainable. We were running ourselves ragged, even without a child. And for what purpose?

I could see her thoughts stretching through the future. Her despair growing, and my anger alongside it, until weariness rolled ahead in a vast wasteland, and death became the only welcomed relief.

She stepped to me again, wrapped her arms around my back, and pressed close. "Please," she said. Eyes looking into mine, fully unguarded for the first time since Eden.

My hands shook as I wrapped my arms around her in return. "All right," I said and nodded, even as fear spread through my belly like cold oil.

Because maybe then she would love me. Maybe then she would be happy.

Chapter 17

I woke the next morning feeling as I did on my first day in Eden. The sun was peering through the slats of the bamboo shelter like those five bright points of Father's fingers, and I was not alone. Eve's arm lay across my belly, and her leg over my thigh. Her head rested in the curve of my shoulder, and her hair tickled my face. I smiled. For the first time in many days.

Maybe she was right, and if she had a child, we would be obeying the Almighty's advice to look forward to the Day of Atonement. Because the relief in my chest after experiencing intimacy with my wife felt like salvation.

The air was warm, and a slight breeze rustled the leaves. Eve's chest rose and fell, a deep rhythm syncing to the ghost of the Music in my mind. The Song of Father, which set everything aright.

I yawned, and the movement woke Eve, who stretched before looking up at me.

"Good morning," I said.

She pushed herself up on one palm and looked around. After a moment, she smiled. "Yes. It is good, isn't it?"

I pulled her into me and we hugged. I kissed the crown of

her head, and her voice was muffled as she said, "What must we do today?"

We sat up and washed our faces in the bowl I'd left the night before. "Well, this morning is a comfortable enough temperature, but lately the nights have been growing colder." I motioned toward our clothing, which were the same animal skins Father had crafted. "We will need new clothes soon. And perhaps extra coverings at night. Also,"—I patted the hard bamboo slats—"it would be good to find something soft to lay on."

She nodded. "How is the wheat growing?"

"If I understand what Father told me in Eden, it is nearly ready for harvest."

"By the river you'll find a large stone bowl that I hollowed out for us to crush grain in."

"Then we will be nearly ready to make flour," I said. "But how shall we store what we do not eat right away?"

She scratched her head. "I don't know. I have been wondering if perhaps we could find a way to keep it in clay pots."

"Father said that grains rot quickly because they are filled with moisture."

"I have an idea I would like to try," she said.

I stood and twisted my back until it cracked. "If all goes to plan, we will have much to prepare for."

She nodded and leaned over to kiss me on the cheek, though she stumbled and I caught her. We both laughed, and I savored the moment. The rush of excitement at the thought of our salvation on the horizon offered hope for the future we might have together. The dark pall of anxiety that had hung over us for so long seemed distant and thin, like clouds in the sun.

For once, Eve was offering me love and acceptance, and perhaps in return we would both find our redemption. If that meant more work, more pain, more struggle, I would gladly pay the price to feel the relief I did that morning.

Of course, that was only because I didn't know how steep the price would be.

. . .

After tending the different plots in our little garden, and gathering enough food for an early light meal, I set about scouting the land for anything that might be used to craft new coverings. With winter approaching, I perceived that we were in danger. Father had told us the temperature would drop so far that water would turn as hard as stone and many of our plants would be destroyed. If we did not craft more appropriate clothing, perhaps our skin, also, would be destroyed.

No plants I found seemed capable of warming us. Though the large leaves of the fig trees could perhaps be a comfortable covering for the bamboo floor.

As I continued outside of our orchard, I spotted a herd of wild goats grazing on a hillside.

I stared at them for some time. In my right hand, I held a long wooden pole. In my left, my obsidian hatchet. Father had killed the beasts he'd formed our skin tunics from. Still, the thought of approaching a goat and striking it to death made my blood run cold.

I stood there long enough that one of the goats griped and walked closer to investigate me.

I bent down and stared as it sniffed my hatchet, rectangular pupils peering. It bleated again, then turned back to the grass.

This was my opportunity. What I'd spent half the morning searching for.

I buried the hatchet in the soil and rubbed my face.

How could I kill an innocent beast? It had not tried to harm me as the wolves had. Indeed, it felt safe enough in my presence to turn its back to me and eat. To make more clothing, I would need to betray that confidence.

I patted the goat's shoulder, and it looked up at me before bleating again and walking off to its brethren. I returned and washed the hatchet in the stream that ran through our little garden. Eve saw and yelled from farther upstream near the stone fruit trees, "Did you find anything?"

I shook my head.

She grimaced. "Then can you help me move this?"

"What is it?"

"Come."

I jogged from my spot up the hill and saw that she'd been weaving large leaves into a mat.

"You lift it by that corner and I will lift it by this corner," she said.

I did. It did not fold well, and was tricky to move even together. "How did you weave this so quickly?"

"You were gone for some time."

We carefully maneuvered between uneven rows of trees and bushes, following the line of bamboo back to our shelter. We laid it on the floor and found that it hung over the edge a bit. "You sized this well."

"I thought I had sized it perfectly." She glared at it, bending back the leaves that hung over the edge. "And it is not all that we need to fix." She pointed to her tunic by her knee, then pulled at it to show me it was fraying open.

My belly sank and I nodded. "I will make us new clothing soon. I promise."

"We need to take better care of ourselves." She cleared her throat and stretched. "But first, let us try the new bedding."

She crawled into the shelter and laid on her back with a sigh of relief. "I like it." She twisted and grimaced. "Though it could be better."

I crawled up beside her. The cushion offered by the soft, thick leaves was enough to dull the ache from the nodules in the bamboo. "I am happy with it."

"Why didn't we make this weeks ago?" she said.

"Comfort seems a small thing when you fear you may not survive."

"Still, for how much time we spent with these bamboo rods digging into our backs, I can't believe we didn't think of it sooner." She reached her arm around me.

I pulled strands of hair from her face and breathed deep as the warmth of her presence filled me. "We are making up for lost time," I said.

She smiled and kissed me. "Yes. We are."

Chapter 18

Three days passed without another chance to make better coverings. Without better clothing, we would not survive winter, which stood like an impassable bulwark between us and the Day of Atonement mid-spring.

Because aside from clothing, food was an even greater issue. What we harvested would rot. What we didn't harvest would die in the frost.

But we could only focus on so much. And my previous cowardice when attempting to kill a goat made me hesitant to try again.

Until I could delay no longer without risking Eve's ire and found myself staring at a herd of sheep on a blank hillside with a long pole in one hand and my hatchet in the other. I tried to approach the animals, but they were wary of my presence.

I waited instead for them to come to me.

But the sheep were edging away. I took several steps closer and waited. *Father, if you can hear my thoughts, give me success today.*

I took several more steps and stopped.

One of the sheep lifted its head, but did not flee.

I waited, and in this way, slowly came within reach. Until I rested my hand on its head while it chewed and examined me with interest.

I held my breath and considered what I must do. Eve was in desperate need of new coverings. Yet how could I strike this innocent beast? I thought of the tasks ahead of me and shivered. Tried to imagine myself running through each step.

First, I would need to kill it quickly. Perhaps a single axe blow to the neck at full force would do the trick.

But what if it didn't?

Perhaps two or three hits.

Nausea grew in my belly.

Afterward, I would need to take hold of the dead beast and cut its skin from the muscle. Then I would need to put the skin on a rack and scrape it clean so it would not rot.

No clean process.

The sheep nuzzled my palm with its nose, and I closed my eyes and shook my head.

I dropped my weapons and clutched its fur, laying my forehead on its back. "I am sorry, my friend."

My fingers rolled the rough fibers of its wool, and the warmth emanating from the beast's body sparked an idea. I looked down at the beast and realized it was chewing slowly, completely comfortable with my presence.

What if it need not let me take its skin? What if it could just let me take its fur?

I reached up and grabbed my own hair, which had grown and now fell into my eyes.

Surely the sheep's fur might regrow as mine did. But if I took its skin, it would die.

I grabbed hold of my obsidian axe perhaps a bit too violently, and it scooted a step and bleated.

I patted it gently. "No, no. You're all right. This is a better way."

I grabbed a lock of my own hair and sliced it through with the axe. "See?" I held out the severed hair, and the beast sniffed it before going back to chewing. "It does not hurt."

Several of the other animals were now grazing beside me, as well. I considered how I had planned to slay them and realized how much of a waste that now seemed.

"I only need your fur," I said. "May I take some?"

None of the beasts answered. But of course they wouldn't. They were not like the serpent.

I grabbed hold of the fur at the top of the beast's shoulder and set the axe head against it at an angle. With a soft scraping motion, the fur came loose in large clumps that held together.

I nearly leapt and ran in a circle, I was so elated. I continued to scrape carefully, until I'd removed the majority of the first sheep's fur. I lifted the pile and considered what we might do with it. At the very least, we might be able to form better bedding with it, or perhaps some sort of covering to warm us at night.

But for it to be truly useful, we would need much more. I counted the sheep around me.

Seven, twelve, fifteen, twenty-two sheep in all. Each with a mound of wool on its back.

I closed my eyes and thanked Father, then set about cutting the fur from two more sheep. It took me two trips to carry the wool back. It would have taken more if the wool hadn't had such a way of clinging to itself.

I piled it in our shelter so it would not get covered with dirt. Then I sat and considered what might be done with it. Perhaps we could sew fig leaves together and stuff the wool into the pockets between leaves?

No, that was foolish. The leaves would rip and the cold fibers would steal any warmth the wool might offer.

We could lay the wool out beneath us, but what would keep it from being blown in the wind? Could there be some way of weaving it? It seemed an impossible task as I pulled apart the fibers and looked at the individual hairs.

Footsteps sounded as Eve rounded the shelter and saw me staring at the pile of fur. "There you are," she said. "What is—"

Her brows furrowed.

"Adam, what is that?"

"I thought of a way we can make better coverings."

She lifted the hunks of wool and looked at me. "This is no covering. This is . . ."

"From a sheep."

"You were supposed to get skins."

I shook my head. "I couldn't." My face reddened, and I scratched the back of my head and averted my eyes. "If you had been there, you would understand."

She cleared her throat and folded her arms, taking in the mound of wool.

"Besides, skins won't keep us warm like this fur might. Taking it did the beasts no harm. Their fur will grow back, in time, I think. And we might now have a way to warm ourselves better. If only we can think of how to work it."

She pulled apart the fibers, seeing how they responded to her touch. With a gentle tugging motion, she began to form the hunk in her hands into a thin sheet.

She set the sheet down and stared at it with a frown. "I don't know what to do with this."

I shrugged. "There must be some way to turn it to good use."

She rubbed her face. "Well, it is time to eat. Come, help me start a fire. The other went out."

I did, and soon the fire crackled, and we set clay pots filled with water on the coals. With smaller obsidian knives, we cut vegetables and tossed them in the pot.

Eve stirred the soup with a long stick and pulled apart leaves of parsley and tossed them in.

When the soup was finished, we took the pots off the coals to cool, then poured the soup into clay cups and filled other cups with cool water from the stream. Then we returned to our shelter and ate.

As we stared at the surroundings, like we had countless times, Eve spilled her cup of water on some of the wool. "Oh no." She glared and swiped the moisture from the sheet of wool she'd formed, setting the cup upright again.

"Do you need me to get you more water?"

She stared at the wool. "No." She dipped and looked closely at the fibers. Then blew on them to dry them.

"What are you doing?"

"Hush," she said and continued blowing.

As the wool dried, it looked slightly matted.

She lifted the sheet and bent it. It remained fairly uniform. She tugged lightly on it, and it started to come apart. She set it back down and stared more.

"What is—"

She lifted her hand to silence me. "I might have thought of a way to use this."

She picked up another lump of fur and began that same gentle tugging motion, forming it into a second sheet of roughly similar shape and size. She layered the second sheet on the first, at an angle, and wetted her hands with some of the hot water from the soup, gritting her teeth despite the discomfort. She swept her hands across the fur, matting the sheets together with long strokes from her fingernails at angles.

After finishing, she blew across the fibers again until they were dry. When she lifted the two sheets, they held together. She pulled on the fibers and found it held together much better. She nodded. "I will get to work. Can you gather more wool?"

I nodded. "The herd is not far, and perhaps I can coax them closer."

She lifted another hunk of wool and began to tug it into a sheet.

"What about your food?" I said.

"It can wait. If we get more wool, I can sew tunics for us and broad coverings to pull over us at night. This changes everything."

"How much more will you need?"

She shrugged and began to motion with her hands as if counting. "Perhaps thrice this amount, assuming I don't make too many mistakes. But already my mind is bursting with ideas, and many of them may not work."

I nodded. "If they don't, you will think of a way."

She smirked. "Will I?"

"Finding this today has given me hope."

Her expression sobered. "Thank you, Adam." Her dark eyes seemed to peer through and steal my breath.

I cleared my throat and said, "Thank you."

"Many days I have not wanted to live. Lately, however, I have been looking toward the next sunrise with expectancy. With hope."

I reached my arm around her and said, "Then let us live while hope remains."

She looked down at the wool and nodded. "Yes. Let us live."

Chapter 19

I found the herd of sheep again, and with my long stick, gently urged them back to the orchard. They had plenty of grass to graze on near us, for Father had turned much of the desert wasteland into prairie. Yet we would need to work hard to keep them from our vegetables.

I thought little, then, of the miracle of Father's provision. From the little we have shared of Eden, many believe that after we sinned, we were on our own. But that could not be further from the truth. We would have died without him. We still would. Every day that the sun rises is an act of his mercy, even when it seems a punishment to endure.

Yet in the ensuing weeks, the moroseness that hovered over Eve passed away like a storm cloud that never released its rain. After we gathered enough wool, she formed rough tunics and pants for us by sewing patches of matted wool together with stripped reeds.

Her long, nimble fingers worked deftly, trying new techniques that she invented day by day. Overlapping squares here, trimming them there to fit the curves of our bodies.

Some of the wool was ruined in the process, though most could be reworked in time. From this and the excess left after our clothing, she formed large covers for us to pull over ourselves at night. In the day, we folded them and tied them carefully to the inside of the shelter so they would not blow away when the winds rose.

I added more palm fronds to the roof of our shelter, and then set about thinking of a way to expand and improve upon our lean-to. It seemed that a shelter with closed walls and a roof might protect us better from the growing chill. Now that the desert wasteland had been transformed into prairie, the temperature did not drop so violently at night.

Yet the seasons were changing, and from what Father taught me, soon we might see flakes of snow on the wind. What would we do if the weather worsened and our vegetables died or our fruit trees bore no fruit?

A pall of anxiety returned as we worked. Eve was surprisingly happy. Though I was satisfied with the change in her, now I worried I might not be able to provide for her as I should. When I thought of the approach of unknown dangers, I felt powerless. The idea of introducing a child into such a world overwhelmed me.

Yet she would not give up attempting to become pregnant. Every night, she rolled close and kissed me. Every morning I awoke with a pit in my stomach, wondering if soon her belly would grow with child.

After a month passed, Eve's excitement dwindled, and the space between our times of intimacy lengthened. She took to wandering the hills alone in the evenings. When she began bleeding again, as she did every month, she sat in discomfort and quiet anger until it passed.

I did not speak to her during this time, for I knew that the discomfort made her temperamental, and she was rightly disappointed that she did not yet have a child growing within her.

Still, I could not help but embrace the hope that it might not happen.

. . .

I waited until the timing felt right. Then, one morning, as we arose and she stared at the beautiful sunrise in the distance, I slipped my fingers into her hand and waited.

"What shall we do today?" she said.

"The grain is ready for harvest," I said. "Perhaps it is time to try your idea for storing it. Without that, we might not make it to the Day of Atonement."

She took a deep breath and let it out slow. Nodded.

I pushed back the wool covering that still lay over our legs. "I am sorry."

She scoffed and shook her head. "For what?"

"I know the frustration not having a child has caused you."

"It has been seven weeks, Adam. Will it never happen?"

I nodded. "It will, eventually. Father promised it."

She snorted. "Father."

My expression darkened. She saw the question in my eyes.

"Where is he now?" She waved her hand as if in dismissal. "He is not helping me. Why should I trust distant words I can hardly even remember?"

"Because he is our Maker. Our Father. The one who gave us this orchard and provided for our needs. The one who formed skins for us to wear when our nakedness shamed us."

She chewed the inside of her cheek and looked at the ground.

"As much as it has frustrated you," I said, "I believe it is a mercy."

She glared at me. "Don't speak to me of mercy."

"The seasons are changing. We have not yet even weathered a full cycle."

"Why do we need to weather anything at all?"

"You know why . . ."

"Do I?" She pushed back her hair and hugged her knees to her chest.

"We do not know how difficult it will be to keep ourselves fed and protected. Having a child in such times seems foolish."

"Without a child," she said, "what reason is there to continue?"

"Eve," I said. "Don't be so——"

"So what? Face what lies before us! Day after day of monotonous existence. And for what? Look at my hands." She held them out. The bruises and blisters and cuts and calluses shone in the morning light. "What sort of life is this? Without the hope of everything changing?"

"The only hope you have for change is the trust you put in Father's promise that he will deliver us from the curse the serpent convinced us to receive. Is that not why you long for a child so badly? For the one who would crush the serpent's head?"

She shrugged and averted her gaze. "I want many things."

"And yet we have much now. We must live. Is that not what you said?"

She rubbed her face and groaned. "Yes, we must live . . ." She stood, and wandered toward the orchard, running her hands across the trees as though she expected the friction to spark in her the desire to do just that.

Chapter 20

Over the next few weeks, we worked toward Eve's plan to store our grain, which was drying on stalks in the late summer breeze. Autumn approached. Leaves turned color and the wind blew cold and dry in the night. Grasses gained tassels that tossed and shimmered like amber feathers.

With a crude stone shovel, I dug into the hillside and found a large deposit of clay. It was just what we needed to build our threshing floor. I dug up and piled the clay next to a hole dug beside our little river. For two days we prepared for the mountain of work that lay before us.

Eve used our axe to cut and pile dried straw bound with reed fibers in bunches. I mixed the clay with sandy soil in the hole as Eve poured water from the stream with large clay pitchers. We crunched up straw in our hands and sprinkled it in, then mashed it together with our feet and turned it up with our hands.

I tossed lumps of the new building material beside the hole, and Eve grabbed globs and tossed them into little wooden molds we had prepared. She wetted her hands, smoothed the tops, and wiggled the molds loose, leaving a rectangular brick to dry in the sun.

Before the bricks were fully dry, we set them in overlapping circular rows with a diameter of my height. Then we patched the holes. For five days we added to this structure, then built beside it brick stairs to reach the top, where a small opening remained for tossing fuel. At the bottom remained two exits. One for placing large pieces of clay for firing, and another to guard a little structure holding in place a paddle fan that we would use to coax the flames hotter than would otherwise be possible.

Finally we built a brick floor near our old shelter. This took the better part of two days, for we wanted to build a floor large enough to lay a sufficient amount of grain on. After several more days, it was fully dry. As cracks formed, we patched them, so that in the end we were left with a relatively smooth and consistent floor that little bits of grain would not get lost in.

Over the next week, we harvested as much grain as we could. Blisters formed on our hands from wielding the rough wooden tools that I'd formed with primitive skill. At night we sat around the fire and soaked our hands in water warmed over the coals to ward off infection and sooth the pain.

We talked little, for there was little to talk about. We knew what we must do. All that remained was to do it. Eve still hoped to conceive; yet another week went by and she bled again as before. I could say nothing to soothe her, nor offer comfort to temper her anger.

Still, we remained intimate with one another, for she would not give up. Once she set her mind to achieve something, she continued until she attained it. I would not complain, but for the current of rage beneath the surface of her skin. I felt a dark foreboding. More than ever I wished to stop her, but I couldn't. Not without destroying the last bit of openness she'd given me.

That was how, nearly a month after beginning our work, we finished the threshing floor to dry our grain on and had harvested and processed enough grain to fill two large clay containers nearly the size of Eve, which we had fired in our new large furnace. We stopped their tops with clay and stored them on the threshing floor.

The rest of the grain lay drying on the floor, and a third container waited to the side to keep through winter. We ground a bit of what was left and cooked flat cakes in our smaller furnace. They were bitter, but they filled our bellies and gave us the energy we needed to finish the last of our work before winter.

In the mornings, when we woke, frost tinged the tips of leaves and burned our ears and noses. Luckily, the wool blankets and tunics we'd formed kept us warm enough, though our feet hurt as we walked the cold ground.

I stripped pieces off the worn-out tunics that Father had made and formed them into sandals for our feet. Eve helped me sew them together with extremely thin strips of animal skin taken from the tunics, and we stuffed the insides with wool pads for warmth.

The ground was beginning to harden and become difficult to work with. Still, when the sun was high, I was able to form more bricks and build walls around part of our threshing floor, to form a small home to keep out the wind.

We built the roof with long, thin beams of wood. This was the trickiest part, because finding the right materials became challenging and time consuming. After laying enough beams across the roof, we placed more rows of wet bricks atop them, embedding the beams in clay, and covering the rest of the wood with bricks as well. This wasn't as easy, and the bricks dried uneven and cracked. Many times I patched them, and before completely finishing, a late storm rolled in with a stark drop in temperature.

The clouds piled high like black boulders in the sky. We huddled in our new home as lightning split the air and thunder rattled the pottery lining the walls. The open doorway was the only source of gray light. Rain shot through and soaked the floor. We lifted the wool coverings and tried to push the water back to keep it from soaking the grain pots.

"What is that?" Eve said and stood listening.

In the distance it sounded as though many stones were falling to the earth.

The skin down the back of my neck prickled, and I peered out the door. Then quickly backed up as sheets of hail fell toward us. One bounced off the brick and rolled toward me. I picked it up between my fingers. It measured approximately the size of my thumbnail and melted in my hand.

"It is water," I said.

"But it is like a stone."

"Feel it."

She dipped her finger into the growing pool in my palm and brought it to her tongue. Her eyes widened. "What has caused such a strange storm? Is Father angry with us?"

I stared at the open doorway. "I do not know."

"It is good that we harvested our grain," she said.

"I wonder what this will do to our garden."

"Our vegetables must be getting beaten."

I nodded, and as the air continued to chill, we huddled under the wool covering. The hail did not last long, but so much of it fell that when the storm passed and we carefully exited our home, we found the ground covered in a sheet of ice, for the hail had melded into a hard, slick surface. Even with our makeshift boots, we slipped, and Eve fell and bruised her elbow.

We made it to our little vegetable patch and saw some of our squash lying with newly dug scars. The leaves of all the plants lay bent and punctured. I squatted and examined the branches.

"Will everything survive?" Eve said.

"I do not know. The plants will suffer, and some of the fruit we must eat in the next few days, before it rots."

"What if another storm like this comes?"

"That is what I fear," I said.

I stood and faced west, as if to catch a glimpse of Father's expression in the distance. I did not understand for what reason he would send such a storm. Yet I was only pondering what I already knew was coming. Soon snow would fall, and the cold weather would destroy most of what we'd labored to tend.

A cycle of life and death. This was how Father intended the world to be. Yet suddenly I did not care whether Father's decree was a response to our evil. The mere fact that he had commanded the world to work so brought a clutching anxiety that stifled my breathing.

Eve saw my expression and laid a hand to my shoulder. "Are you all right?"

I swallowed hard and closed my eyes. "Yes. I am only weary."

We made our way carefully back to our new home and lay on the floor with our covering over us for a midday nap. Eve remained restless. Exhaustion lay heavy across my shoulders, but every time I nearly fell asleep, anxiety woke me like hands around my throat.

After some time, Eve sat and stared out the open door. Then she stood and exited. I tried to stay and rest, but it was no use. Too much weighed on my mind.

I found her just outside, sitting on the edge of our threshing floor. The hail had melted, though the holes it left in the leaves remained.

I sat next to her.

"Can't sleep?" she said.

I shook my head.

"I am hungry, but I cannot eat."

I looked at her. "Didn't you eat this morning?"

"No," she said. "I managed to eat a bit of the green squash yesterday. That is all."

I considered her. Her eyes were clear and intense, and seemed to be peering at something in the far distance. Her jaw flexed, as though chewing on each word before letting it fly. There was something resolute in her expression. A slight upturn at the corners of her mouth that hinted at hope.

"It has been long," she said.

I knew what she meant.

She took a deep breath and closed her eyes as if to savor it. "I am trying not to become too hopeful. But——"

"You believe a child grows within you," I said, and my own abdomen filled with cold darkness.

She glanced at me and suppressed a smile. "I do."

I cleared my throat and tried to push back the anxiety that rose like a wild beast in my chest.

Her mouth turned downward. "You are afraid."

I tipped my head as though I did not know. "How can I know what this will bring?"

She looked down and stared at her feet, covered in those scavenged boots.

"I am happy for you," I said.

"But not for yourself."

"I don't know, Eve."

She stared, and her frown deepened. She stood and entered the house again. I remained for a while, wondering if she would return.

After a moment, I heard her crack open a clay container.

I shot to my feet and entered to find her opening the fourth, smallest container of grain. "What are you doing?"

"The bread went down well enough the other day."

"We must not waste any grain prematurely."

"I need food," she said, and her eyes gained a hard edge. She took a clay cup and dipped it into the grain, pouring it into a grinding bowl. Then she set about crushing it with a rough, round stone.

I let her work, for I knew she was right. She was thin. Much thinner than when we walked in the garden. At that time, she had been healthy and thick. Now, her dark arms and legs were sinuous. If she truly had a child growing in her belly . . .

She would need even more food than I had eaten.

I walked back out, and she exited and started a fire in the furnace with dry wood we had stored in our home. She made more of those bitter cakes; only this time she tore dried figs and sprinkled them through the dough.

When the cakes were finished, she nibbled them slowly, until she managed to eat nearly two of them. The remnants she gave to me.

As I tried it, the sweet bread filled my mouth with such unusual flavor that my tongue tingled and my stomach ached.

"Did you make anymore?" I said.

She shook her head. "You said not to waste it. After that storm, we must use up the damaged squash. But I cannot eat it."

She was right, of course.

I went out and harvested two. I returned, stoked the fire in the furnace, and baked the squash. The fire got too hot and charred the outside. I retrieved them from the furnace, and broke them open, but the insides were only partially cooked.

I forced it down, for I was hungry and did not want to be wasteful, lest Eve point out my hypocrisy. Eve went to bed early, leaving me alone as the sun dipped beneath the cloud cover and shot color across the billowing clouds. A sheet of rain fell in the distance like a slow-moving shadow.

The anxiety that had come in waves seemed to turn everything I had eaten rotten. I steadied myself on my palms and knees and breathed deep to fight the urge to vomit. I could not afford to lose any nutrients. Neither of us could.

Yet the thought of Eve bearing a child through the most difficult season we had yet faced . . .

The days would grow shorter as our work grew longer. I would need to gather much firewood and store it inside so it would not be wetted by the weather and so grow impossible to work with. But my hands already bled with blisters from our rushed work storing the grain and building the new structures.

The late summer rains had given us cold nights already. I could not imagine what would happen in the middle of winter.

Would our coverings be enough? Would the food we stored be enough to get us through?

I did not know how long winter would last. I had neglected

to ask Father. Now I wished I could go back to him and ask so many questions.

But he had told us he would be with us. Had he not?

Yet he felt so distant, and we no longer heard his footsteps or felt his touch. So it was true that he was not with us—at least, not in the way he had been.

Still, sometimes in my dreams, I thought I heard his voice. And the memory of his smile brought warmth in my chest on the coldest of days.

Was it possible his Light was hidden, however dimly, in the light of the sunrise and the reflection of the moon?

When I considered his unending wisdom, his ability to see when he was not even present, I became certain he saw us now. I had only thought of it a few times since leaving Eden, but as I sat there pondering our chance of survival, I wondered again if he could hear my thoughts.

For he had crafted the universe with his words. Words were how he worked, were they not? It stood to reason that he cared for the words I thought as much as he cared for the words I spoke.

I closed my eyes to see his fingers bright before my eyes when I woke for the first time. He said he would always be with us. Perhaps that was a promise that he could hear my prayers now.

I stood and faced west with arms outstretched as if to receive his fatherly embrace. "Almighty," I said. "I believe that you are able to help us." I paused, remembering the depth of evil that gripped my soul at the foot of the Tree of the Knowledge of Good and Evil. The sound of the serpent hissing as Eve and I tasted the forbidden fruit.

We deserved death and cold pain and the lonely wakefulness of endless darkness. What right did I have to ask him for anything?

"Please," I breathed. "Tell me how long this winter will last. Tell me whether we will survive it."

Silence. No answer but the wind shaking the trees as darkness fell complete.

No stars tonight. The clouds were too thick.

The darkness seemed answer enough.

I crawled back beside Eve, who was sleeping soundly, and lay quaking and sleepless until, hours later, I finally succumbed to dark dreams.

Chapter 21

In my dream, we were hiding again in Eden with fig leaves covering us. When Father called us from the brush, a great pit opened beneath my feet, and I fell alone into a black shaft. My insides churned as the wind whipped my hair. I screamed, but all sound was swallowed by the hungry hollow gaping infinite below me. The tendrils of a great serpent's tail coiled around me and—

I woke with a start as a terrible noise erupted from my throat.

Eve shook me hard. "Stop, Adam, stop!"

I gasped for breath and clutched at my throat, feeling for the serpent that had moments before been strangling me, but it was gone.

It was not yet light, but I could see enough to catch the gleam of Eve's eyes staring into mine. I swallowed, lay back, and rubbed my face.

"What was that about? Say something."

"I am awake," I said.

Eve stared at me as she sat cross-legged. I was on my back, coverings tossed in a furrowed pile. Cold sweat matted my hair to my skin. I shivered and held myself. Eve pulled the covers back over me. "Was it a nightmare?"

I nodded.

She did not ask what I dreamed. Perhaps because she did not want to know, lest it sully the hope she'd taken hold of the day before. For she knew as well as I did that the Almighty had spoken to me in dreams before. I prayed he had not done so again just now.

For it was the fourth night in a row that the same dream had assaulted me. Each night, the dream went further before I awoke.

"I still have not bled," she said after a moment of wakeful silence.

I groaned and twisted. The animal fear conjured by my nightmare still pulsed through my veins, and her words only added more. Knowing the dream was a lie helped little, for I felt that the serpent, a physical being in the garden, now stalked me at night. Whether the dream was real or not, what was the difference? I was suffering. And I would continue to suffer until the serpent's head was crushed.

Eve believed our child would do that. But foreboding weighed on my shoulders like a layer of brick. It made me wonder if the child inside her was an omen of doom. For amidst the promise of good, had not Father promised that the serpent would strike our progeny's heel?

What did that mean? And how did the prophecy intertwine with the nightmares? The unknowns seemed impossible to work through.

I struggled to my feet and exited the door.

"Adam," Eve said. "What are you—"

But I could not answer her. I needed to feel the wind rush over my skin and blow away the storm that churned inside me.

I strode through our orchard, past our vegetable patch to the pasture that our sheep grazed in, like slow-moving stones on the hillside. I dropped to my knees with my face to the sky. Light was growing on the horizon, chasing away the stars.

Eve was excited. Hopeful for our future, as she should be. It was unfair to not return her enthusiasm. But I did not know how to change. It seemed as though my emotions were held captive, forced into some evil labor they did not want to perform.

The sheep dipped their heads and tore little bits of grass. Their feet softly struck the earth.

Being out here, I finally felt a sense of relief.

I breathed in.

Then out.

"She needs me," I whispered.

The sheep directly in front of me raised its head and stared at me. Chewing slowly.

I stood and forced myself back.

When I returned, I found her gathering dry leaves and grasses to start a fire.

"I am sorry," I said.

"For what?" Her voice was cold as she bundled twigs beneath her arm to grasp at more leaves.

"For leaving like that."

She shrugged.

I laid a hand on her shoulder, and she glanced at me. I could see the hurt in her eyes. "I will not leave you," I said. "No matter what happens, I will help you care for our child."

She nodded and turned back to her work.

"I do not understand why I feel the way I do."

"Neither do I. But what does it matter? You feel it."

"I'm trying to feel something else. Something different."

"Don't," she said. And when she looked up, her eyes were rimmed with red.

"Eve—" I reached for her, but she did not allow me to touch her.

"It's the curse."

I ran my nails across my scalp. She was right, of course.

"That is why we cannot love each other, no matter what we try."

I squinted. "But I do love you," I said.

She nodded and chewed her bottom lip. "Think of how our lives have gone since Father forced us from the garden."

I stared in silence.

"Every joy has been met with an equal pain," she said. "We are chasing the wind. Clutching rain. Longing for a dream that's long changed into a nightmare."

"I will always love you," I said.

"No."

"Stop."

"If you love me, why aren't you happy for me?" she said.

"I am, it's just—"

"I can see it in your face every time I mention it. Feel it in the hesitation of your touch at night. I practically had to pull you to me in order to find intimacy with you." Tears flowed from her eyes, and she turned away, hardening herself.

I turned away as well. When she spoke next, her words were no more than a whisper.

"Do you think me so blind? I am not a fool."

"I know you are not," I said.

"Then have you become one?"

I opened my mouth, then thought better of it. Anger charred my throat.

"Speak!" she said.

"I don't know what to say!"

She dropped the twigs and leaves and brush and shoved her palm into my shoulder. "Say something, anything! Stop standing there staring like that!"

I opened my mouth but all that came was a conflicted croak.

She growled and struck me again, until I grabbed her wrist and forced it down, feeling a rush of fire in my veins. "Stop striking me!"

She tried to jerk herself out of my grip, but I held her firm. Fear flittered across her eyes, and she gritted her teeth. "Let me go."

"No. I won't let you strike me again."

She lifted her heel and smashed it into my thigh. I grunted as she slipped out of my grip. My leg seemed to turn to stone, and I stumbled to the ground.

She gathered up the twigs and brush and rushed away, breathing hard and swiping at the moisture in her eyes.

I waited on the ground until the throbbing lessened in my leg. When I finally stood, the muscle ached. I pulled back my tunic and found a growing bruise.

The sun rose cold and distant, its red hues barely reaching my skin.

Through the bamboo, the fire Eve started flickered and hissed as the moisture in the wood fled like the spirits of the dead. I walked slowly around the bend and stopped when I felt its heat on my face.

Eve would not look at me as she turned up the coals and placed another split piece of wood on the fire.

She disappeared and came back with more flour in her grinding bowl. She worked it slowly, the snap of stone on stone joining the crackle of the flames. She worked the flour into dough and cooked little cakes in a clay bowl over the fire, turning them slowly with a flat piece of wood. "I am sorry," she said. "For hurting you."

She said no more, and I didn't see any reason to respond. After she gave me bread, we went our separate ways and tended our duties until night fell and she entered our home to sleep.

I stood, went to a tree near the bamboo, took up a stone, and scratched a notch into the bark. Because I longed for the Day of Atonement, when all our anger would be dissipated.

Chapter 22

The following week, snow fell sparkling through the sky. We spent half the morning catching flakes in our hands and watching them melt.

Eve still had not bled, and she rose to retch nightly because of the pregnancy. The sound woke me every time and left me struggling to fall back asleep.

In addition, I was beginning to fear sleep, for the nightmares were worsening. The pit dream returned every week. In another dream, Eve ate the forbidden fruit and vomited blood. In a third that was growing in frequency as the month continued, Eve gave birth to a baby whose face was mine and whose fat fist clutched a living gray serpent.

My anxiety grew daily.

Father had explained that bearing a child takes time, yet neglected to tell us how much time. Eve had been pregnant for weeks, but we did not know precisely how many, for our only marker was her lack of bleeding and the difficulty that she'd developed in eating. I expected her belly to grow. When it didn't, I tried to hold on to the idea that maybe she would not bear a child after all.

But this was a false hope quickly dashed.

As winter arrived with a slow-falling snow, we decided to perform one last sheep shearing to make additional clothing.

This time I tried to help. I succeeded in matting squares of wool together, but my sewing skills were poor, and I nearly ruined the first pair of pants. As I tried them on, I realized they were too large, and they fell off regardless of how I adjusted them.

Eve re-sewed them, then had me try again. They were still too large, so she performed a second adjustment and made them stay on my hips with the aid of a braided rope sewed through the top and knotted at my belly.

Father had been right. It was not good for me to be alone. Without Eve's skill and clever hands, I would not have weathered the winter.

Yet in the coming weeks her nausea grew, and she often retched through the day as well as the night.

"You must eat," I told her.

"I am," she said as she nibbled on the edge of bread dotted with the last of the dried fruit we'd prepared for winter.

But after tending the weeds that sprang up around the kale, I found half of her bread hidden in a clay bowl in the corner of our home.

I offered her bits of greens to chew on as she worked. She did what she could, but day after day, her arms and legs withered.

"You have to eat more."

"I'm doing all I can. Leave me be."

I couldn't, because I feared that if I left her to her own devices, she would starve to death, and I would be left alone.

Her belly was finally rounding out. At night, by the fire, we pulled up her tunic and felt her stomach, imagining our child only inches away.

"What a strange experience," I said.

She nodded. "Sometimes, I think that I can feel a fluttering in my belly."

"Do you think you are feeling our child move?"

"I don't know." She held her belly with both hands. "But already, I feel more love for it than for anything I've yet encountered." Her eyes seemed to peer down into a deep well and grow clear and focused. "It is a ravenous love. Consuming, fiery, intense."

I put my hand atop hers over her belly. I nodded. "I, too, feel a strangely growing love. Like a bamboo shoot, rising from the ground." But I also felt an equal amount of anxiety, that the child was not well within her. That when it emerged, I would not love it like Eve loved it.

The gap between our emotions grew. She was fixated on the child, and though I longed to meet it, the process fixed my focus too closely on our fears.

Our fruit trees stopped bearing. Our vegetables shriveled, scarred by frost. Little remained but hardy greens, leeks, and root vegetables that we dug slowly, so as not to use them all right away.

Our small container of grain was gone, and we decided we needed to use one of the three large containers left in storage.

As Eve went off to gather water, I cracked the lid and pulled the massive clay jar into the pale winter sunlight. As I stuck my nose in the opening, a foul odor choked me. I recoiled and stared into the opening, which even in the sunlight remained dim. I grabbed a clay cup and scooped some of the grain. It was black and oily.

I stared at the soiled grain and tried to slow my breathing. My pulse pounded as my thoughts rolled forward.

Eve came around the bend and stopped short when she saw me. "Adam?"

I swallowed hard and gripped the container to keep from tipping sideways.

"What is wrong?"

"Come see." I lifted the cup of rotted grain. "It is unusable."

She peered into the cup, then stared at the container. Her dark skin paled, and her face seemed to grow even thinner. Her voice came shrill, "We still have two containers left."

I threw the clay cup against the side of our home, and it shattered and made Eve jump. "An entire container is rotten!"

She chewed the inside of her cheek. "Check the others."

"I can't check the others without exposing them to the weather."

"Then check only one." Her eyes hardened. "If this one won't provide us food, we'll need the next one to."

I ran my hands through my hair. "And if that one is rotten as well?"

Eve coughed into her arm. "Then you will open the third one." Her words gained a subtle growl at their edges.

"And if that one is worthless?"

She straightened and stared with bitter intensity. "Then you can say that I killed us."

I gritted my teeth. "You said it would work."

She tossed her hands. "*You* didn't have any ideas for storing the grain."

I wanted to rage at her, for her mistake very well could be the death of us. But what good would come of it? I knew it would only push her away.

I stepped to the containers to decide which one to open. If only one still held good grain, I didn't want to know it.

I didn't think I could handle it.

Eve exited the home and fell into a coughing fit. I dragged the container on the left out and cracked open the top. When I peered within and breathed deeply, no foul scent assaulted me.

I closed my eyes and held my face in my hands as emotion rose and burned my eyes. I took a deep breath and blew it out slowly.

"What?" she said. "Is it rotten?"

I shook my head and gathered some of the grain in my hand to show her.

She pushed the kernels in my palm and sighed, the lines in her face seeming to smoothen and disappear. "It seems I did not fail so completely as you feared."

I ran my tongue across my teeth and turned away, dropping

the grain in her grinding bowl. "Just make some bread and let us continue. I want to build a door today, and if we don't get started, I won't have enough time to finish before night comes."

She snorted and took the grain as I went off. She ground it into flour and baked little cakes in the furnace. But her coughing continued, and as we chewed our bitter bread, I said, "What is wrong with you?"

"Nothing," she said.

But I knew it was not nothing.

I chewed my next bite for as long as it had taken me to eat the first half. The only way I managed to urge it down was to chase it with a gulp of cold water from the stream.

"Here," I said and offered the rest of my bread to her. "You need this more than I do."

She stared at it, then said, "I can't."

"Then eat it later." I dropped it into her hands, grabbed my obsidian axe, and went to the hills to find a tree to cut down.

As I left, I tried to ignore the echo of her coughs through the orchard.

. . .

By the next day, I had cut enough wood and shaped it flat to lash together a crude door to keep the snow from entering while we took shelter in our dark, cold home. The cool seemed to leach through the brick floor faster than ever, and we took to huddling atop one of our wool coverings and pulling the other atop us.

In the following days, her cough grew worse. At night, when she pressed her head to my neck, heat radiated from her skin.

One morning I woke to her shaking with fever. Sweat matted her coarse hair to her skin, her dark skin was pale, and she moaned in discomfort.

"What is wrong?" I said.

"Everything."

"Do you have pain?"

"Everything that touches me hurts me. Even the wool covering. And I am cold. Colder than I've ever felt before."

I felt her face. "You are burning with heat."

She moaned and coughed into her arm.

"Are you hungry?"

She shook her head.

"I will make you food." I stood and pulled on my wool pants.

"I can't eat."

"You need to. Look at you. You are wasting away."

She rose on her elbow and bit her lip. "I know what I need."

"You are not well because you have not been eating. And this child growing within you is taking the last of you."

Her eyes darkened. "Don't talk like that."

"I am only speaking the truth. Would this have happened if you hadn't gotten pregnant?"

"This is not our child's fault."

"But if—"

"No," she said. "I forbid you to speak thus."

I let a slow breath hiss between my clenched teeth, then grabbed a bowl and went to the stream where I filled it with clear, glistening water. I came to find her pulling her pants on and tossing back sweat-drenched hair.

"What are you doing?" I said.

"I am going to look for fruit."

I grabbed her wrist and said, "Are you mad? No, drink this and lie down."

She ripped her arm free and said, "I will do as I please."

I shoved the bowl toward her, splattering her feet with half the water.

She grabbed it, drank it slowly and with pain, for her throat was sore, then tossed it back at me.

I fumbled to catch it, but it slipped through my fingers and clattered across the brick floor. By the time I retrieved it, she was gone. Off to find fruit that both of us knew was long done growing.

There was nothing for me to do but cut wood, tend the fire, and make a meal for when she returned. If she felt well enough to walk, perhaps I should let her. But I was growing tired of her resistant attitude.

I tended my duties, tossed split wood on the coals, and grumbled as I waited for the bread to cook. We hadn't found any reason to use the large furnace in many weeks. I stared at it as I chewed on the bitter bread, wondering if it would make sense to search for ore.

Come spring, I would be able to do little without metal tools. Stone and wood broke easily when I tried to till the ground. If I didn't have any metal tools, I would waste too much time repairing and preparing new tools. It would set us back and keep us from pulling as large of a harvest as we could.

It hadn't snowed all day, and the air was warmer than it had been the previous week. Eve had still not returned, so I found no reason to stay back. If I tried to find her and urge her back, she would only refuse and grow angry.

I retrieved my thick, wooden stick, useful for turning loose soil, and also a carved stone hand tool that I used for carefully working hard earth. Then I retreated to the rocky hills where I'd found deposits of oddly colored stones.

I worked for hours breaking stones, tracing wavy lines of green, brown, yellow, and black, looking for traces of metal. Father had shown me how to attain copper and iron by smelting ores. But none of the stones here looked like those of Eden. There were so many varieties that I ended up carrying back seven smaller stones that each represented a different potential.

When I returned, I found Eve asleep in our home beneath a mound of wool blankets. I did not wake her, but instead tossed my tools and brought the ore to the large furnace.

It took some time to get the fire started, and even longer to get the furnace hot enough to be used. Working the furnace alone was difficult. I tossed wood in the top of the furnace, then spun the rod attached to the fan toward the back.

When at last I thought it hot enough, I put the small chunks on wide, clay plates and pushed them in with a rod of stone, because the fire was too hot to use wood. I went back to the fan and kept the air flowing, tossing additional fuel as needed.

Then I let the heat die, and as the sun set, was finally able to pull the clay plates out. Four of the seven ores had slumped and bubbled. Two split and became useless. The last was too far from the heat, and only looked charred. I set it aside, then examined the others.

There was no copper or iron that I could tell. Still, the lumps that were there seemed interesting. I tested their hardness with my stone tool, but all were useless.

Disgusted with the wasted time, I stacked the ruined plates and considered how to explain to Eve that I had destroyed so many. She would be irritated unless my search led to any legitimate usefulness. Which meant I would have to go back first thing in the morning.

But night was growing, and I had neither seen nor spoken with Eve since morning.

I returned to our home quietly, careful not to wake her. I crept beside her and slid under the covers. Her chest crackled as she breathed, and from time to time, she coughed as she turned to a new position.

Heat radiated from her as the cold grew through the wooden door I'd built. Sleep came slow and difficult, and I woke to her coughing at least six times.

Then came another nightmare.

Chapter 23

In my dream, I stood next to Eve in a barren wilderness, blinking up at stars so bright they seemed close enough to touch. Blue and yellow and red stars, the light casting a kaleidoscope of hues across our skin.

Eve's belly protruded so far it seemed she would burst. She smiled and said, "The children are coming."

"Children?" I said. "There is more than one?"

She lay down as if we were suddenly in our home and not in the wilderness. The stars seemed to swing through the sky with the rapid passage of time. When they stopped, I looked down, and in Eve's arms were two children. One looked like me, with pure, brown skin. The other was very dark, and very beautiful, like Eve.

Eve smiled at the brown one. "My little lion cub." Then at the very dark one. "And you, my dark lamb."

I frowned. For I was suddenly so hungry that my bones ached. I grabbed at the skin of my stomach, and Eve looked up at me through glazed eyes and said, "You feel that?" Her smile looked like fired clay. "There's no food left." She indicated the wilderness around us.

I spun in a full circle. There were no trees, no fruit, no vegetable patches, no grain, not even any cactuses or sagebrush. Only sharp pebbles stretching infinite in all directions.

"We only need one," she said, and lifted the children to indicate them.

My eyesight dimmed and narrowed until her smiling face seemed a bright pinprick at the end of a long tunnel. "What?" I said, but the sound was distant and echoed strangely.

"A lion is no good for food, but a lamb is different. Father killed a lamb to cover us. Come, eat with me."

I shook my head as the knowledge of what she was about to do sped my pulse. "No!"

Her mouth opened, revealing rows and rows of teeth. Now it gaped, and I ran toward her as she lifted that dark little baby. But she was so far away and was only growing farther as the path broadened between us.

The baby was wailing as Eve's laugh changed into the slow hissing of the serpent.

...

I awoke with a scream dying in my throat.

Eve lay next to me, breath labored as she slept fitfully. I stared at her, horrified, but thankful she was herself. I wiped my eyes to clear my mind of the vision of her mouth gaping with rows of teeth, but doing so only seemed to bring it back brighter. I shivered and tossed the covering from myself.

I pulled on pants and slipped from the house. The door creaked as it fell into place. I waited and listened. Her breathing sounded within, but she didn't seem to be waking.

A few monkeys swung through the bamboo outside our home and glanced at me before swooping away. I jogged to the stream and knelt to splash my face with the icy water.

What evil haunted me? I felt certain that the dream held more than subconscious fears. Eve was no monster. She was my love, my life partner whom Father had given to me. And she would never devour our child.

Yet even the fact that I had to comfort myself with this truth disturbed me.

I had experienced enough nightmares for a lifetime. I did not need another to make me worry.

Yet I could not deny that I now wondered how many children grew within her belly.

I rubbed my eyes. I needed to expend my energy preparing for our future. Not fearing that the serpent was somehow creeping back into our family.

Still, I couldn't stop feeling it was somehow true. Because Eve's love for me had changed, and there was distance and difficulty between us, no matter what I did.

Light grew as the sun rose above the edge of the horizon. I looked at my reflection in the water and saw something glimmer in the riverbed. Narrowing my eyes, I stuck my hand in and pulled it from the muck.

It was a chunk of metal in the rough, uneven shape of a freshly dug ginger root. I spun it and shook my head. I set it on the ground and stood, peering into the water farther upstream. Father had said that if there was one chunk of metal, there were more.

Roughly three paces up, I thought I saw another glimmer. I stepped into the stream and reached, but it was only a rock made of stone and quartz. Several more paces and my feet lost their feeling from the chill.

There was another glimmer up ahead.

No, more like a cluster of glimmers. I reached and pulled up another hunk of metal. Then another, and another.

I splashed up the shore and tossed the metal in a heap.

I had expended all my energy the day before looking for ore when whole hunks of metal had been hiding in the very stream we drank from.

More glimmers dotting the riverbed. There was enough to build many tools. With my hands on my hips, I began to wonder if that was the reason for the nightmare. Without the dream, I would not have run out to the stream as I had. And perhaps the glimmer was only noticeable in certain lighting. Maybe that was why I had not noticed them before. For how many times had I stared into the stream at sunrise? Not often.

Eve would wake soon. I should gather some water for her to drink and start a fire to dry myself and warm my feet. Then I could share with her the good news.

I looked back one last time, then smiled and splashed into the stream for more.

. . .

The fire crackled hot, but the heat did little to cure my feet of the chill that took hold. I had been so excited to find what seemed more proof of Father's providential care that I had risked too much time in the cold.

My feet ached, and I shivered and had difficulty walking. The soles of my feet had discolored, and I began to worry I had done irreparable damage.

The sun had risen, and as I stacked the hunks of metal and counted them, I heard Eve scream. I held my breath and twisted to discern whether she was in danger.

It sounded like she was struggling with something.

I grabbed my obsidian axe and hobbled back toward our home.

"Help!" Eve screamed. "They're taking it!"

As I rounded the bamboo, I saw the door of our home had been torn from its place, and grain was spilled everywhere. Eve was on her hands and knees and struggled to stand while three of the large monkeys that had been swinging by our home earlier dragged off our container of grain.

I yelled and threw myself at them. They were nearly as large as me, and their dark eyes shifted as they bared their teeth and screeched. I swung at the first but it was too fast and slid out of the way. The axe swung through empty air and threw me off-balance. At the same moment, the beast shoved me with terrifying strength, and the blow crushed the breath from my chest.

But I managed to clutch its fur, and the momentum swung me around. I smashed the axe into its back, and it howled and hobbled away as I clutched my abdomen and wheezed. The other two monkeys hopped back and beat the dust, yelling and pointing at me.

I stumbled and swung at them like a drunkard. The two retreated a step, while the wounded one made a full retreat holding its bleeding shoulder.

As my last swing went wide, the nearest monkey grabbed my arm and shook me so hard that everything went dark. It tossed me away and my axe fell to the ground, skittering.

I can't be sure how much time went by, but when I blinked and raised my head, I saw the other two monkeys dragging off our container of grain.

The wounded monkey had stopped some ways away and was touching its bleeding shoulder and staring at the fluid on its fingers as if it couldn't believe what had happened.

My axe lay in the dirt between us. Carefully, I crawled to it. But the beast noticed me and hobbled off, hollering and pointing as if to warn its brethren that I was dangerous.

The other monkeys were dragging the grain so quickly that I could hardly believe it. They were now far away and had spilled grain the entire way. A solitary bird alighted on the path and pecked at the bits. More monkeys joined the first two and helped them pull.

I felt unsteady, shaken by the fight, and lucky to have wounded the first one at all. It was only because the animal had not tried to kill me that I was alive. The thought made me feel ill, as I considered what they could have done to Eve and me both.

Still . . . without food, we were as good as dead. And they had just taken half of what we had left.

Eve was on her feet watching me. "Are you all right?"

I nodded and motioned at the grain littered across the ground. "Get bowls and save what you can."

Her eyes narrowed. "Where were you? I was calling you for some time."

"At the river." I tossed my axe on the ground and hobbled past her, wincing at the throbbing in my feet and the ache in my head and chest.

As I stacked bowls and brought them in my arms, I saw her bending double and coughing so hard that she shook. Over and again she coughed, with no time between attacks to breathe, until she fell to her knees, wheezing.

I dropped the bowls and rushed to her, grabbing her shoulders. "Eve," I said.

She gasped for breath, but whatever fit had attacked her seemed to be passing.

"You must lay down."

Her eyes were squinted shut in discomfort. "Wait," she said. "Give me a moment."

I let go. "You are too weak for all of this."

She raised a hand to silence me as she took three deep breaths through pursed lips. Finally, she retched what little was left in her stomach—nothing but foam. She wiped her face and straightened, eyes closed, nodding. "All right, can you help me inside now?"

I steadied her against my shoulder as we walked back inside. After laying her down, I sat beside her and pulled up my clothing to see a growing dark bruise.

"What are we going to do?" With weak fingers she pushed some of the grain that had spilled in our home.

I shook my head. "We must survive until the Day of Atonement."

She moaned and turned to her side. Her hips had been paining her lately. "We only have one container of grain left. There is no other food."

"I know."

She lifted her head and stared at me.

I ignored her.

It seemed clear that life would never be easy, never be simple. Still, I believed Father had offered little gifts along the way, like those chunks of metal in the stream. Because what could the metal be but a token of his love still burning in the distance? It seemed as though his gift called me home, to Eden. Away from the difficulty and constant striving to please Eve or fill our stomachs.

I stood. "Stay here."

"What are you going to do? You're not going after those—"

"No. But I have work to do."

"What about our food?"

"I found chunks of copper in the stream today."

Her eyes widened slightly. She knew as well as I the usefulness of that metal.

"I believe it a gift from Father."

Her voice came thin and brittle. "If that is true, why did he let those beasts steal our food?"

"I . . ." My hands clenched into fists. "I don't know." Then I walked out before she could say anything else.

. . .

I started a fire in the small furnace after gathering enough wood—which steadily grew more difficult to find in the wilderness. Soon, if I did not discover a new clutch of trees, I would need to cannibalize our fruit trees.

I worked the pile of clay we'd stored and formed several rough shapes. My goal was to craft receptacles for the molten metal that would allow me to form tools. I built an oddly shaped bowl that would form a shovelhead. Then the form of a small wood splitter, and an axe head. Finally, a hoe and a scythe for harvesting.

I didn't have enough metal to make every tool, of course, but that hardly mattered. I wanted to understand what was possible before choosing which tools to build.

After firing the clay molds, I started up the large furnace and worked it into a blaze. I placed the rough amount of metal into the molds that I thought might be needed for three of the tools, the hoe, the axe, and the shovel—though I came up short on the axe. I shoved them into the heat of the furnace with a long stick that caught fire as I did so.

I ran up the stairs, tossed in fuel, and fanned it hotter and hotter. Smoke churned from the top like a billowing tower standing on its head. I worked until the sun set and painful blisters formed on my hands from spinning the wooden fan.

I let the blaze cool and carefully worked the molds from their place in the furnace.

The metal had melted unevenly. The shovel would need another firing. And the axe-head was not sharp. But the hoe had been formed well enough. Too much metal had been placed in that mold, and it bubbled over the side. But the molds had done their job, and I would be able to re-use the excess.

I thought of showing Eve, but she would not share my excitement. She knew the usefulness of tools, but she was impatient when ill, and the recent events had been more than enough to cope with.

Add to that her reaction when I mentioned my belief that Father had given us this as a gift, and it was easy to see she did not want to be reminded of any connection we had to our Father.

Besides, with my stomach growling, I was reminded it was time to check the final container of grain.

· · ·

She was staring at the doorway when I returned.

"I thought you were going to rest," I said.

"I did." She raised herself, then coughed into her shaking hand.

I knelt and urged her to lay again. "You obviously need more."

She cleared her throat and closed her eyes. "I need food, as much as I don't want to eat anything. You were gone so long that I wondered if something had happened. Those beasts were not kind to you."

"Sorry. I should have come sooner. You checked the grain, then?"

"No." She waved her hands to indicate her condition.

I cleared my throat and walked to the tall container in the corner. Light bled brighter with the door hanging broken.

Just one more task to pile atop the others.

I placed my palm on the rough exterior of the granary and paused. I broke the seal at the top and tipped it to peer inside. A fetid, yeasty scent assaulted my nostrils. I turned my head and ground my teeth.

Eve met my gaze.

I lowered my eyes.

She laid her head back and croaked, "The beasts have killed us, then."

"It is too early to say that."

"Then I will say nothing at all." She turned to her side and pulled the covers over her head.

"We still have grain left."

"Two small bowls of it. Winter is barely halfway done, and I can't—" She coughed again, and it set off an attack worse than any of the previous ones. She groaned and held her chest. "Why do I feel as though death would be a mercy? The pain is incredible."

"I will keep us alive," I said, voice low yet firm. "And you will get better."

She let a breath hiss slowly through her nostrils. She didn't believe me, but that hardly mattered. She was bedridden. She couldn't stop me from trying.

"You will see." I stood and brushed myself off.

"Where will you find food?"

"I will find it."

"Where?"

"It does not matter."

She snorted. "What if I worsen?"

I stood like a broken branch, picturing her eyes swollen and dim, face motionless and cold. The words were sapped from my tongue. I picked up one of the two bowls of grain and walked to the door. "I will be back soon with bread."

Chapter 24

We used up the rest of our bread in several days.

It took that long to rebuild the door, for we were running out of trees, and I didn't want to use up our nearest supply. Which meant I had to travel farther and farther for the materials.

The first morning that I woke to sunlight peering through the cracks in the new door, my stomach gnawed at my insides.

I sat up and saw Eve lying on her side, limbs tangled in front of her. I felt her forehead with the back of my hand. Her skin no longer burned, but her breath still crackled while she slept.

I quietly worked myself out of the covers and stared at the wall where the granaries previously stood. By my crude estimation, we still had eight weeks left of winter. It was not so cold as it had been, but snow still fell, and frost coated the trees.

Eve's belly was growing, but her body seemed to wither at an even quicker pace. If I did not find a good source of food, she would die, consumed from within by the demands of growing a child.

Or, if my dream was true, two children.

I pulled on my matted wool clothing and crudely insulated boots, then opened the creaking door.

As it creaked into place behind me, the cold breeze tugged

at the breath in my chest. Bamboo rattled, and dead leaves danced across the frosted ground.

"Adam?" Eve called.

I winced, irritated that the door had woken her. I wanted to finish working the tools, then scour the region for food. Not that I'd found any in my previous searching. But perhaps Father had commanded something new to grow.

"Adam!"

I opened the door and peered within.

"Lay with me?" she said. Then she coughed into her arm and cleared the mucus in her throat.

"I need to work," I said.

"My back hurts."

I sighed. I had refused to rub her back for several days, though she claimed it brought relief.

"It's early," she said. "You have the whole day. Why not come be with me first?"

"I have no comfort to give."

"What if I offered you myself?" she said.

I sighed again, and my fists began to twitch. "If you think me so selfish, why not just say so."

"That is not what I meant."

"It is," I said and let the door shut again behind me. I stayed standing with my arms crossed and back to the door.

After a few moments, she coughed again and groaned.

I scratched my head, then swung the door open.

She was sitting on the heels of her hands, surprised.

"Lie on your side," I said.

"What about your work?"

"I changed my mind."

She stared at me.

"I could change my mind again." I raised my arms as if to weigh the alternatives.

She rolled her eyes and lowered herself to the bed. "Thank you."

I knelt and carefully worked the muscles beside the bones in her back. She groaned in a mixture of comfort and pain. Her long shirt was off, for it nearly failed to fit her now and she found it uncomfortable to sleep in. I stared at her belly and imagined the child within her. She placed her hand over her belly and smiled.

"Here," she said and pulled my hand to the spot.

Her belly rolled and twisted beneath my fingers.

"Say hello." She smiled up at me, and in that moment, she seemed as beautiful as I remembered in Eden. It brought a pang of longing so deep I thought I might break.

"Hello," I whispered and kissed her so that she would not see the emotion in my eyes.

She kissed me back and pulled me to her. She turned toward me, and her belly pressed mine. I felt the child kick my ribs, and the fear of loss and the bitterness I'd harbored against her for pushing me to have a child returned like a wall that separated my lips from hers.

"What?" she said.

I stared into her eyes. So dark and beautiful. I did not want to lose her, this woman who was falling to nothing in my arms. I nearly wouldn't have recognized her, had I seen her walking the paths in Eden. "I have much to do."

"Yes. Begin by being with me." She pulled me toward her again, but I placed my palms on the floor.

"I need to finish working the tools, then—"

"Then what? Find food? We're going to die, Adam. We might as well enjoy each other until then."

She kissed me again, passionately, but I pulled away and glared at her. "Is that where this is coming from?"

"Why do you care?" She tried to kiss me once more, but I put my hand over her mouth and forced her head down. She glared at me. "Don't push me away."

"Stop saying that we're going to die."

She sniffed. "I see no food."

I sat up and scooted back. "I will find some."

"There's nothing out there. Except the sheep."

"What?"

"I had a dream two nights ago. Did I not tell you?"

I shook my head.

"In it, we killed and ate a black sheep."

My belly chilled at how her words resonated with my dream of our two children. Could it be she had the same dream as me?

No. That couldn't be so.

Her eyebrow arced. "What?"

"Nothing," I said.

"Isn't there a black sheep in the herd outside?"

"Several," I said. "But we are not to eat any beasts."

"Father killed a sheep for us in Eden," she said.

"Never did he say we could eat the flesh of another living creature. He gave us only the fruit bearing trees and plants."

"You tried to eat a scorpion, remember?"

"Yes, and nearly perished for it."

"Sheep don't have stingers," she said. "But the ache in my stomach does."

"No. I will not let you eat a living creature." My veins seemed flooded with cold water. If she began to eat living beasts, how much closer would such disobedience lead us to my nightmare?

I must be clear, Enoch. I was not insane. I did not actually consider it possible that my wife would one day devour our child. I knew it to be a symbol of something. Still, ever since Father began speaking to me in dreams, I feared also my nightmares. Her behavior in my dream resonated too closely with the madness that overtook her after our departure from Eden.

"You do not command me," Eve said.

"Why did you want to be intimate with me?"

She blinked. Turned her head. "Why does it matter?"

I reached and slid my hand into hers.

She rubbed my hand with her thumb. Looked into my eyes. "When I looked up at you, before you kissed me, you seemed to me like you had in Eden."

I nodded. "I am sorry."

She chewed the inside of her cheek. "Yes, well . . ."

"But I must work. I fear for you." I grabbed her thinning arm.

"Go, then. And find us food. Or we are doomed."

"After I find you food, I promise I will be with you."

She squeezed my hand and let go. "Then you'd best hurry."

Chapter 25

I scoured the land. Not a seed in sight.

I walked until my feet ached. The sun hung precarious, burning like a great eye peeking over the edge of the world. My pulse quickened. I didn't want to return to Eve with nothing to offer.

I also didn't want to risk hunger once again setting off her madness.

Yet I had nothing to offer but the very thing she'd asked for. The flesh of a beast.

I looked at the shimmering, jagged form of my obsidian axe. The only time I had used a weapon to harm another creature was when defending myself from the monkeys that stole our grain. If I could do it then, I could do it now. Desperation had been my ally in that moment, and I had not regretted my actions.

But this was different. The sun set as I approached the sheep huddled for warmth in the cleft of a stony outcropping that left their dark forms hard to differentiate.

I applied Eve's reasoning and agreed that if I did not bring one of these beasts to Eve as food, we would likely suffer death through starvation.

But that was the problem, it was still so unsure.

Eve disbelieved that Father would rescue us. I was not convinced.

"Then why hasn't he yet?" she would say.

"Because he is testing us," I replied out loud, and several sheep raised their heads.

"When shall we pass? When we perish?"

"No," I said. "We shall pass when . . ."

I did not know. And that terrified me. Already, the weakness of hunger had settled on me like a stone covering. I did not know whether I had the strength to drag a dead beast home. Especially as the dark around me deepened.

Yet it was all I could do.

I raised my hatchet, pulled one of the sheep from its herd, and slayed it as quickly as I could.

It took three blows, and with the sound of each strike, my bones become more brittle.

I stood over the beast's motionless form and felt that the violence had displaced my soul. As though my eyes were windows far off, and my limbs not mine but another's.

The wind blew clouds away from the moon, and as the light grew, I noticed for the first time the color of the sheep's fur.

Black.

Tears came to my eyes. It seems now unreasonable, or juvenile, but I felt in that moment that the dark sheep symbolized my unborn child. That my axe had fallen thrice not to gain food, but to devour my own flesh and blood. Not that the sheep was actually my child, but that my mistake of murdering that innocent beast would somehow bear the terrible consequence my nightmare hinted at.

"Father," I moaned. "Why did you never give us the right to eat another living beast?"

There was no answer.

Yet now that it was dead, could I let my mistake be in vain?

I dragged it home, fingers aching with the weight of its heft. Fur tearing loose as I tugged it over rocks.

I let the body drop outside our home. "Eve," I called between breaths. "Food."

The door creaked open, and she peered out with squinted eyes. She coughed with her mouth closed, attempting to fight an attack.

I motioned toward the beast. "Do not tell me that I don't keep my word."

She cleared her throat. "You killed it?"

I turned away, not wanting to answer.

"We won't be able to eat it like that." Her tone was thin and accusatory.

I offered her the hatchet. "Would you be willing to prepare it?"

"I ca—" Another coughing attack overcame her, and she bent to one side and covered her mouth.

I caught her. "All right," I said. "I will do it."

I helped her down. She leaned back and held her belly, wincing with the pain as the attack finally subsided.

"Will it never end?" She looked at me with rare, unfiltered transparency.

"It must."

She pushed her hair back, some of which had stuck in her mouth as she coughed. "Are you going to eat as well?"

I'd hoped she wouldn't ask. I didn't want to start another fight.

"I don't know."

She grimaced. "That means you won't."

"It means what I said."

"Are you afraid of Father?"

I remained silent. Eyes averted. Jaw clenched.

"Adam, he doesn't care."

"He does," I said.

"No, he doesn't."

"Then how are we still alive?" I said.

"Because of you. Because of me. We kept ourselves alive. We chose to live, just like you said."

"Did I also choose to have these fruit trees grow from nothing?"

"You know what I mean," she said. "Our Father abandoned us. He threw us out to die. What did he offer but parting gifts?" Her hand slid over my shoulder, but I shrugged it away.

"Soon, we will return to him. He has called us home. And I will go. He offered much more than parting gifts." I began cutting into the dead beast and stripped it of tissue. Eve tested some of the meat, but it made her gag. So we tossed it into a clay plate over the fire.

When it was finished, she ate her fill, and I got up to search for more food as she worked more meat from the bones. The smell of sizzling flesh wafted from the fire on the wind as I left.

But I found nothing more.

I returned to find her laying in bed and joined her.

...

The next morning, I snuck out of our home, for I had an unusual task to finish, and thankfully the creak of the door did not wake her. The air seemed a bit warmer, though frost still covered the soil and the last bits of grain we hadn't cleaned up. My stomach had turned to a yawning chasm, and I did not know how much longer I could continue.

Of course, I had no choice. There was no food growing in this region. In Eden, maybe, but that was out of reach.

The dead sheep lay beside the bamboo, its shoulder stripped of flesh and fur. Some blood lay frozen in clay bowls. The sight of it made me wish I had listened to Eve and eaten my fill.

Because how else would I survive?

I shook my head and reminded myself of my task. Regardless of whether I filled my belly, I needed to make things right.

I walked back over the hills to where I'd found the herd huddled against the stony outcropping. They were still there, migrated from when I brought them back, for we had not tended them well through winter and had let them wander.

The sheep watched me with their rectangular eyes, and I bowed and said, "I am sorry. It was a terrible mistake, to take one of your own. I had no right, and I am sorry."

I pressed my face to the ground and put my palms to the earth. The sheep, of course, were unimpressed. But I had to do this, for my own sake.

"Father God, forgive me. For doubting you. For disobeying and forgetting you. I feel ashamed. Do not let my heart become hardened."

As I sat up, my hands slid across the ground, and I felt little pieces of something roll between my fingers. They didn't feel like rocks. In the dim light, I grabbed one and brought it to my face.

My eyes widened.

I placed it between my teeth and bit.

The nutty flavor of grain spread across my tongue. A shiver ran down my neck as I saw more littering the ground. I stood and followed a trail through the sheep toward the rocky outcropping.

Finally, there between two boulders, I found the remains of the container of grain the monkeys had stolen. The top had been shattered, but the body remained intact, and it was still filled with grain.

I scooped a handful and smelled it.

No rot.

I fell to my knees. "Thank you," I said, my voice no more than a whisper. Then I rushed to my feet and leapt into the air. "Thank you!"

The sheep looked at me like I was mad.

I laughed and grabbed the container carefully so as to avoid cutting myself on the broken edges. Then I dragged it all the way home and placed it beside the dead sheep. The frost had disappeared, and I saw little flies fluttering about the carcass, so I dragged the grain farther and set it on the threshing floor.

I did not see Eve, so I decided to start a fire in the small furnace and grind grain. I had no sweet fruit to put in the bread, but that hardly mattered.

I formed little patties and cooked them in the furnace before bringing them in a bowl and setting them just outside the door.

Then I waited.

And waited.

Until finally the door creaked open, and Eve waddled out, squinting in the light. She saw me and stepped forward, spilling the bowl of bread and nearly falling.

"What—?" She glared down, then blinked. "Bread? Wait, am I . . .?" She looked at me.

I smiled. "You're not dreaming."

"But where did you—"

I clapped my hands. "Father provided." I pointed at the broken granary, and she followed my finger and stared wide-eyed.

"The grain that was stolen? You found it?"

"Apparently those beasts didn't find much use for it."

"But how?"

"I went back this morning to the sheep to ask for forgiveness from Father. As I prayed, my fingers found grain in the dirt. I followed a fresh trail to where the granary was hidden among stones. Then I brought it home and made you bread." I laughed, so overjoyed to finally find hope.

She looked between me and the granary and the bread. Then she smiled. "Thank you."

I ran to her and swung her carefully in my arms. "We are saved! We'll survive this winter, and our children will be born."

She gave me a puzzled look. "Children?"

I stopped, and my smile fell. I stepped back and shrugged. "Perhaps you have more than one child within you."

She placed a hand to her belly, mind clearly working through thoughts. "Is that possible?"

"I don't know. Perhaps. But we will have more children in the future, I am sure."

She pulled her disheveled hair behind her ears. "We could still die."

"We won't," I said. "Don't you see? Our Father has provided."

She chewed the inside of her cheek. "So you said."

"You will see. One day, you will believe like me."

She dipped, grabbed a bit of the bread, and took a bite. "As long as we have food, I am content."

I smiled and pulled her close. "As long as you are content, I am content."

She smiled with difficulty. I kissed her, and she kissed back.

PART III

Parents

Chapter 26

"So," Enoch said as he and Adam sat around the fire and watched the sun rise. "Did she grow to trust the Father again?"

Adam took a deep breath. "For a long time, I held out hope. Until the birth, when everything changed."

"Changed?" Enoch said. "How?"

"In the ensuing months, as her belly grew, winter fled and I began to work the fields with my new copper tools. Thankfully, her sickness finally left, but it took weeks. After she was back to health, I enlarged our garden, doubled the size of the wheat fields, and tended to everything as best as I could."

"How much did she work?" Enoch said.

"Little. She was in great discomfort. Her bones ached. Her muscles throbbed. She was weak and easily set off-balance. Once, she nearly fell on her belly while raising her arms to help me prune a tree. From then on, we agreed she should limit herself."

"Was your second year as difficult as the first?"

"No," Adam said. "But for Eve, it was still miserable. Whenever I tried to speak to her of Father, she would find a way to change the subject or minimize my words. Until the day her labor pains began and my fears were proved true."

"How did it happen?"

"It was nearly time to return to Father when I remember waking in the middle of the night to her groaning and tapping my shoulder."

Chapter 27

"Something is wrong," she said.

I opened my eyes, disoriented in the dark. The door was a dim shadow to my right, and Eve lay like a black hill to my left near the wall of our home. "What?" I reached and found her wrist. Her tendons were taut as she drew in a sharp breath and clutched the covers.

Another groan. "It hurts so bad." Her body trembled, and her words came as a pinched whisper.

"Have you injured yourself?" I tossed back the covers and knelt to search for wounds, though the darkness was too great. "I can hardly see. What is happening?"

"Our child."

My pulse sped, and my breaths became ravenous. "Is everything all right?"

"I think I am in labor."

She groaned again and pushed herself to her knees. She blew a harsh breath out as the wave of pain passed. "I need to move. Help me up."

I did. "Did it just begin?"

"No," she said.

"How long has it been happening?"

"I don't know."

I steadied her, then waited as she paced in slow, hobbling circles. Every so often she placed one hand on the wall and another on her back, breathing and struggling to remain standing as waves of pain wracked her body.

I followed her closely, fearful she would fall.

She pushed me away and said, "Stop fawning."

"I'm trying to help."

"I can take care of myself. If I feel that I will fall, I'll kneel."

I watched as she paced through the house, until a powerful wave of pain overwhelmed her, and she cried out and fell to her knees. When it passed, she whimpered with her hands and forehead against the cold brick wall.

"I will get you water." I rushed out toward the stream with a bowl in hand. Mostly because I didn't know what else to do.

The stars were covered by a thick layer of clouds, and the moon was lost. I had considered lighting a fire so I could examine her, yet in such darkness, I would not be able to find the flint.

I stopped, legs suddenly turned to fired clay. Was not today the day we had planned to journey back to Eden?

Sweat beaded on my forehead. I could hear the stream and just make out its shimmering surface. I scooped up some water and hurried back. My foot caught the edge of the threshing floor and I stumbled. Cold water splashed my feet, but enough remained for a quick drink.

I tossed the door wide and stepped in but didn't see her. "Eve?"

"Shh—" she commanded from my left, and grunted.

She was curled on her side in the corner. I knelt beside her. "Here. Water."

But she was holding her breath, fighting another wave of pain. When it passed, she took the bowl and drained its contents. She gasped and wiped her face.

I set the bowl on the ground and waited with my back to the wall.

The waves of pain seemed to come indefinitely, until I wondered when the sun would rise. Her chest heaved like a wounded animal's, and the intensity of her behavior frightened me. I could not imagine what sort of pain would render her so ragged.

She looked as thin as the sheep carcass outside our home. I worried with pain so intense, it would somehow break her bones.

I remembered then that it had been Father who commanded her pain in childbirth to grow. This experience would harden her resolve against Father, because she had not for a moment forgotten his curse.

What would we do after the child was born? Would Eve refuse to return to the edge of Eden with me?

Eve stood and liquid dripped into a puddle beneath her. "Fluid is seeping from within me."

I steadied her by the arm. "Is it blood?"

She pulled out of my grip. "No, I . . . I do not know what it is."

I could see the dim gleam of the liquid as light began to grow outside. From what I could tell, it was colorless and thick.

"Do you think that is supposed to happen?" she said.

I rubbed her back with my palm and tried to keep my voice level. "I think . . ."

But she looked at me with such fear that my words were stopped. I wrapped my arms around her. She rested her head on my shoulder as tears flowed. The waves of pain came closer together now. We leaned into each other and swayed on our feet as the sun rose.

As a surge of pain departed and she let out the breath she'd been holding, I said, "One moment."

I left her to open the door so I could see, for the first time, the state of my wife. Light spilled in and revealed her dark face pale and beaded with sweat. Her hair matted and frozen wild and uneven. Her belly protruded painfully, and compassion washed over me. My soul yearned to help her finish. Finally, after a year of viewing her as my helper, I realized it was my task to be hers, and nothing else.

Yet what could I do?

A wave of pain sent her to her knees. "Adam—" She leaned forward on her palms and spoke through a grimace. Her belly hardened and protruded even more.

"I will hold you, don't worry. Let me just put a covering beneath you. We do not want our child to fall and be injured." I jammed a large stone under the door to let enough light in so that I could see.

She nodded and shook. "Hurry."

I ran to our bedding, grabbed one of the wool blankets, and worked it under her knees. After, she placed her arms around my shoulders.

"Thank you, it is more comfortable for my knees too."

My heart swelled. "Do you want to stand or remain on your knees?"

"Remain," she said.

She breathed deep and held her breath when the pain rose like a wave trying to drown her. I realized after a while that my breathing matched hers, and when her hands clenched my skin, mine clutched hers with equal strength.

"Something is happening," she said.

"What?" I tried to look at her, but she held me too tightly.

"Stay. I need you."

Warmth spread through my chest and stung my eyes. "Okay," I said. My fear reached its pitch. Would anything go wrong? With such pain, surely this process was harming her. I contemplated whether I might lose her as she held her breath and began to push.

I realized I was squeezing her perhaps too hard and tried to loosen my grip.

She pushed again and growled with pain. After several manic breaths, she pushed again. And again.

Now she screamed, and I began to shake.

"It's okay," I whispered through fearful tears. "You're strong." I rubbed her back. "You can finish this."

She pushed one final time, and our first child slid out of her and landed on the wool, still attached to the inside of her by a long fleshy cord. "Oh," she moaned as she looked down at our new infant boy covered in blood and mucus. Our tears fell like rain in a storm. A mixture of relief, elation, joy, fear, and exhaustion.

Our baby had some mucus around his face, and his mouth was wide, but no sound came out. I wiped his face with the wool covering and held him upright. Finally, he reached with little fists and croaked.

He was a healthy, brown color, much like me. And his tiny fingers were little mirrors of mine. He clutched my thumb, and I sobbed with joy.

Eve lay back to rest, and I offered him to her. She took him and cooed and put his face to her breast. He seemed to realize that she intended to feed him, and after a few moments of struggle, he latched and began to drink.

Eve wiped her face and shook her head. "Look at him!"

I laid my hand on his tiny back. Eve's fingers found mine and squeezed. "What would you like to name him?" I said.

Her eyes widened and shone. "You think I should be the one?"

"Of course," I said. "Don't you remember?"

She stared at the wall and shook her head.

"I was given the gift of naming the animals in Eden, and you were not. Here, now you have brought forth our child. What would you name him?"

She stared down at his little face and said, "He will be called Cain. For he came like a spear." She smiled and nodded. "Yes, with the Lord's help, I have gotten a man."

My eyes widened, for I had forgotten that with the curse had come a promise. I had been too distracted by my fears.

What she had spoken was true. This was our firstborn son. A male descendant. Could he be the one to set us free? To undo our curse and crush the head of the serpent that stalked our dreams?

She bent and kissed Cain on the head. "My little lion cub."

My throat went cold, and the walls bent around me. "What did you say?"

Eve looked up. "Huh?"

"Nothing." Against the canvas of my eyelids, I saw her in my dream, smiling, mouth opening wide to rows of teeth. I opened my eyes and cleared my throat.

It's not real. It was all a dream. A foolish nightmare.

She grimaced and laid a hand on her belly, taking no notice of me. Her eyes narrowed, and her brow furrowed.

"What is wrong?" I said.

"I don't know."

I watched her belly harden again, and she sucked air through clenched teeth. "Mmmm . . . it hurts."

I stared at rivulets of blood that followed Cain out of her womb. The entire experience suddenly seemed grotesque, too close to my nightmare for comfort. Could it be, perhaps, that another child resided in her womb?

No. It was all too strange. I knew it to be impossible.

But she had said it, hadn't she? *My little lion cub.*

I shivered and took Cain from her as her labor pains returned. For it was true. She would bear another.

Yet the second child did not come like the first.

In the span of what seemed a moment, I held two infant boys in my arms. One brown like me, the other dark like Eve. My vision spun, and my fingers tingled. Fearful that I would fall, I handed them to her. "Here," I said. "They may want to nurse."

She accepted them awkwardly, arms weak, hair matted with sweat. "Help me," she said, for she could not maneuver them both and also support their heads.

Finally from her womb issued two bags of bloody tissue. I tried not to look as I helped both children latch to eat. I grabbed an obsidian knife and cut the cords of flesh connecting the children to the bags of tissue. They did not cry when I did so, and I was thankful.

"What are we going to name him?" Eve said and thrust her chin toward the new, dark baby.

Grimacing, I worked the bags of tissue into a deep clay bowl and began to clean up the mess with the wool blanket that had been soiled during birthing. "I don't know," I said. In truth, I wanted to get out of our home as quickly as I could, so that I would not hear her say what I feared.

"He's so dark," she said, and my legs turned to wood.

"Yes," I cleared my throat and forced the few steps toward the door.

"You know, he looks like a little lamb."

I swung open the door and smashed it into my toe, stumbling and nearly dropping the bags of tissue in the clay bowl.

"He came quick, like a breath. Perhaps we should name him Abel."

"Abel," I said, feeling the name ride across my lips.

"Yes, Abel." She scrunched her nose and kissed him. "My little, dark lamb. The one who came quick, like a breath."

The brick seemed to crumble beneath my feet, and I steadied myself against the wall. Then I left the home to dig a hole and bury the bloody remains.

Afterward I sat beside the stream in hopes that the moving water would salve the panic that tugged at my soul. Because no matter how I tallied the days, my memory would not let me escape the truth that today was the day we were to return to Eden.

How had we let time slip by? I had told Father that we would return. And yet I had become so distracted by daily life that I had let the days pass unnoticed.

If we left now, perhaps we would reach Eden and find him still waiting.

I stood, vision blurring as my panic grew.

But what would Eve say? She was in no condition to travel. Her body had been ravaged by childbirth.

Perhaps she would be willing to try.

I thought of the blood, of her weakness, and of the vulnerability of our boys. They would not survive a sandstorm like the one I had faced wandering the wilderness last year. Neither would they survive being in the harsh cold for long.

I groaned and held my head in my hands. What choice did we have? He had told us to return. If we didn't, when would we have the chance to see him again? It was possible that we would never be invited a second time.

To have sinned against Father the first time was enough. To fail him again was more than I could bear. We had spent every moment of the last year longing for redemption and forgiveness. But as I stood beside that stream, I felt we had thrown away our only chance to undo the ruining.

I rushed back and threw open the door. Eve jumped, and her eyes flashed with anger. But when she saw the fear in my face and my fingers clenched to fists, her eyes narrowed. "What happened? Are you unwell?"

"We are late," I said.

"Late . . ." Her expression flattened. "For what?"

"For Eden."

She looked down at our boys nursing at her breasts, nearly asleep. Wool coverings partially obscuring her lower half. "You are sure?"

"As certain as I have been of anything."

She shivered, and I crossed to pull her covering higher.

"Then," she said slowly, "we are without hope, but for the hope we have in our children."

"No."

She repositioned so that Abel was not in danger of falling out of her arms. "'No,' what?"

"We could still go."

Her eyes widened. "Have you lost your mind?"

"Perhaps Father is still waiting," I said, "and if we hurry we might speak with him again."

"I cannot." She indicated the tiny forms of Cain and Abel.

"If we attempted to make the journey, we would not all survive it."

I knelt beside her and pushed the loose hair from my face. "My love—" I slipped my hand into hers, but she pulled her hand away. "Please, we must try."

"I refuse."

"What you said when Cain was born is true. With Father's help, you have gotten a man. Two men. A double fulfillment to his promise. How can we refuse him now?"

"Because it is not possible to accept."

"Can you walk?" I said.

"Perhaps. But not far. I doubt I will ever be the same after this day. Come, see my wound." She pulled back the wool covering, and I saw the growing pool of blood beneath her.

She was right. She was in no state to travel.

I placed my palms over my eyes and breathed deep to calm my rushing thoughts. "There must be a way. I just do not see it yet."

"There is no way." Eve punctuated each word slowly and clearly.

I stood and paced.

"If Father truly cares to see us, why would he not come here?"

"Don't speak like a fool," I said.

"Explain why we cannot meet here," she said. "There is no lack of beauty in this garden we have crafted for ourselves."

"How could I know? Perhaps he wants to invite us back into Eden."

"Then he would not have sent us from it and guarded it with that flaming . . ." She shivered. "No, we will never again walk in Eden. He only wants us to be reminded of everything he won't let us have."

"He wants to be with us."

She shrugged. "And yet an entire year has passed and I've not seen him."

I stopped and stared at her. She matched the resolve in my

eyes, until I felt my shoulders slump in defeat. "Must I go by myself?"

She blinked several times. "You would leave me?"

"I would return to him, but you refuse over and again."

"I can't!" Her face reddened. "Have you gone blind? Do you not think of our children?"

"It is for their sakes that I would return."

"At my expense," she said, tone scornful.

I stood and considered her. I knew that if I left now, she would need my help. She could not gather food for herself. Neither could she retrieve water. Even dressing herself would be difficult.

I did not know what to do.

I wish now I would have chosen differently. Perhaps our lives would have been changed.

As it was, I saw no way of convincing her. And to leave seemed a guarantee that all I had done to win her love would be for nothing.

So, instead of leaving, I gathered up grain, crushed it in a bowl, and went to make my wife food.

. . .

Life with two new infants proved infinitely more difficult.

The first day, Eve could do nothing but hold and nurse them. I gathered water, held them while she ate, then passed them back to her as I went to check on our animals.

Some of the sheep had not made it through winter. They died not long after I killed the one for Eve's food, and their bodies had been picked apart, leaving no more than tattered bones in their wake. Those that survived had been rendered so thin by lack of food that a strong wind seemed ready to break them.

When I returned from the fields, Abel soiled himself. I used a bowl of water and a square of wool to clean him as best as I could. Then I cleaned the wool in the cold creek until my fingers ached.

I returned to rest, but tears wetted Eve's cheeks. "Is something wrong?" I said.

"Shh, do not wake them."

Cain's little lips were slightly parted, and Abel's round cheek was squished against Eve's side. Their eyelids were still partly swollen from the violence of the birthing process, and their heads oblong.

"Why do you cry?" I whispered.

"Because they are so precious to me."

I nodded and crossed to her. I reached down and stroked their backs with my index finger. Then kissed their little shoulders.

My boys. My children.

It felt strange to know that I now had responsibility over two human beings. I knew nothing about children, other than that they needed to nurse as often as possible. Father had told us that newborn children are vulnerable and weak for years.

I had been formed by the hand of my Maker as a fully-functioning adult, so I had no memories of childhood. The idea that I would need to follow these boys through their entire lives and teach them how to live seemed unreasonable. How could I? Especially now that I no longer had Father to advise me.

Tears welled in my eyes, and I retreated into the corner to rest so that Eve would not see. With eyes closed and the mid-day light filtering through the cracks in the door, I listened as Eve cooed softly to our children, and then I fell into a new dream that brought excitement and heartache in equal proportion.

Chapter 28

Father was standing outside Eden. The wind blew his white tunic, still stained brown from when he slew the beast a year ago to clothe my nakedness. I viewed him from high above, as though I clung to the wings of an eagle that swooped in, slowed, and circled him an arm's-length away.

I saw the muscles of his jaw working beneath his beard and heard the warm rumble of his voice as he said, "My son, where are you?" His eyes were rimmed with red, as though he had been weeping.

"I'm here," I tried to say. *"I'm right here."*

But my voice was no more than a distant echo.

"My son," he whispered, and tears grew in his eyes. "My son."

"I will come," I said. "I promise, I will come."

Father looked at me then. Eyes following my movement until I knew he not only saw me, but heard my very thoughts. "I will wait," he said, reaching for me with his scarred wrist shining in the sunlight.

And just as I tried to grab hold of his hand, I awoke.

. . .

Eve was asleep. Night had fallen. Cain and Abel lay sleeping beside her.

I rose to a seated position, no longer tired because my Father had beckoned me home, and I had promised I would come.

Eve had borne two boys, one brown, the other dark, just like in my nightmare. She'd even spoken the same words, and that made me fearful. However, as I watched her in the dark, I knew there was no chance that she would devour Abel. I was convinced the nightmare had been a symbol of something important. I was also convinced I would not find the significance on my own.

Only one choice seemed apparent. I needed to leave before Eve woke and questioned me. I had failed to convince her to come with me. And if I told her I was to leave, she would grow angry and try to persuade me to stay. Or otherwise, in spite, tell me to leave.

I needed to see my Lord, and I believed that if I obeyed him, it would go well with us. Though I did not think it so clearly at the time, I hoped that somehow going to him would fix my relationship with Eve.

I realize now just how naïve I was.

I pulled on my clothes, grabbed my shoes, and snuck out the door. I tied the cloth around my feet and ran over hills, past dead trees, and across the barren wilderness that stretched between our home and Eden.

After being thrust from the garden, we had wandered long and slow in the wilderness to our new home. But we had not made our way in a straight path. We had accepted the new home the Almighty provided us. To attempt to live anywhere else seemed foolish, if not profane. And it left us only a short journey away from Eden.

So, I was able to make quick time in a direct line and arrived at Eden as the sun rose. When I saw Father standing in that stained white tunic, tears blurred my vision. I crouched and cried into my hands. I was so overcome with emotion that I could not even make it to him.

Instead, he came to me.

His footsteps brought back the memory of cold fear and the scrape of branches as I hid from him in Eden. My weeping intensified as he slid his arms under mine and urged me up.

I found my footing with shaky legs and leaned into him. My tears soaked his shoulder. But I was most surprised when I realized my hair was wetted with tears of his own.

"My son," he whispered, voice strained.

I clutched his back. The warmth of his Light was gone, but the warmth of his body was as real as anything I'd ever felt before.

My Father. The one who brought me into being.

He had waited for me. Just as he'd promised.

I became suddenly convinced that he was who had been giving me dreams. That in my nightmares, he had been warning me of the serpent's influence. That he had provided for us all along, offering us food and keeping us alive.

And everything he had done in the past year was for this moment. So that we might be together again.

We disentangled, and he held my shoulders and stared soberly. "Where is your sacrifice?"

My smile flattened. A chill ran up my neck, and I averted my eyes. "I forgot."

"You forgot? Or you chose not to bring it?"

"I did not want to miss you," I said.

"I told you that I would wait." He looked over my shoulder, back the way I'd come. "And you came alone."

I nodded.

He took a deep breath and let it out. "There can be no forgiveness of sins without the shedding of blood."

"I know. I—"

"There can be no intimate relationship without evil being purged. Because evil destroys love. This fact has swallowed your life since leaving, hasn't it?"

I thought of Eve's bitter resentment. Of the difficulty of winning back her love. I nodded. "It has."

He let go of me and turned. "I will provide a sacrifice." He pointed, and I saw a lamb standing just outside the entrance to Eden, which was still guarded by swirling flames. The beast stood and stared at us dumbly.

Father picked it up and brought it to me. I received it from him with my arms under its legs. At last, he slipped a knife into my hand. I recognized the iron blade. It was the same weapon he'd used to slay that first beast a year ago.

"This is the cost of your sin," he said. "I slew a living creature on your behalf a year ago, to cover your nakedness. Now, you must slay this beast to cover your family."

"My family . . ."

"Why do you think they did not come?"

I tried not to look at the sheep, who was staring at me. "Because . . ."

"Because you did not trust me," he said, and his voice pleaded. "You did not tell Eve of your dream and again urge her to come. You did not tell her that I would wait for her. You doubted you had the strength to resist her reasoning and feared your sin more than you trusted my word." There was pain in his eyes.

He was right. I had sinned against him. As had Eve. Yet Eve was not here to offer penance for herself. I knew what I needed to do. But it all felt horribly wrong, and it set my hands shaking.

"I am sorry, Father. Please, forgive me. Forgive us all."

He placed a hand on my shoulder and squeezed.

I placed the sheep on the ground and hugged its shoulder, the flat of the knife pressing into its fur. I'd faced this task before. First, when I nearly slew a sheep for clothing as winter approached. Second, out of desperation, and in the madness of starvation, when I'd slaughtered a sheep for food.

Now, finally, was when I truly did need to shed innocent blood. Not for the sake of food or sustenance, but for the sake of love. To avoid the punishment of death that we deserved.

"Every year that you return here, you alone will offer up a sacrifice to atone for your family's sins," Father said. "This is to teach you the weight of your evil. The price of sin. But it is a temporary atonement, nothing more."

"Temporary?"

He nodded. "You think of my promise?"

"We have longed for its fulfillment ever since leaving Eden."

Father knelt and laid a hand on the sheep. "I will fulfill my promise. It is for that very reason that I forgive you today. Your sacrifice today is no more than a symbol of the coming atonement, and an act of love and obedience."

"But when will our sons participate?"

"Only One will fulfill the prophecy."

"But I have two sons."

Father took a deep breath and stared into the distance as if weighing each word in the scales of eternity. "When your boys have grown to adulthood, I will offer them a test. Then, everyone will see who pleases me. But that is not for you to worry about. You must only obey and return every year. For if you do not return, I will no longer meet you here, and you will lose your intimacy with me. You will be on your own."

Fear ran its fingers down my neck. I nodded, grabbed the fur on the back of the sheep's neck, and steeled myself for the task ahead of me.

This was the payment for every sin this past year. And a low payment at that, for each mistake deserved death.

I would not fail. I would do this painful thing to buy back the time. To give us another year.

So, as quickly as I could, I pulled the blade deep through the sheep's throat. Blood splattered across the ground, and I held the beast as tears burned my eyes. It struggled, and its gaze met mine, frozen in terror. "I'm sorry," I whispered.

Regret and sorrow over the beast's pain pierced me like a spear. I buried my face into its warm fur until its movement stopped and the heat slowly faded.

I shook with horror. Feeling the cold chill of evil. Of wrongfulness.

For everything about this was wrong. Even as I knew it was

how it must be—precisely because *we* were wrong, and our wrongfulness had made the entire world go wrong.

"I will stop sinning," I said, "if this is what it means."

Father stood and raised his hands. "Arise."

I obeyed.

"Now follow just behind me."

I trailed him as we crossed toward the swirling flames. He broke a limb off a tree and held it out to the flames. Instantly, it caught fire. He brought it back toward the sheep, crackling and hissing as moisture escaped the fresh green wood. When he touched the burning branch to the dead lamb, its body went up in flames that consumed and consumed and would not be quenched.

He knelt and held his hands up to the sky, and I mirrored him.

"Almighty, be pleased with this sacrifice, as a symbol for the full redemption that I will see fulfilled."

I nodded and closed my eyes, thinking of the promise. Which of our boys would be the One? "Please," I said. "Forgive us."

When we opened our eyes again, the sheep had been reduced to ash that the wind slowly scattered.

Father's hand alighted on my shoulder. "You must return now. And quickly."

I paused. "Wait. When should we return next year?"

"This very day. Bring Eve, and do not forget."

"I will not let you down," I said. But that was what I'd said about the sacrifice, and I had failed to bring it.

"Remember that I am with you. I am for you."

"I love you," I said.

"I love you too."

Chapter 29

I made my way home as though chased by the fire outside Eden. Without my Father's steadying presence, I felt cold foreboding growing ahead of me. The icy fury of my wife building like a rolling storm.

My breaths came painfully hard. I had abandoned Eve with newborn twins to take hold of the promise of a God she wanted little to do with. I held no delusions of a warm reception.

But I hadn't anticipated the cost, nor how long I would pay for my mistakes. After all, had I not just sacrificed an innocent sheep to cover her sins? To experience the washing blood of atonement?

But I'd forgotten that my wife was not God. And her fury bent to different winds.

I returned by nightfall. The wind was gone. The stars illuminated the square form of our home in silver lines. As though the serpent had lain its body across it.

I entered to soft snuffling sounds as Cain attempted to nurse, and Abel fussed on the floor beside Eve. I could see the gleam of her eyes but couldn't tell whether she looked at me.

"I'm sorry," I said, for I did not know what else to say.

The only sound was of Cain's sucking noises, and Abel rustling.

I crossed to her and held out my hand.

"Why would I want to touch you?" she said.

My fingers closed on empty air. I pulled back and sat cross-legged. "I met him. He was there, waiting for us."

"For you," she said.

"He wanted to see you."

"You didn't tell me. I was here, alone. I cleaned up both boys after they soiled themselves. I couldn't even wash the rags because it was too cold to bring them out." She pointed at the corner where she'd piled them. "Also, I haven't stopped bleeding."

I swallowed hard and prayed for the silence after her words to break. It seemed clear now that I had done her evil in my attempt to please Father, and managed to fail both. God, I knew, had forgiven me. But she was not yet willing.

"I didn't think you would—"

"No, you didn't think of anyone but yourself."

"I was frightened that we wouldn't see him again," I said.

"But he was there."

"I thought he might not be."

"If you believe so much in him, why wouldn't he be?"

"Because . . ." How could I explain it? "It does not matter. I went, and he was there, and he promised he would return again next year, but only if you and the boys come with."

"And if we don't?"

"We will never see him again," I said.

"Just like we would die if we touched the forbidden fruit?" she said.

The cold gleam of her eyes seemed like a spear in the dark.

"Why should I trust your word?" she said. "When you've lied to me so much in the past?"

"I made a mistake."

She lay a sated Cain down and picked up fussy Abel to feed him.

"A lot of them," I said. "And I went back in the hopes of undoing them."

"Our sons are our hope of undoing your mistakes." The emphasis she put on the word *your* thrust like the jab of a dagger.

"The only hope we have in our sons is based on the word of our Father."

"Yes, and he spoke his word," she said. "There is no danger that he will make himself a liar."

"But we must return every year."

"Why?"

"Because when they grow old enough, he will offer them a test, and they will prove themselves at that time."

Her mind worked through the implications. "So, if we do not go next year, you think our boys will never be offered such a test."

"I will not alienate my sons from the source of all life," I said.

A pregnant pause. "No, instead you abandoned them for a dream. A distant God that you treasure more than your present family." She lay with her back to me and spoke no more as Abel nursed.

I did the same, but found no sleep, even after she began to softly snore. Because as I told you before, Enoch, I knew that I'd damaged her. In the coming months she would act as though all were fine, even as the pain of that wound and the root of her bitterness remained. I could see no way out but to return to the Almighty and hope that seeing him would salve her heart, and restore her love toward me.

PART IV

Family Trouble

Chapter 30

"So," Enoch said, "how did she learn to love you again?"

Adam stood and stretched, old bones cracking. The sun had started to rise, and the light of the sun had dimmed the light of the fire fallen to glowing coals. "I am thirsty from all this storytelling. Are you not as well?"

Enoch nodded. "What do you have?"

"A bit of old wine."

A woman carrying dirty clothing to the river hailed them, and Adam raised his hand in greeting and lowered his voice for Enoch. "In truth, I would feel more comfortable continuing in private."

"Then lead on," Enoch said.

Adam took him through the village back to one of the mundane, circular mud huts and pulling back the heavy curtain over the doorway, motioned him in.

Enoch entered the small home and sat cross-legged beside Adam's bed in the dark as Adam left to light a lantern. When Adam returned, the little flame cast a glowing radius big enough to light both of their faces as they sat facing each other.

Adam swept his hand to indicate the home as he filled

Enoch's cup. "After Eve passed, I had to leave that home. The memories . . ." He shook his head.

"I am interested by how much you miss her. You still love her greatly, do you not?"

"Yes, of course. She was my passion." He poured wine into his own cup before setting aside the wineskin and holding the cup in shaking hands. "I couldn't sleep, after she passed. I still can't."

Enoch raised his eyebrow at Adam as he sipped. Fruity and complex. "Why not?"

"Isn't it obvious?"

"Not completely," Enoch said.

"Every pain I caused and failed to apologize for . . ."

"I thought she passed in peace?"

"She did. But after she died, the memories I'd suppressed surfaced like sharks in open water. She had forgiven me, but I . . ."

Enoch nodded. "I see."

"I was prideful." He drained his little cup of wine and reached for the wineskin.

Enoch held out his hand. "Don't drink too much. You have much left to tell, do you not?"

Adam laughed. "Don't worry about me, boy." And he poured another cup.

"Why did you choose such a small home?" Enoch said.

"This one?"

Enoch nodded.

"I have no need for more," he said.

"You still work diligently," Enoch said. "In your old age, I assumed you would want to rest."

Adam sniffed. "If I stay busy, I don't remember."

"So, stay busy and choose a better home."

Adam's right eye twitched. "I'm the reason for your pain. Why should I find special escape? Because I'm old?" He scoffed. "Running from my past only reminds me I can't distance myself from it. This feels like a sort of small penance. It helps me feel better about it all."

In that moment, it seemed clearer than ever that every choice in Adam's life was an attempt to offer up penance for his mistakes. "Adam," Enoch said. "You know you'll never pay the price for your sin."

He took another sip. Nails digging into his legs.

Enoch stared at the flickering flame on the lamp and cleared his throat. "Did you return to the Almighty the following year?"

Adam ran his tongue over his teeth and closed his eyes. "Of course."

"And Eve went with you?"

"Yes."

"What happened? Did her opinion change when she saw him?"

"When she felt Father's arms around her, she broke. It was beautiful. Frightening. Relieving."

"To see that she still loved him?"

Adam nodded. "It revived my hope that not everything was yet out of reach. I sacrificed a sheep from our flock. The boys were too young to realize what was happening, but the experience brought the light back to Eve's eyes for a while. Of course, several days after returning, everything went back to how it always was."

"And that was?"

"Troubled. Even with two children, Eve was unhappy, and so was I. Because even though I gave her what she asked for, she remained hollow, and her bitterness grew like cysts on a tree. She was frustrated at her inability to find satisfaction in what she hoped for. At the time, I thought it stemmed from her hate of me. Because of that, for a long time, I blamed her for what happened."

"What do you mean?" Enoch said.

"As Cain and Abel grew older, I was quite busy tending our garden, fixing our home, and building tools. They were alone with their mother quite often in those early years. I heard only what my boys repeated to me. The first time I realized the extent of her bitterness was when Cain was three years old . . ."

Chapter 31

We were traveling to see the Almighty for the third year as a family. The blue sky and warm breeze was pleasant enough for travel, though we had experienced little rain yet, and I worried for the crops.

Eve was holding our boys' hands to keep them from lagging behind while I carried our lamb. Though the boys were strong and coordinated, we had tried to prepare too much of the garden before leaving, and now needed to rush to not risk missing the appointed time.

The Almighty was waiting outside Eden in that stained tunic, as always. When our boys saw him, they squealed and ran to him. Father laughed and scooped them into his arms. He kissed and held them as I set down our lamb and knelt before him.

Father set down our boys and threw his arms around me.

"I have missed you," I said.

"I missed you, as well."

Eve waited with crossed arms, but a smile lifted her eyes. Father rose and kissed her on the forehead as I set down the bag I'd held over my shoulder containing grain and honey in a clay jar.

"My daughter," he said, and she swiped her hair back.

When it came time to offer our lamb as a sacrifice, the boys said their goodbyes to the beast with many tears. They remembered what had happened last time, for every time they watched as I spilled the sacrifice's blood. They did not understand what was happening, but we thought the experience would help them understand the weight of their own sin when they grew older.

After all was over, the Almighty built a fire and cooked us sweetened bread from the ground grain we brought. We ate together, yet as always, Father's frown returned, and as the sun set, he bid us goodbye and returned through fire to the inside of Eden.

The ache of Father's absence bled the joy from our spirits like the lamb's wound spilled its blood to the soil we'd been formed from.

We made our way back by starlight, carrying our sleeping boys in our arms, their cheeks on our shoulders, their breath on our necks.

Abel woke in my arms partway through the night and rubbed his eyes. I hushed him, for I did not want him to wake Cain. Travel was easier when they slept.

"Daddy," he whispered.

"We are not home yet," I said. "Go back to sleep."

He nodded but kept his head up, staring at the trees like dark skeletons around us and the moon in the clear sky.

"Something wrong?" I whispered.

He shook his head, but I could tell he was thinking.

"Tell me."

"Mmm," he said and scrunched his face as if trying to think of how to say it. "Daddy, why you do that?"

"Do what?"

"Why you hurt the sheep?"

"Well . . ." I thought hard of how to explain it to such a young mind. But how could I? "Do you remember what mommy and I told you? How we used to live with Father before you were born?"

"In Eden," he said.

"Yes, in Eden."

"The fire didn't ouch you?"

"The fire wasn't there, then," I said, and looked back to see Eve was far enough away. She probably couldn't hear our whispered conversation, but I lowered my voice anyways. "We made Father mad by doing something bad, and that's when the fire came."

"Mommy said you made her do it," Abel whispered.

I looked back again as my arms tightened around Abel.

"If I'm real bad, you won't kill me, right?" he said.

I stopped and looked into his eyes. "What?"

"Right?" His voice searching, worried.

"Of course not," I said. "What gave you that idea?"

"Cain said if I was real bad you would kill me."

"That's ridiculous."

"Mommy calls me little lamb."

My world seemed to spin as I remembered my nightmare from years earlier. The horror of it never left me, and instantly it came back thick enough to stop my throat. I wondered at how the ritual of sacrifice, which was meant to cover our evil, could be used to twist my little boy's fears into distrust. "I will never let anything bad happen to you," I said. "I will protect you."

"Always?"

"Always."

My feet crunched scraggly desert grass. Bats flitted through the sky, swooping at insects.

"I didn't make her do it," I said.

Abel rested his head in the crook of my neck. "Why mommy say you did?"

"I don't know," I said. "But it's not true."

Chapter 32

The following day, I started up the furnace to recast the bronze hoe that had grown dull from overuse. Cain kicked a wadded ball of wool back and forth, and Abel joined, though he was never as quick or as strong as his elder brother.

I placed the metal in the furnace and instructed the boys not to touch it. I needed to gather tools for working the hot metal once it began to cool. I could not afford to have them move anything and risk spilling the molten metal.

"Promise me," I said.

They nodded and said in unison, "We won't."

I went back to our home and found Eve there, weaving reeds into a basket.

"Where are the boys?" she said.

"By the furnace."

"You left them unattended?"

"I need to grab some tools." I found what I needed and just barely held them all in my arms.

"You know how Cain is," she said.

When I returned, Cain was crouching by the furnace.

"Hey!" I yelled, and he jumped and walked away as though

he hadn't been doing anything. "What were you doing?" I set the tools down and faced him.

"Nothing," he said.

"He was being naughty," Abel said.

Cain struck him in the arm.

"Leave your brother alone," I said.

"I will," Cain said.

When I crouched and peered into the furnace, I saw he had overturned the mold and the metal had spilled.

Fury ignited my veins. Cain was laughing and kicking the ball past Abel.

"Cain!" I yelled.

He gave me one look and sprinted away, yelling for Eve.

. . .

In those days, the familiar shadow of discontent came over Eve, and she convinced me that she wanted to bear another child. I consented, and in time her belly grew, and she gave birth to a beautiful little girl.

"Her name will be Sarah," Eve said with a smile.

Though Eve gloried in her little girl, Sarah failed to permanently stave off the moods Eve was subject to. I always knew the shadow was returning when she pulled away from me and whispered too much to our children. In those seasons, Cain always became especially defiant.

Time would fail to regale you with all of my eldest son's misdeeds, so I will tell you of just one additional event, to show you that he was that way from the beginning.

When the boys were five, I began to give them true responsibility. Eve's hands were full taking care of Sarah, who was now toddling. That often left the boys under my care as I worked.

One day, I assigned Cain to watching over the herd of sheep while I taught Abel about pruning fruit trees. The sheep were hemmed in by a fence, so it was by far the easiest job I could have given him.

I spent hours with Abel, and when I returned to the pasture, I found the fence broken and the sheep gone.

"Uh-oh," Abel said.

"Go back to mother," I said as my eyesight dimmed. "I need to find Cain and remind him what happens when he disobeys."

Abel ran back without a word.

I searched the hills and found Cain chasing the sheep, laughing as he struck them with a stick.

"Cain!" I screamed, and he jumped and turned.

He tried to straighten and act as though I hadn't frightened him. "Hello."

"What do you think you're doing?"

"Taking care of the sheep." A wicked smirk twisted his face, and I saw in it the worst reflection of myself.

I grabbed him by the wrist hard enough to make him cry out. "You little liar," I said and jerked the stick out of his hand and struck him across the back with it.

"Owe!" he said.

"You think that's funny?" I struck him again. "To beat innocent creatures?"

"Leave me alone!" He tried to jerk himself out of my grasp.

I tossed the stick and grabbed him by both arms and shook him hard as I screamed, "What's wrong with you!"

"Nothing!"

"I give you one job and you intentionally ruin it. Do you realize what you could have done to us if you had lost our entire herd or gotten them killed?"

"It was just a joke," he said.

"Just a joke? To risk destroying our only source of clothing? You want Sarah to die this winter? What possessed you to do such a foolish thing?"

He wrenched his arm out of my grip. "You took Abel instead of me."

Fury washed my vision. "Because he listens! You do nothing but waste my time!"

Tears grew in Cain's angry face. "You give me the worst jobs."

"Everything I tell you to do, you do the opposite. And what is forbidden, you do with impunity. Should I reward defiance? Should I try to teach you to do work when you refuse to obey the simplest of commands?"

"Nothing I do is good enough for you," he said.

"Because you just keep doing wrong on purpose!"

"The Almighty doesn't think so. He hugs me when he sees me. All you do is hurt me!"

"Do good, and I won't have to hurt you," I said.

"It's all your fault anyway."

"What?"

"Mom says it's your fault. I'm naughty because you were naughty," Cain said.

Fury darkened my vision, and I continued speaking in low, controlled tones to avoid screaming. "You're naughty because you want to be naughty. You just remember if she says that again, she's a liar, like you. It's not my fault. It's yours, and yours alone."

"She said we didn't used to be naughty, but you broke everything and now we have to live out here."

I grabbed him again, bent him over, and beat his backside until he stopped talking.

Then I pulled him home by the arm, which remained bruised for a week.

That evening, after the children fell asleep, I knelt beside the river and listened to its chortle. Eve found and faced me with hands on hips.

"Care to tell me why Cain came home with bleeding welts on his back?"

"It's none of your concern how I discipline my son," I said.

"Of course it is. He's *our* son."

I stood and lifted my chin at her. "Then tell me what you've been whispering into his ear behind my back."

"I tell him nothing I wouldn't say to your face," Eve said.

I laughed humorlessly. "He said today that it's my fault he's naughty."

Eve shrugged. "I didn't say that."

"No, you just said something designed to make him think that."

"His arm is black and blue," she said. "You think what he did is worth such a beating?"

"I'm tired of my family fighting me. All he does is disobey and ruin the work I've put into keeping us alive and happy. And all you do is complain and make it worse."

"Nothing you've done has made me happy," Eve said.

"That's such a lie. As much of a lie as everything Cain told me today."

"It's true. I'm never happy. And it *is* your fault. Don't act like you don't hold responsibility in this."

"Stop saying it to our children!"

"I will speak the truth as long as I live."

"You're poisoning them," I said. "You are teaching them that they are not responsible for their behavior."

"If you had not—" Her breath hissed between her teeth, and she held up both hands as if to stop herself. "You know what? It's not worth it. We both know what you did. And that's enough for me."

She left me beside the river in bitter anger.

I was desperately tired of the quiet war I felt she was waging against me through our children. I felt that all she wanted was to have more children so she could use them as arrows against me. To push me away and make me feel the pain I'd pierced her with.

I realize now that wasn't true. But what could I do? I could not convince her that it wasn't my fault. And I could not with-hold from her the ability to have more children without making her hate me, which would only spill over into my children's attitudes toward me.

I needed to find another way to cope. To patiently endure this trial.

I knew Father would want that. And perhaps if I did, the following year he would be willing to address the situation.

I determined to no longer beat Cain. Neither would I address Eve's bitterness. So that when we returned to the Almighty, and I spoke to him, he would clear whatever discomfort remained between us.

Yet several weeks after she left me beside the stream, she told me she was pregnant, and a profound darkness settled over my heart.

Chapter 33

The third pregnancy felt longer than the previous two, yet
ended sooner. Sarah was beginning to speak in complete
sentences, and the boys were difficult to contain. They rarely
fought openly, and for that I was thankful. But Cain was spiteful
and secretive. It was hard to catch him elbowing Abel or passing
quiet insults.

I tried to punish him in what ways seemed best. But it was
difficult not to grow physical, for he responded to little else.

If not for my decision to never beat him, I would have struck
him time and again. But I could not allow Eve to hold my mistakes
over me when we faced Father. For I wanted peace with her and
my children, and if I failed in that search, they would never learn
obedience. Then, when Father offered his test, our boys would fail
and forfeit the fulfillment of our greatest hopes and dreams.

For the first portion of her pregnancy, Eve did not have the
same nausea she'd had with the other two. But halfway through
her pregnancy, she began to feel light-headed and to have pain
in her head.

One day, she collapsed in front of Abel.

Abel ran to me right away and said, "Mom needs help!"

"Where? Show me!"

He sprinted off, and I followed.

She was awake by the time we arrived, though she was confused and did not remember what had happened. I carried her into the home and commanded her to rest.

She nodded. "Thank you, I will."

"Do you need water?"

She nodded. "I would drink."

I brought her some, and she drank the bowl dry before giving it back to me. I handed it to Abel. "Please, son, fill this again for your mother."

He nodded and ran off.

"You will be all right?" I said.

She nodded and assumed a more comfortable position. "I am certain that after resting, I will regain my health."

But in the ensuing days, her headaches worsened, and she confessed to me after the children were asleep that she'd periodically had difficulty seeing clearly.

She was worried. And that made me worried. I did not know what was happening. I understood birth to be a frightening, painful experience. But pregnancy, prior to that year, had seemed less so.

The day the bleeding started, Eve lay napping with Sarah. Cain was playing a game with Abel where they set sticks in patterns on the ground and jumped them in succession. I was tending our vegetable patch and harvesting summer squash. As I lifted my woven basket with ripe squash inside, I heard Eve calling for me.

Her voice sounded thin and harsh. A moment later, Cain called, "Father!"

I dropped my basket and ran home, wondering if something had happened to Sarah.

As I rounded the bamboo and spotted the boys, Cain said, "She's calling for you." His face was pale, and I could tell he was frightened.

I swallowed and offered them a smile. "I will see what she needs."

I swung open the door and passed within. Sarah's tiny voice droned on. "Mommy, you okay? Mommy? You okay?"

My legs felt unsteady beneath me. "What is going on? Cain said you were calling for me."

"Look," she said and raised her hand. Something wet glistened on her fingers.

I neared and tried to see what it was.

"Blood," she said.

Prickles ran down my scalp. "Are you all right?"

"I worry for our baby," she said.

"It's not time, is it?"

"I do not think so."

"How long has it been?"

"The child should be growing another two months." She winced and leaned back on her palms as if her abdomen hurt.

Cold sweat wetted my palms. "Are you having labor pains?"

"I don't know. I hope not." She winced again and groaned as one hand slid to cover her belly. "Maybe."

"Come," I said to Sarah, and she crossed to me with arms outspread, eager for comfort. I picked her up and she clung to me and kissed my shoulder. I kissed her back. "It's fine. You stay out with the boys. Mommy might be having the baby."

"Now?" she said.

"Wait with the boys."

I brought her outside and set her down. Cain held Sarah's hand. "Is she okay?" he said.

I stared at him a moment, wondering if he could handle the truth. "I don't know."

I turned back inside and tended to Eve as her labor pains increased. Several times, I had Abel fetch water. But I did not let the boys see her.

At one point, Cain knocked on the door.

"I said stay out." My voice grew angry, for Eve was in pain and she needed to focus.

"Is mom going to die?"

The worry in his voice sapped my anger.

"If she's going to die," Cain continued, "we want to say goodbye."

How could I say no to that?

"Eve," I whispered.

"What?"

"Can they come in?"

"Of course. Just cover me first."

I pulled a wool covering over her legs, and she rested with her back to the wall as the boys came in with Sarah clinging to their hands.

"Mom," Cain said.

"Hush," I said. "She is in labor. Don't distract her."

He held his tongue, but looked like he might begin to cry.

I placed my hand on his shoulder and met his gaze. "Son, she is very distracted, but she is alive, do you see? She's not going to die, I promise."

"How do you know?" Cain said.

"Yes," Abel said. "How do you know?"

"Our Father, the Almighty, will take care of us," I said.

"What if he doesn't?" Cain said.

"He will."

We stared at each other, both well aware of the blind corners in my faith. But I had neither the time nor the margin to consider the possibilities. I needed to support my wife and keep my children calm.

"Son, I need you and Abel to take care of Sarah. Can you do that?"

They nodded.

"I love you," Cain said.

"I love you too," I said.

They turned and left, aware that I could offer them no more.

Eve arced her back and slid to the floor as the birthing pains overtook her. I propped her up in my lap with her cheek against my chest. She groaned and clawed at my tunic as each contraction wracked her body, followed by a respite just long enough for her to wipe the tears from her eyes.

"Breathe," I said as the pain returned. She held her breath and shook, and I squeezed her as if doing so could press the pain from her body.

When it passed, she whimpered, "I'm frightened."

"It's all right. It will be over soon. You're doing well."

Another wave of pain came, and she moved to her knees and said, "I think it is time."

I held her as she began to push.

But it only took her three tries.

When the baby slid out from her, I knew something was wrong. It was motionless and pale and tiny enough to fit in my palm. I lifted our precious little baby in my hands. "It's a girl," I said.

"Is she alive? Let me see her."

How could I speak the terrible truth? I brought her to Eve and laid our stillborn child on my wife's chest. We wept and kissed her, but this time, Eve did not name her.

After a while, another knock sounded on the door. "Dad?" Cain said.

"Come in."

Cain, Abel, and Sarah entered together.

"Is everything all right?" Cain said.

"Your mother is fine."

Eve silently wept and clutched our dead daughter. "What happened?" she said. "Did I make a mistake?"

"No," I said. "Of course not."

"I walked to the stream yesterday."

"You rested more than enough," I said.

"Then why did this happen?"

Cain touched the little baby on Eve's chest, then retracted his hand as if the touch had burned him. "What's wrong with it?"

"She is no longer alive," I said.

"Dead?" Cain whispered as he stepped back slowly.

"Hush," I said. "Give us some time."

Their feet padded softly out, and the door creaked back into place. Eve wept, but I stayed strong. I didn't feel I had the luxury of breaking, lest she see my weakness and despair. Later I realized the toll that detachment took.

. . .

That evening I took our nameless daughter to the roots of the fig trees the Almighty first made grow. I set her swaddled in a wool covering beside the hole as I dug. With each shovelful flung, I felt the numbness inside me crack. Soon, I would no longer have the sight of her—only the memory of her face.

I had not had the same time to grieve as Eve had. Yet no amount of time is enough when you lose a child.

As my family joined me, I lifted our stillborn daughter, pulled back the wool, and stared at her beautiful little face as I set her in the hole. Moisture dripped across my hands as I brushed her cheeks and dipped to kiss her. It was only as I climbed out of the hole that I realized I was weeping.

Eve stood like a block of stone. As I pushed the dirt over our dead child, I cried so hard I thought I would break open and my innards would spill out. Cain, Abel, and Sarah watched me with tears in their own eyes. They did not understand the full import of what happened, but they wept for the pain they saw in me, and for the wrongfulness of losing a sibling they had longed for.

Finally, when the mound was back in place, Eve and I lay across it and wailed until she had to take the children to sleep. As the moon returned and a slight breeze turned up the dust, my tears dried, and I knelt alone with my face to the stars.

Emotion roiled within me, but the pain was so great that it could no longer escape. I felt my soul was bleeding. To lose a precious little child that you never knew felt like having a part of your soul that you didn't know existed torn from you like flesh from flesh.

For the first time since the beginning of everything, I wanted to die. It reminded me of Eve's despair in the wilderness, and then her bitter emotions when we lost our food and teetered on starvation.

I had chastised her for her weakness, but if this was like anything she had felt, I was sorry for it.

I stood and faced our home. "I lied to you, Eve," I whispered. "We aren't all right. It isn't going to end soon. It is just beginning."

. . .

Morning came, and the children woke early. I went with them to let Eve rest because she would still be healing for the next two weeks and was in no state to take care of our children.

Then again, neither was I.

My children were talking, but their words seemed disjointed. Sarah tugged on my tunic several times before I realized she was asking me to make bread.

"Sorry," I said. "Sure."

As I ground the flour, I realized I'd been staring at the dust and hadn't noticed that Cain and Abel were arguing.

"Boys," I said. "Stop that right now."

Cain wrenched a wooden staff out of Abel's hands, and Abel rubbed the back of his own head.

I finished making the dough and cooked little patties in the small furnace on clay plates. Sarah spun in circles around me and stumbled, giggling. Cain struck at weeds with the rod, and Abel sat drawing in the dust with his fingers.

I brought the food to the children, and they ate while I stared at nothing. Because all I could see was our unnamed daughter's precious little face. So beautiful, yet so terribly motionless.

I hated myself for the mistakes I had made. When I tasted the forbidden fruit in Eden, I had thought of no one else. Only my own pain. Yet she had died because of me and Eve.

And what was Eve thinking? I worried for her, about what this would do to her.

Sarah's little hand tugged at my tunic again. "Where's Mommy?"

"She's resting," I said.

"Hey," Abel said, and the irritation in his voice alerted me that something was happening.

I glanced up and saw Cain shoving a piece of bread in his own mouth. But he was already holding his own serving, and Abel had nothing left in his hands.

"He just ate my bread," Abel said.

"Cain," I said, and Cain stared at me, defiant. "Give your brother your bread."

"It was just one bite," he said.

I stared at him. Too tired and numb to fight. Instead, I shook my head and made my way back to check on Eve.

"Dad?" Cain called. "Are you all right?"

I ignored him and, as I entered our home, saw Eve sitting with her back to the wall, staring at the cracks in the brick. She did not acknowledge me as I sat beside her and placed my hand on hers.

"Are you hungry?" I said.

She shook her head.

"Have you slept anymore?"

She shook her head.

"The boys miss you."

She slid her hand out from underneath mine.

"Can you come out?"

She shook her head again.

I stared with her at the cracks between the bricks until the silence grew stifling. Finally, I took a deep breath, stood, and left her to herself.

Chapter 34

A week passed in disconnected misery, but we could do nothing but trudge on, to the next Day of Atonement, when we would return to Father and experience the joy of togetherness for one more day.

More than ever, I looked forward to the ultimate Day of Atonement, when all our pain would be removed. One of our sons was to be our savior, but first he would need to prove himself when he reached adulthood. Because once he was approved, and Father showed himself pleased, he would crush the head of the serpent and redeem us all.

How would it happen? Would Father call the serpent back and command him to stay motionless as our child stomped on his head? Or was it a symbol of something? Maybe our boy would enter Eden and burn the forbidden tree, and find a way to remove the fire at the entrance so that we could live there again as a family.

Whatever happened, I clung to the hope of it like a dying man. And so did Eve.

One morning, I woke before the sun rose and found the space beside me empty. Carefully, I pulled on my clothes and left our children sleeping.

I looked through the orchard, but found nothing. Finally, I walked down the edge of the stream and found her wading in the water.

Moonlight illuminated her form. She'd discarded her tunic and spread her arms to the heavens as she spun with closed eyes. I said nothing as she stopped and knelt in the stream, letting the cold water wash her skin.

It was the first time I had seen her smile in weeks. I did not understand what was happening, but I did not want to break any small joy, however momentary, so I kept myself back in the shadows.

When at last she finished, she climbed out of the stream and paused as she noticed me before pulling her tunic on.

"How long have you been there?" she said, and her smile vanished.

"A while. Are you well?"

She smiled again at me as the tunic settled around her. "Better now."

"What were you doing?" I pointed at the stream.

"Waking up," she said. "I have much to do today."

"What?"

"I've been sitting around too much."

"Have you healed so soon?"

"Enough," she said and then walked back to our home.

I followed her. She did not go inside, but rather passed around the back and grabbed several dirtied clay vessels and brought them to the stream to wash them.

I followed at a distance and watched her scrub and hum to herself before I returned to the threshing floor outside our home, scratching the back of my head.

And then Sarah called for us from inside, and I entered our home to calm her.

. . .

The next day, I found Eve talking to Cain alone in the

orchard. She knelt in front of him, and he stood with straight posture, staring with all the intensity and sincerity a five-year-old can muster. I heard no words, but when I caught sight of her expression, she was smiling as she had been the morning before.

She noticed me and patted Cain on the shoulder. He nodded and ran off, and Eve turned and walked through the trees, picking fruit and snacking as she went.

Later, Sarah accidentally made a mess during her nap, and I cleaned up after her with one of the spare wool rags we'd formed for daily tasks such as scrubbing pots.

Sarah was sniffing away tears, trying to maintain her dignity. I pulled her into a gentle embrace. "It's all right, dear. Cain did the same until he was three."

"Why?"

My smile dulled. "Because."

"Why?" she said again.

My grip tightened on the dirtied rag. How could I be so easily annoyed at her repetitive whining? I patted her on the head and said, "You will grow out of it soon."

I reached for the door as she asked that dreadful question again, but it swung open and Eve rushed in, nearly knocking me over.

"Oh!" she said. "Sorry. I didn't think you would be right there."

"It's all right. I was just taking this rag to the stream to wash it."

"What happened?"

I lowered my voice for Sarah's sake. "She had an accident."

Eve mouthed, "Oh!" then said, "I can take care of that."

"I was already planning to."

"I don't mind," she said and smiled that smile again.

I narrowed my eyes. "Very well. So long as you truly want to. Are you thirsty, as well?"

She shook her head and held out her hand for the rag.

I stared at her, then slowly offered it. "How are you feeling?"

She grabbed the rag and swung open the door again.

"Good."

The door slammed shut behind her. I stared at it, disturbed. But why?

Was it not good that she was doing well? That she was happy? I should be relieved, and yet a part of me was shaken by the shift in her.

Did not the ache of our loss remain so central in my soul that I could not smile? She could not be free of the mortal wound of losing our child so soon, could she? No, for she seemed to feel things even more deeply than me.

"Daddy?" Sarah said.

"Yes?"

"Can I be awake now?"

"Of course."

. . .

That night, I lay in bed half the night while my mind tended the image of our unnamed daughter's precious face, rendered in ultimate detail by my perfect memory.

My memory, at first a gift, now had been twisted against me like a curse. All I wanted to do was forget. But I couldn't. I still can't.

I did not cry for her. Instead, I ached like an arm aches for the hand that has been severed from it.

When I considered why I felt so strongly for a child I never truly knew, I did not understand it. It seemed unreasonable. But when mixed with the guilt of knowing that I had been the reason for her death—it was like a deadly poison.

I had been lying stone still for quite some time, and the children were asleep. Eve shifted and lifted her head as if peering through the darkness to see whether I was asleep. I did not move and tried to keep my breathing slow and consistent. After a moment, she rose and snuck out the door.

I thought that perhaps she needed some time alone. That maybe the memory of our daughter was bothering her, as well, and she needed privacy to deal with it. I shifted in bed, searching for comfort, but my mind would not allow it.

Then it began. A cold, high-pitched wailing.

I pulled the covers over my head to try to block out the sound, but even muffled, it pierced my soul. I sat up and considered the children. If this continued, she might wake them. And the unpredictability of her behavior worried me.

I could not keep our children from pain, and I could not cure Eve of hers. But whenever possible, I wanted to keep my family from carrying the weights I believed were mine to bear.

I rose quietly and exited our home.

The soil was cold under my feet, and the breeze raised little bumps across my skin. I found her by the river, kneeling with her face to the ground and hands outstretched. I waited, watching until she breathed deep and sat up.

I walked to her, no longer caring to hide my presence.

As I knelt, she nodded. "You weren't asleep after all."

I shook my head.

She sighed and wiped the tears from her cheeks. "I save it for the nights, when no one can hear."

"I understand."

She glanced at me. "I suppose you do."

I slid my hand into hers and squeezed. She squeezed back.

"It's all right, though," she said. "I realized something, several days ago. When you saw me here, in the stream."

I watched her face with wonder as her sorrow bled away, and in its place came the look of bliss.

She laughed. "How I didn't see it earlier, I have no idea."

"What?"

"It all goes back to Eden."

I swallowed the saliva that pooled in my mouth. "What about that gives you hope? We will all die because of what happened in Eden."

"We die because of the curse," she said. "That means that when the promise Father gave us in the garden is fulfilled, all those we have lost will be returned to us."

I narrowed my eyes. "We die because we sin. Each one of us."

"Do we?" She shook her head and smiled wider. "Or do we die because he cursed us?"

"I don't think the promise will return our daughter to us."

"What do you know?" she said, and her frown returned.

"As much as you do," I said.

"I need to believe it. I don't know if I can survive if it isn't true."

I stared at her. "I'm sorry, Eve."

She waved me away. "Sorry won't bring my daughter back to life."

"I know it is hard to hear, but I have a feeling that when we see Father next year, all will seem very different."

"I'm not going," she said.

I straightened. Then scooted to face her more directly. "What?"

"I'm never going back to him."

"You have to," I said. "He commanded it."

"I don't have to do anything."

My mind raced. If she didn't go, what would Father do?

"Stop worrying for yourself. Father won't abandon you. This is my choice."

"He's the only one who offers us hope," I said. "Do you not believe that?"

"I do. He also took my daughter from me."

"But . . ."

She stood and brushed herself off. "I'll go back to him the moment he gives me my daughter back."

I grabbed her wrist to stop her. "I will not let our children stay back for your sake."

"Why would I want them to stay here? One day, when they're older—if what you said is true—our boys will need to sacrifice for themselves and prove their worth to the Almighty. So long as they remain true, my choices do not matter."

"But they do. They influence our boys."

"Then so be it."

Her words made an unnerving sort of sense. As I thought of our nameless daughter's motionless face, the temptation to convince myself she would one day be returned nearly overwhelmed me.

Yet was this not the same reasoning she was using on our boys, to convince them that they were not responsible for other people's pain? "This is like when you lied to our boys."

She pulled her arm from my grasp and groaned. "It's late. We need to get some sleep before sunrise."

"This is not only my fault. Each of us is responsible. How could it be any other way?"

"I'm done talking," she said and walked home.

Instead of following her, I sat for a while beside the stream.

I did not think she would come to believe anything other than what she had determined to believe. And even if I could convince her, I feared she would not be able to continue on.

The bond between mother and child is unique, for a mother's womb caresses a baby for months as it grows inside her. If her pain were double mine—and I believed it was—I understood her inability to accept the truth.

But if I let her believe this lie and infect our children with it, what would happen? Her goals seemed to align with my own. We needed to teach our children to be faithful to Father. If they appeased him, and he chose one of them for the task of reversing our curse, the entire world would benefit.

If they failed, the world would suffer.

Was it possible that her belief in a lie could lead to the hope we tended ever since leaving Eden? Could her words be enough to convince Cain to finally behave? For if our sons believed that by being good, they could return their dead sister to us, perhaps that would help them feel the weight of what rested on their shoulders.

I thought back to when I found Eve speaking with Cain. Had she been telling him of this even then?

I considered what might happen if she had told him that the

resurrection of his sister rested on his shoulders. I thought to the resolve I had seen in his face. And the way he had nodded so definitely.

Eve had a way with Cain that I did not. Whenever she spoke to him, he obeyed her. Yet when I tried to command him, he resisted to the point of pain.

What if I simply did not convince him otherwise?

What fruit would that bear but greater obedience?

I moaned and rubbed my face. I did not know what to do. And truthfully, who was I to say it was not possible?

Father was the Almighty Creator, was he not? If he wished to, he could bring our daughter back, could he not?

I wish I'd sensed the danger in what was happening in my mind. For Eve's words had taken root, and to my shame, I decided that I would let her do what she wanted, for I did not believe I could dissuade her. If that meant letting her teach our children that they controlled their sister's fate, I would let her. And, if necessary, I would join her.

I was mortally tired, Enoch. I could no longer endure this cursed world. I longed for us to be set free, same as her. To return to Eden and be with our Lord, free from the ache of this broken life.

And I would do anything to get us there.

. . .

I spoke no more about Eden or Eve's hopes for our daughter to be returned. Yet as the long months of Cain and Abel's fifth year wore on, the pain from our loss hardly dulled. There were days when I worked hard enough to forget. But at night—every night—I saw her nameless face.

Until finally, I said to Eve, "It is not right that she has no name."

Eve stared at me. "I will not name her until I can kiss her face again."

"Can I, for my own sake?"

She shrugged. "Do what you need." But her eyes told a different story.

"If I name her, do you want to know?"

She pressed her lips together and tapped them with her fingers. "I don't know. No."

I spoke no more to her of our daughter, but after she left me, I closed my eyes and whispered the name I thought fit her precious face. "Ayah."

At the sound of her name rolling from my lips, warmth bled down my body. I smiled and closed my eyes, imagining it was her arms reaching for me from beyond the veil between life and death.

Proof that she forgave me.

Hot tears fell down my face.

In the distance, I heard the boys' chattering coming closer. I wiped away the evidence, sniffed hard, and cleared my throat.

As they came into view and met my eyes, I waved, and they waved back.

"What are you doing, Dad?" Abel said.

"I was talking to your mother."

"Where is she?"

"She was going to take Sarah to the water," I said.

"Oh, we were supposed to weave baskets," Abel said. He seemed disappointed.

Cain smiled. "Come on, let's hide by the water and jump out to frighten them."

Abel shook his head, but Cain took him by the arm and led him away.

"It will cheer you up," Cain said. "Trust me."

I returned to tending the weeds in our garden and worked hard all day without a twinge of sorrow.

Finally, as the sun set, I laid in bed and fell into a sleep so deep that I didn't remember anything until the morning light broke through the cracks in the door.

Chapter 35

When the time came for us to return to Eden and sacrifice to the Almighty, Eve gathered the children in our home and readied them for the journey. Sarah was old enough now that she could walk for the first time holding the boys' hands.

Eve tied little makeshift boots to Sarah's feet. "These will protect you," she said with a smile.

Sarah stamped her boots on the brick floor of our home. "Mommy, are you coming?"

"No," Eve said. "We talked about this, remember?"

"Why?" Sarah's lower lip jutted with genuine emotion.

Eve gently grabbed her shoulders and kissed her on the cheek. "This is your chance to walk the whole way like a big girl. Aren't you excited to show your brothers how strong you are?"

"Yes." Sarah glanced at Cain and Abel, who were peering into the bag of food and trying to pilfer dried fruit.

Eve stood and snapped her fingers at the boys before dusting herself off.

"But Mommy?" Sarah said.

"Yes?"

"I just want you."

Eve nodded and pulled disheveled hair behind her ears. "I know."

I stepped forward and scooped Sarah up in my arms. She leaned into me for comfort as I said to Eve, "It will be a long journey without your help."

"It will be what it is." Eve turned to meet my gaze. *Don't push me,* she mouthed.

I sighed.

"What?" Sarah said.

"Nothing," I said.

Eve knelt and seized both Cain and Abel by the shoulder. The boys sobered and stared up at her. "Boys," she said. "You know what to do."

They nodded.

"We won't let you down," Cain said as his chest puffed slightly.

"What if he doesn't choose one of us?" Abel said.

"Hush," Eve said. "You know he will not choose this year. There is no need to fear."

"I know," Abel said. "But what if he never chooses either—"

"You are the ones," Eve said. "On your shoulders rests our hope."

I placed my hand on Eve's shoulder. "Your mother is right. Without you, the world would forever be lost. Because on you rests the promises of our Father himself."

Cain nodded hard. Abel stared, wide eyed.

"It is a great honor," I said.

Abel glanced at his brother, then nodded.

"Now," I said and planted Sarah on her feet. "Until we arrive, I'm going to need you to look after your sister. Ready yourselves, because as soon as I return with our sacrifice, we will depart."

Sarah kicked her legs and said, "These boots feel funny."

"You will grow accustomed to them," I said.

"You don't want to cut your feet on any rocks," Cain said.

"Or get stung." Abel rubbed his backside where he'd been stung by a ground wasp the year before after sitting on its nest.

"You should drink before you leave too." Eve grabbed the water jug and filled some cups.

"I already did," Cain said.

"Then drink more." Eve passed the cups.

I exited our home and let the door slam as Cain grumbled and Sarah fussed with her boots and spilled some water. Months earlier, we had moved the sheep pen to a new pasture. I walked north to grab the lamb we'd set aside the day before and examined him in great detail one final time. His fur, skin, eyes, legs—everything about him was flawless.

I smiled at those odd little eyes. "Thank you for giving your life to us. It means another year to work toward the promise of redemption. To crush the head of the serpent who poisoned our lives. You will be the covering we need to be with our Father at least one more day."

And I hugged him and brought him back to our home before we set off.

. . .

The journey took longer than I'd expected. We began in the early morning the day before we were to meet him, but we needed to stop multiple times because Sarah's legs grew tired, and I had to carry the lamb.

Abel had carried Sarah as much as he could, and that sped our journey along. But Cain refused, and I didn't think it worth pushing him. We needed our time with Father to go smoothly. I could not risk causing more friction than necessary. Because of this, when we did walk, it was at such a slow pace that we had to stop and sleep under the stars.

We tied the lamb to a small tree and huddled together on the dusty ground to sleep fitfully. Sarah woke in the middle of the night calling for Eve. "Hush," I said and held her against my chest and kissed her until she calmed. The boys woke in intervals to relieve themselves in the brush. I lay awake until the sun crept over the horizon.

As we rose and stretched, Sarah asked for help to relieve herself. I walked her off into the brush and cleaned her.

Then it was time to eat. We broke out the dried fruit the boys had tried to pilfer, but I could not eat because anxiety had sapped my appetite. The boys were hungry, so I gave them my share so they would not be tempted to take Sarah's, for she was a slow eater.

And then we continued on. When we finally arrived at the entrance to Eden and faced those twisting flames, it was midday, and Father was nowhere to be seen. To arrive so close to the final hour worried me. Had I miscalculated the time and missed him?

I brought the lamb as close to the entrance as I dared and waited.

"Where is he?" Abel said.

"I don't know."

"Hasn't he always waited outside for us?" Abel said.

"Is your memory broken?" Cain said. "Of course."

"Hush," I said because I thought I saw movement through the flames. I squinted and held my hand over my forehead to guard myself from a bit of the brightness.

Sarah's little hand found mine.

"What would happen if we missed him?" Abel said.

"You'd be cursed forever," Cain said.

Abel's voice rose in pitch as he said, "We would have gotten here sooner if you would have helped carry Sarah."

"You hardly carried her yourself," Cain said.

"I carried her until my arms felt like they would fall off," Abel said.

I thought I heard footsteps. "Quiet, boys." I cupped my hands around my ears to hear better—though the roar of the flames made it difficult to tell.

"The Almighty sees all. He'll see your weakness, for sure," Cain said, voice sneering.

"If he does, he'll see you're cruel and petty!"

Cain struck Abel, who cried out, "Father, Cain hit me!"

Cain grabbed and shook him. "Close your mouth, you little fool."

"Quiet!" I said, my face reddening as I let go of Sarah's hands and forced them apart.

"Daddy?" Sarah said.

I followed her pointed finger to the dark form of a man walking through the blinding flames. As he walked toward us, the conflagration seemed to peel back from his skin and tunic, and he escaped the blaze unscathed.

For he was our great Father, the Almighty Creator, who had commanded those flames to spring forth from nothing. They could do nothing to harm their Maker.

I breathed a sigh of relief at the sight of his face, then felt my anxiety return as I realized he wasn't smiling.

I bowed, and my children did the same. "Great Father, Almighty Creator," I said, and my children echoed me. "We bring an offering, a spotless lamb, as you commanded. Please forgive us, and let this symbol cover us until the final day of atonement."

When he did not answer, we straightened. He stared at each of us in turn. "Where is Eve, the mother of your children, and the wife I formed to be your helper?"

I swallowed hard and struggled to talk. "She . . . gave birth to our second daughter. We buried her by the fig trees." Tears threatened my eyes, but I stared at the flames to distract myself. "I named her Ayah, for she was very beautiful, and precious, and small."

Father nodded. "Cain," he said.

Cain raised his chin haughtily and said, "Yes, Lord."

"Watch yourself. I have seen your bitter resentment and selfish desire. Such evil, if tended, will put you in danger of giving up your birthright as the firstborn from Eve's womb."

Cain straightened and held his fists at his side, shaking with anger and embarrassment. He knew, even as young as he was, that the Almighty was referring to more than what duties he would inherit when I passed away.

"Speak," the Almighty said, but his voice was gentle.

"Yes, Lord. I am sorry. Forgive me." He bowed, but his movements were stiff.

The Almighty knelt and stared at Cain as he straightened. It seemed as though the Almighty was offering him an embrace. Cain lifted one arm subtly, then flexed his hands into fists and turned away.

So, instead, the Almighty turned his gaze to Abel. "Abel."

Abel stepped forward, shaking even harder than Cain. "Yes, Lord." Then he remembered to bow and nearly fell for how unsteady his legs were.

"I appreciate your gentle heart."

Abel's dark face slowly widened in a grin as he dared to peer up.

"You desire to prove yourself. And so you have. But you are in danger, as well. Resist the temptation to grasp what isn't yours. Stop provoking your brother to anger."

Abel straightened as his smile fell. He nodded. "Yes, Lord. Forgive me." He bowed again.

"Sarah?" the Almighty said, then smiled and opened his arms in invitation.

Sarah smiled and ran to him, and he scooped her up and spun with her in his arms. She giggled, and he laughed in return and kissed her. She kissed him back and wrapped her arms tightly around his neck. He whispered in her ear, and she nodded and kissed him once more before scooting out of his arms and running back to us.

"Adam," he said.

I bowed, my own feet now unsteady. "Yes, Lord."

"Because you have failed to lead your wife, and she has refused to come, her womb is closed. You will try to bear children, and you will fail until she returns and pays penance both in her heart and in deed."

I knelt and pressed my forehead to the soil as my anxiety

reached its pitch. "Lord, have mercy on us. I have brought a sacrifice. Let it cover our sins."

"I have spoken," the Almighty said. "Now arise and perform your duty."

I rose and took the lamb, and the boys watched—though Sarah turned away—as I spilled its blood on the soil and raised my hands in worship to the Almighty.

"Father, we love you. We are sorry. We worship you for your goodness. Have mercy on us, and do not see our sins."

Father stepped near and lifted me by the hand. I faced him, not knowing what to expect. His face was sober, mouth lined with sorrow. But he pulled me into a gentle embrace and whispered in my ear, "I love you, my son."

"I love you too." But for the first time since tasting the forbidden fruit, I worried whether that love would remain. I felt the weight of our mistakes and realized the tenuousness of our relationship to him. At any moment, we could shatter this intimacy and risk losing much more than our ability to have children.

Our lives hung in the balance, as did the hope for our future redemption and the redemption of every person to come after us. It was enough to make my mind spin.

But the heat of his body so present, warm, and gentle pushed my uneasiness to the side. I squeezed him back and felt emotion rise as he kissed my head. "I have missed you," I said.

"I have missed you, as well. Yet remember that even when I am distant, I see all. I hear all. I know all."

I let go and searched his eyes for what he meant by that. But I saw no anger or resentment. Only welcome. "I know," I said. "You count every hair and number every thought."

He nodded. "I know your heart, so you need not tell me anything." He smiled again. "But when you tell me anyway, it makes my heart glad. Come, I will make you food, and we will eat together."

He passed back through the flames and brought out some of the fruit of Eden. Not the fruit of the Tree of Life—for he had forbidden us to eat of that tree. But Eden held much more variety than we grew in our new smaller garden. And he brought to us a more bountiful feast than he had in any of the previous years.

We ate until our stomachs ached, then sang and danced in purity and joy until night fell and the flames stood like a mountainous lamp.

"You may sleep here, by the entrance," the Almighty said. "You will be safe from any wild animals. In the morning, you must leave, for I will not come out of Eden again until next year."

"Yes, Father," I said.

"Remember, if you do not return as I have commanded, you will forfeit this joy for all who come after you. Eve knew this, and yet she stayed. So now the weight rests on your shoulders, Adam. Do not fail."

"I won't," I said. "I promise you, I won't."

But he looked at me as if he knew it was a lie. Even as my heart swelled in absolute assurance that I would never let him down.

Chapter 36

Cain was silent our whole trip home. Abel chatted with Sarah about the diversity and color of the wildflowers now blooming. But all I could think about was the weight of Father's words.

How could I explain everything to Eve without her hardening her heart toward him? Surely he knew that punishing her would provoke her wrath.

Yet he had sent me back, as his messenger, to carry the painful word of truth and to bear her contempt.

In her mind, I had been the one to push for meeting the Almighty outside the entrance to Eden, and she would think that if I had not begun this yearly ritual, she would not have garnered this additional curse. It would not matter that it was her choice that led to it. Her perspective was distorted by pain. And nothing I could say would convince her otherwise.

When Sarah became tired, Abel attempted to carry her as best he could. But when Abel grew exhausted, Cain finally agreed to help her along—likely because of the Almighty's warning. Cain had grown strong and tall for his age, while Sarah was petite by comparison. He carried her quicker than Abel had, but spoke no word to us.

I was too distracted with the fear of facing Eve to consider what pressures my eldest son was facing. I wish now that I would have thought to praise him for his helpfulness, but as I fear I've illustrated all too well, I failed him. Besides, a portion of my frustration was aimed at him for foolishly exposing his cruelty to the Almighty.

Of course, I knew that the Almighty saw everything and knew Cain's heart without seeing him strike his brother. But perhaps if Cain had not done so in front of the entrance to Eden, the Almighty would have spoken more kindly to him. And he would have avoided the warning that revealed what we all feared too much already.

That the promise in Eden of the reversal of our curse very well could slip from our fingers.

Though perhaps it was good that he had been warned and would harden his resolve even more.

Night fell, yet I knew we were close, so we pressed on until we saw the light of the fire Eve had kept burning to welcome us home. She sat cross-legged beside it, a dark shadow blocking a shaft of firelight.

We spoke no word as we approached, though it was the second day since we left.

She nodded as I stepped into the ring of orange light. I nodded back.

Cain stood with fists clenched as tightly as his lips. Abel held Sarah's hand and let go as she ran to Eve.

"I missed you, Mommy," Sarah said.

Eve kissed the top of Sarah's head, but her face was tight with anxiety as she stared at me. I tried to look away to avoid what I knew I must speak.

"Well?" Eve said.

"He wasn't there," I said, and Eve's eyes registered shock, "when we first arrived."

"What do you mean?"

"He has waited for us every year. But not this year. At first I thought I had calculated wrong. But now I believe that he walked out at the exact time we had agreed to meet. I think . . ."

But I did not voice my worry that the change in his behavior had been because Eve had refused to come.

"Cain was naughty," Sarah said.

Eve raised one brow. "Was he?"

Abel nodded but averted his eyes.

Cain mumbled, "Keep your mouth closed."

"I didn't say anything," Abel said, but his voice was soft and low. It reminded me of the warning the Almighty had given Abel. At the time, my heart swelled with pride that he was already attempting to obey.

I should have realized right then that my feelings were a sign of the favoritism I had shown Abel.

Instead, I glared at Cain, who took one look at me and stared at the ground. "The Almighty warned Cain that he was in danger of forfeiting his birthright."

Eve's mouth hung open in shock. "He said that?" She glanced between the two of us, as if wanting proof.

"He warned me too," Abel said.

"Hardly," Cain mumbled.

"He's not taking back his promise, is he?" Eve said.

"I don't believe our boys have lost anything."

"How do you know? Will one of them still be chosen?"

I sat beside her and stared into the fire. "Yes. But there is more."

Eve stood and brushed herself off. "Tell me. Enough dawdling, be quick about it."

I scratched the side of my head and tried to ignore her clenched fist shaking within view. "When Father saw that you had not come, he commanded that your womb would remain closed until you returned to him with an offering of penitence."

We listened to the crackling flames and the sound of Sarah's dress scraping against Eve's as she tried to nuzzle her mother for comfort.

Eve laughed, and Sarah jumped and looked up at her. "So," Eve said. "If I can't bear any more sons, one of our boys must be chosen, for there will be no more sons to fulfill the promise."

"Unless," I began, but she cut me off.

"I will not go back to him. He knows it. And he knows that I know it."

I looked up at her. "What is the point?" I tried to keep the irritation out of my voice, but I was growing weary of her stubbornness.

"I won't go crawling back to him, begging for forgiveness. He's trying to force my hand. But I can force his, as well. Unless he comes to me, I have nothing for him. And he is bound by his word. Lest he make himself a liar." She smiled.

I blinked. "You would go to war with him," I said, warning in my tone.

"I would show him this is my life, and I will live it how I desire."

"You have gone as mad as you were in the desert years ago."

"I know what I want," she said.

"But what if he does go back on his word?"

Eve tipped her head at me. "Losing faith in Father now, are you?"

"If you try to force his hand, and he unravels his own promise, you will have killed us all."

Eve snapped her fingers. "Cain, come here, now."

Cain walked forward tentatively. Eyebrows low and angled with caution.

"You know your duty," she said.

Cain did not respond. He twisted the edge of his tunic in his fist.

"Speak," Eve barked, her voice so loud that he jumped. "Do you remember your duty?"

Tears threatened his eyes. "I can't do it," he said.

She grabbed him by the shoulders and shook him. Sarah fell back and cried out, and Cain gritted his teeth together and looked ready to run away. "You can! And you will! I will not have you destroy our lives for lack of obedience. Now promise me you will obey his commands."

"I . . ."

"Promise!"

"I promise!" he said and tried to rip himself out of her grasp.

I watched everything in stunned silence. If I'd had the presence of mind, I would have told her she had no right to pressure him to perform what she herself could not. But I did not understand the workings of sin, nor how deeply our evil desires block our ability to love.

She pushed Cain back and faced me. "The next time you see our *Father*, you can tell him what I told you. If he wants me, if he ever truly loved me at all, he can meet me here. The day he does is the day I'll offer my penance. That is my word. And I will not go back on it. Let's see if he will go back on his."

Tears fell from Cain's face, and he swiped at them and fled into the dark.

"Cain?" Abel said as Sarah grabbed at my tunic, wanting me to lift her.

I picked Sarah up and let her sniff into my shoulder as Eve walked back to our home.

"Abel," I said. "You should find Cain and bring him back."

"Can you come with?" Abel said.

"No, I have to stay and take care of Sarah."

Sarah sniffed away her tears. "Why is Mommy mad?"

"Hush," I said. "Don't worry about Mommy."

"But—"

"I said don't worry. Abel?"

Abel nodded and sighed. "All right. I will find him."

"Good, now hurry. It is late and tomorrow we have much work to do. We need to get to bed."

But as Abel walked away, I stood holding Sarah for several moments, considering what had just happened. Eve had decided to wage a quiet war against our Father and pushed Cain to carry the weight of the redemption of the entire human race.

I shook my head. Yet she was right about one thing. If our sons failed, we were doomed.

Chapter 37

The next year, when we went to see Father again, Eve remained at our home and kept her fire burning. The journey was laborious, and when we arrived and Father saw that Eve was not with us, his countenance fell. He did not speak of her. But I could see that her disobedience hit like a spear through his heart, for he loved her as much as he loved any of us.

After we sacrificed, Father told us again of the importance of our obedience. He warned us of violence, bitterness, and the temptation to lose hope. It was a sweet time, but my worries sullied my joy in it.

On our way home, I realized that the only thing I could do to fix the chaos we were in was to raise up our boys to be what Father demanded, in the hopes they would be deemed fit to become the fulfillment of his promise.

. . .

Time would fail to elucidate every mundane hour spent grappling toward the end of that season of our lives. The days ground on like seeds in a mortar and pestle. The months like the low grind of stone and stone.

Our children grew. The boys gained responsibility. Though I spent more time teaching Abel the tasks necessary to keep us alive, Cain's abilities soon outstripped Abel's, for he worked harder to prove his worth. He took more than his share of labor in the garden while Abel spent most of his time tending our sheep. Abel loved them, their tender presence and soft manner. They suited him, while the hard soil suited Cain.

I remember seeing proof of the profound change in Cain shortly after we returned from the Almighty and witnessed Eve's pronouncement on the quiet war she planned to wage against him. That day we had little work, and Abel wanted to pass the time.

"Come on, let's catch fish in the stream," Abel said.

Cain stood and stared at Abel as if he had just requested that they sever their own legs. "Why would we do that?"

"We always do," Abel said.

"There are no fish in the stream," Cain said.

Abel's six-year-old eyes narrowed. "I know. We imagine them. Are you ill?"

"No," Cain said and walked off without another word.

Abel stood bending his fingers with furrowed brow.

"Don't worry," I said. "He will get over it soon."

Abel nodded, then walked off, as well, clearly disturbed.

But Cain didn't soon get over it. He merely hardened like clay in the sun. We had formed him into the mold we needed, and he would remain unmoving until he broke.

He knew he was holding the weight of our hopes. Even at so young an age, he had faced our words and decided his only choice was to plunge forward, to try harder, to do what we demanded.

What else could such a headstrong child do? He could not leave us, for there was no one else who would receive him. He could not disappoint us, for why then would we love him?

Do you see, Enoch? The impossible maze we built for him? And all roads in that infernal puzzle only led inward, until he scraped and bled and hurried along like a boy falling headfirst into a black hole at the very center of himself.

He walked about, face flat, eyes sharp, aware but cold. He worked harder than any of us. His arms and legs grew strong and lean, and his face thin and hard. As a teenager, I began to see in him the weathered reflection of my own face, which I still spied from time to time in the shimmering stream when the wind was low.

But even though he was distant, he was no longer cruel. Indeed, he formed a habit of serving us all. When he perceived that we needed water for cooking, the water would appear in a large jar. When he heard Abel complain about the difficulty of fixing the sheep pen, he would silently repair it while Abel watched.

I was pleased with this change in behavior. It encouraged me.

However, from time to time, when Sarah was about twelve, I would find her crying alone late at night. The first time, I thought nothing of it. But when it happened for a third time in a single month, I began to wonder if Cain were involved.

I stepped out to show her that I was present.

As she heard my footsteps, she tried to hide her emotion.

I touched her shoulder and said, "What has been bothering you, my dear?"

She pulled her tunic up tight around herself and turned away. "I just have been having a hard time sleeping. That is all."

"Would you like me to sit with you?"

"No, thank you," she said and stood and returned to our home to sleep.

For several months afterward, I didn't find any sign of those late outpourings of emotion. But the boys were now fifteen years of age, and our family was outgrowing our small home.

So, after we visited the Almighty and he still did not choose one of the two boys to represent our family with his own sacrifice, we returned and began to build a second home near the first.

We formed the foundation of brick, just like the first, and built it slightly larger, though we did not form another threshing floor. My boys worked with me, though Cain finished the walls while we rested and ate. It seemed something had possessed him, and he rejected even food or drink while we labored. He would only rest when exhaustion so seized him that he could not continue.

I tried to tell him that he should take a day off, but he would not listen to me.

"I am fine," was all he said.

"But you will become ill if you continue thus."

"I am fine."

"Yes, but you won't be if you continue."

A small smirk grew at the corner of his lips that I wondered was mocking or sincere. "I am fine."

We finished the new home and the boys slept in it while Sarah stayed with Eve and me.

Several days later, in the middle of the night, Eve rolled toward me and said, "Do you not think it time to consider Cain to be a husband to Sarah?"

"Hush," I said, for Sarah was sleeping beside us, and it seemed that at Eve's whispered words Sarah's rhythmic breathing grew uneven. I continued quietly with my lips against Eve's ear. "If we did, what of Abel?"

"Cain is our eldest. You cannot say he hasn't proven himself these many years. He works harder than you do. He serves me well. Even Abel agrees."

"You talked to Abel?"

"Why not?" Eve said. "He is a kind, sensible young man. And he is humble."

"Do you realize what that might have—"

"He does not feel he deserves anything," Eve said.

I paused and considered her. "And did you talk to Sarah as well?"

"Of course."

My voice grew in volume. "When did you plan to speak to me about it?"

Sarah's breathing skipped, then settled.

"I'm talking to you right now."

"How long ago?" I said.

"What?"

"How long ago did you talk to Sarah about this?"

Eve took in a long breath. "It does not matter. When I told her I needed to talk with her about something, she guessed what I was to speak with her about."

"And Abel?"

She shrugged. "A few months ago, perhaps."

I sat up and stared down at her form in the dark. I saw that Sarah had changed positions and worried she might be listening. "Come," I said to Eve.

I stood and crept out; Eve followed. We sat amidst the bamboo and stared at the stars.

"You favor Abel," Eve said. "Even he sees it."

A growl escaped my throat, and I felt a rush of fire to my wrists. My words came sharp and slow. "What else did you talk to my son about behind my back?"

"He was the one to bring it up," Eve said. "You are too hard on Cain."

"Yet you seem impressed by the results," I said.

"He is trying to earn your favor. Has he not achieved it?"

"He is on his way."

"He is burning himself like a spent wick." Eve sighed. "He needs a helper to treat him with tenderness. To be a relief to his struggle. A new focus to distract him from the weight we've put on him."

"It was your idea to pressure our sons," I said.

"Yes. But we must not pressure them too hard. And you have put twice the weight on Cain."

I shrugged. "He is firstborn. Does the promise not rest on him most of all?"

"That is not the only reason."

"His heart is unpredictable. And wild."

She glanced at me as if much more should be said.

"What?" I said.

"Nothing. He just needs to find relief from the pressure from time to time."

I considered her words and grabbed hold of one of the bamboo shafts beside me. I leaned into it, felt its bulk bend but hold me upright. What if we were pressing Cain too hard and somehow broke him? I had not thought much of it. You must understand that we were still hardly older than the children we raised. We were intelligent, but not all in life is intuitive. Still, I thought back to when we were building the new home and realized she was right.

"Very well," I said. "I will consider giving Sarah to him as a wife. But we cannot afford to let him grow lax. Not after we have built so much."

"The Almighty has still not chosen," Eve said, tone cold and distant.

"He will choose soon. I feel it in my bones."

"You know nothing," Eve said.

"You have not returned to the Almighty in years." I pushed myself to my feet. "Had you been there and seen the way he looks at our boys, you would know that the test is coming."

"When?"

I considered whether claiming a day would be worth it. If I were wrong, she would hold that over me. And what would I gain if I were right? Very little. Still . . .

"Next year," I said.

"He will choose?"

"He will send the test. And the following year, I believe he will choose."

"Their seventeenth year," she said.

"Yes. Now you must speak no more behind my back to my sons or do anything that might upset them. They must believe and not waver."

She thought this over a moment. Then nodded. "Very well.

But when shall we tell them? It would be helpful for Cain to know he has a joy to look forward to. He will have much to prepare for before they become one. He has grown cold and distant. It takes time to warm a chilled heart. I know that all too well." And her eyes gleamed in the dark.

"We wait until next year, when we visit the Almighty. On the way to our sacrifice, I will tell them that if they do not displease the Almighty that day, they will be betrothed. Yet they will not marry until the final year."

"The year you believe the Almighty will make his choice."

I nodded.

"And if he doesn't choose?"

I nodded. "They will at least be glad to be married."

Eve nodded and stood with me. "Very well. Let us return before Sarah wakes and wonders where we are."

Chapter 38

The following year, we began our journey to the Almighty in the same way we had so many times before. Our children readied themselves while Eve built a fire outside our home that she would keep burning until we returned.

"Remember," she whispered to me before we left. "Today you will tell them."

We made our way, and Cain carried our sacrifice as Abel walked alongside Sarah. I carried a satchel holding food and three containers of water sealed with clay.

When we were far enough away that none of them would consider turning back, I stopped them. "Children."

Cain stared at me.

"Yes?" Abel said as he and Sarah turned.

"Today is a special day," I said.

"You believe the Almighty will choose?" Abel said.

"No, I speak of something else."

Cain's brow furrowed, and Sarah's face grew red. She turned away.

"Your mother and I have spoken. We deliberated long and decided that if you please the Almighty today, you"—I pointed at Cain—"and Sarah will marry in one year and one day, after we return from visiting the Almighty one more time."

Sarah nodded.

Cain's gaze bounced from her to me, then back again.

Abel stared into the distance, lips thin, face unreadable. "What a wonderful gift," he said.

Cain rearranged the sheep in his arms, then continued walking.

"Cain," I called.

He ignored me.

I glanced at the other two and jogged to catch up to him.

"We must arrive on time," he said.

"Are you not happy?" I whispered.

"I am." But when he looked at me, his eyes still held that same cold distance. "Thank you."

I settled into a well-paced walk behind Cain and tried to read Sarah's face, but any sign of emotion had been wiped away. Though I wasn't sure how, I felt I had misstepped. It seemed all three had known I would speak to them today and had already decided their reactions in advance. That meant only one of two things. Eve had disobeyed me and spoken to them in secret, or they had somehow overheard us speaking.

But I knew that wasn't possible.

I bit my tongue. I would speak to her when we returned. Until then, Cain was right. We needed to get to Eden and face our God.

. . .

We arrived early and spent the night. We ate in a line facing Eden and abided the long hours in silence until Father walked through those twirling flames in the same stained white tunic he'd worn every year since the beginning, bearing marks from every sacrifice we'd ever offered.

Cain set the sacrifice down as the Almighty came and

greeted each of us with an embrace and a kiss. Then he stood and faced us with his hands on his sides.

"My children," he said. "Today is the last day that your father will be the only one to give offerings."

I closed my eyes and reveled in the rush of excitement. It was as I had told Eve. I felt such relief that I almost wept. Finally, we were on the cusp of the fulfillment.

"Next year, my boys, you will all bring an offering."

"What about me?" Sarah said.

The Almighty smiled. "Your father's sacrifice will cover you. After you marry your brother, Cain, his offering will be yours."

Sarah's eyes widened as she realized the Almighty had known of the marriage without being told. She bowed and said, "Thank you, my Lord."

"Now," he said. "You know of blood offerings. But there are other offerings, too, that please me." He looked at Cain. "You may bring to me the bounty of your harvest." And to Abel. "But always, there must be a blood sacrifice to cover your sins. Adam will bring it, for he is your father. Yet that does not mean you cannot bring your own. Do you understand?"

My boys bowed.

"Only remember the reason for your offerings," the Almighty said and stared at Cain. "That they are not for you."

"No," Abel said. "They are for you, and you alone."

The Almighty smiled and lifted Abel to an embrace. "Now," he said, "let us sacrifice and celebrate together."

Chapter 39

The following months passed quickly. Cain's focus only increased as the final day approached. At dawn each morning, the boys set forth to finish their respective tasks. Many times they didn't return until after sunset, drenched in sweat and aching with exhaustion.

I normally started out shortly after dawn, but made certain to enjoy a small meal beforehand. Most days, at the beginning of the year, Sarah joined me and picked at her food, lost in thought. Later, toward winter, she stayed in bed until midday, only venturing out to perform chores or to prepare food or drink.

Still, once a week, we all observed the day of rest, except Cain who continued to trudge through the fields.

I remember one summer day we spent resting beside the stream with the sun burning our backs. We hung our toes in the water, sang songs, and ate special cakes that Eve had made. They were soft and sweet.

"What did you do to make these so delicious?" I said.

She smiled and took a bite. "I talked to a little silver snake."

I felt the blood leave my face. Then she burst out laughing, and I felt my face warm with embarrassment. "That is not funny."

"Oh, relax," Eve said. "It's our day of rest."

Sarah giggled. "His face went so pale I thought *he* might be the serpent."

"Yes," Abel said, "and now his face is as red as the flames outside Eden."

Eve snorted and choked on the bite in her mouth, then coughed and shook her head. "Stop, I am trying to eat!"

I shook my head but smiled at the ease with which my family seemed to be enjoying themselves.

Abel splashed Sarah, and she giggled and jumped into the water to splash him twice as much.

He stood and flung the droplets from his arms.

"Let that teach you to splash your sister!" Eve said as her smile revealed teeth that gleamed like pearls.

As the day wore on, I did relax. In the end, we played and laughed so much that my side hurt.

I slid my fingers between Eve's and kissed her softly while our children waded through the water and whispered to each other.

Eve smiled at me, eyes warm, inviting. Open as she hadn't been in years.

I ran my finger down the side of her face. "I haven't seen you like this since—" I cut myself off.

Her smile dulled, and she looked at the shivering stream. "Yes. I feel good today." Her thumb rubbed the top of my hand.

"Me too," I said.

Cain approached with a bucket to draw water and noticed us with a frown. Sweat dripped from his long, dark hair to the stream. As Abel lifted something slimy from the river, Sarah exclaimed and hopped back, giggling.

Cain's face reddened, and he returned to his fields with his bucket full of sloshing water. Sarah noticed too late and called for him, but he ignored her.

She stayed staring after him. Abel nudged her and said, "Come, let us gather shards of obsidian and build a mountain."

Sarah nodded, but the light had gone from her eyes. After they'd gathered a few, Sarah stepped from the stream and cleared her throat. "I'm feeling tired."

Abel examined her, then glanced at us. "All right. Do you want company?"

"No, I'll be fine; don't worry." She smiled, but the expression was weak, and she returned then to our home, presumably to lie down.

We tried to engage Abel, but after Sarah left, he became sullen and distant. It seemed he felt he had made some sort of mistake.

"It is not your fault," I said.

He sighed and said, "I think I will go to the fields."

"What?" Eve said. "Today is your day of rest."

"I have rested. Now I desire to stretch my limbs." He smiled and squeezed Eve's shoulder.

I watched as he walked away. Weariness seemed to weigh on his shoulders. I leaned toward Eve, whose black skin and slender features mirrored Abel's so well. "He is going to help Cain in the fields."

Eve ran her tongue over her teeth, frown lines deepening in her face. "I fear that is not all."

"Sarah?" I said.

She nodded.

"She is betrothed to Cain. She loves him and will learn to love him more as the years pass, so long as he is good to her."

"Yet she loves Abel too."

"What are you saying?"

She shrugged and tore at the grass beside the stream, tossing the brown blades onto the surface of the water and watching them float away. "Nothing, really."

"You have spoken to Sarah?" I said.

"I have observed tension between our children for some time."

I scoffed. "When hasn't there been tension?"

She nodded. "You are right."

I slid my hand over hers again, and she turned her somber gaze to me. I smiled, and the corner of her mouth tugged upward. "Come," I said, "let us not sully this day."

She nodded and leaned into my shoulder.

I twisted and lay her softly on the grass where we kissed passionately, like we hadn't in years.

. . .

That night, I woke to Sarah slipping out the door of our home. I tried to close my eyes and return to sleep, but my spirit was disturbed. What had happened, that she would rise again in the night to hide her weeping? Had Cain done something to her in retaliation for earlier that day?

I scooted away from Eve and slowly lifted the covers from myself, careful not to disturb her. I still wore a thin tunic and, because we were in the heat of summer, did not put on any additional covering.

I slid out the door and let it close softly behind me. I swept my surroundings for any sign of her and reached with my ears for any noises.

I heard the low rumbles of a quiet conversation by the stream and crept through the bamboo, careful not to crack any twigs. Holding my breath, I found Sarah by the stream, talking to someone. The dark made it hard to see whom it was. But after a few moments, I thought I heard Cain. I watched them for some time, until they kissed. Then I pulled away and returned to Eve.

Something was not right, but I did not want to risk being found watching. The starlight gave enough illumination that they would be able to see my eyes if I stood staring for too long.

I would need to speak to Eve about it in the morning.

Then I lay down beside my wife and, after some struggle, fell back to sleep.

. . .

The morning came too soon. Dim light grew in the cracks of the door, and I rose and dressed myself before noticing that Sarah was gone. Eve groaned and stretched. I pulled on my shoes and knelt beside her. "Eve." I shook her gently.

"What?" Her voice was muffled by the covering.

"Sarah left last night and did not return."

She lifted her head and looked at Sarah's empty bed. "Did you see where she went?"

"By the stream with Cain."

She groaned and buried her head in the covers.

I stood and exited, then walked to our boys' home and peered inside. Both Cain and Abel were already gone. Their bedding neatly stacked in the corner.

I went back and crept through the bamboo one last time, to see if they were still beside the river. But the ground was empty.

I checked the furnaces and found Sarah stoking a blaze in the small furnace. A container of grain sat open beside her, and she had piled herbs in a mortar and pestle. We had taken to adding herbs to our bread to solve the bitterness of the wheat without constant need of honey or other sweeteners.

"Greetings," I said.

She looked up and rubbed tired eyes. "Hello, Father."

"Sleep well?"

She shrugged and tossed a chunk of wood in the furnace before taking up the mortar and pestle and grinding the herbs.

"Have you seen Cain?"

"He's in the fields," she said.

"Have you talked so early already?"

She nodded.

I stood staring for as long as I dared without risking curiosity. Then I went off to the fields to find Cain weeding, and Abel pouring water from buckets to keep the vegetables from the scorching heat. That section of the garden could not be reached by irrigation, so we daily lugged water to it.

I hailed them, and they hailed back. Abel smiled, seeming happy enough. And Cain no longer scowled. Whatever had passed between them the day before seemed to have been settled peacefully.

I did not want to ask the boys what happened and risk churning up resentments. Half the year had nearly disappeared already, and we had little time left to prepare for the final day when the Almighty would choose one of our sons to undo our curse.

Which would it be? Had Cain proved his worth? Or would Abel's meek demeanor win our Father's heart as it had mine?

Chapter 40

For a time, it seemed the joy we found that first Sabbath would be ours. We continued meeting for our days of rest while Cain worked the fields. Until in the late autumn when Cain saw Sarah and Abel tumbling in the leaves together.

Cain stood and stared, and when they saw him, their laughter fell, and they disentangled their arms.

From that day on, Sarah spent her days of rest alone in bed and avoided Abel when he spoke to her.

I tried to talk with my children about it, but they would not abide me speaking of it. I understood that tensions were growing as the day to meet with the Lord approached. Cain was making known his claim on Sarah was complete. He distrusted the time she spent with Abel, and how could I tell him to let go of this? He was right, in one sense, and was always strong in his opinions. To accost him during the final phase of winning the Almighty's approval would only spark additional anger.

. . .

Winter passed like a blanket of frost tossed to the wind, and spring arrived as if lifted from the ground by the sprouting green vegetables that grew in our gardens.

Then came the day for us to leave for Eden. Cain harvested the best of his spring harvest. Leafy greens, garlic, peas, broad beans, turnips, wild flowers, and early apricots.

Abel combed through his flock for a flawless lamb and made his choice.

I brought a lamb as well—a sibling of the one Abel had chosen.

Eve started her fire, which she would keep until we returned, and the rest of us departed early in the morning the day before we were to meet with the Almighty, carrying our sacrifices the long distance to the entrance of our first home, where we spent the night with our sacrifices tied to a tree, and Cain's sacrifice in a broad basket beside us.

None of us slept.

Chapter 41

The Almighty came from the flames in greater splendor than I had seen since we walked with him in Eden. The light in his eyes pierced our own, until we bowed ourselves to the earth.

But when his voice came, it was gentle, and as he spoke, the Light dimmed until we could see without pain. "Today is the day you become your own men. For years, you have labored under the covering of your father. Now, you will offer your own sacrifices, and the Spirit will test your hearts. Then, everyone will know who pleases me." He raised his hands. "Adam, first of men. Offer your sacrifice."

I led my little lamb to the feet of my Father and took hold of the blade he offered me. Wincing, I dragged the blade through its throat and drained its blood on the earth as an offering.

I closed my eyes and prayed not just for myself, but also for Eve and Sarah. "Please, Lord, forgive us."

The Light grew and grew until the pain returned. I cried out and covered myself with my arms, but as quickly as it came, it went. He smiled at me and lifted me into an embrace. "I see your sacrifice, and I forgive you."

I stepped away and motioned for Cain to come forward. He straightened and held his basket in both hands. All the hardness that had marked his face that last year seemed to melt away, and in its place remained only pride. "My Lord, I have gathered a sampling of the greatest spring harvest we have yet received. Please, view my sacrifice and labor with pleasure." He bowed and offered the basket at Father's feet. "And forgive me of any errors."

A long silence passed. Father stared at Cain with an unreadable, blank expression. The Light did not grow—or, at least, I did not see it grow.

I nudged Sarah and whispered, "Did you see the Light when I gave my offering?"

But Sarah did not respond. She was transfixed, eyes narrowed, mouth lined with worry.

Cain looked up, confused.

The Almighty sighed, and his shoulders sagged. He shook his head. "How can I be pleased with a sacrifice meant for your own glory?"

A spasm of anger flashed across Cain's face before he stood, wiped it clean, and smiled a tight smile. He bowed, "My Lord."

He walked away, smile plastered on his face. Sweat beading across his forehead.

Abel stepped forward and swallowed hard. Face thin and haggard. He lifted his fat little lamb, the firstborn of his flock, and set it before his Father. Then looked up, nervous. The Almighty offered him the knife, and he took it and stared at the little beast.

"Here, my Lord. I offer you a sacrifice of the firstborn of my flock, and of the fat portions."

The Almighty nodded.

Abel paused, then glanced up one last time and said, "I never knew it was so difficult." He nodded at me. "Thank you."

"Sin is always a burden," our Father said.

Abel gripped the knife hard and pulled it through the lamb's throat in one, hard motion. Then he clutched the beast and shed tears as its blood wetted its wool and stained his tunic.

Finally, when all was finished, he whispered, "I am sorry." Both to the beast and to the Almighty.

The Light grew and grew until all of us cried out and turned our faces to the ground, yet the Light seemed to reflect off even the earth shadowed beneath us.

Finally, when it passed, the Almighty said, "I see your sacrifice. But for Cain's sacrifice, I have no regard. Abel, your faith lies in me. But Cain trusts only in himself."

I looked at Cain, who still held that same, pained smile. He dug his nails into his wrist until it seemed he might make himself bleed. Heat rose to his cheeks, and he stared at the ground to hide it.

"Why are you angry?" the Almighty said. "And why has your face fallen? If you do well, will you not be accepted? And if you do not do well, sin is crouching at the door. Its desire is to consume you, but you must rule over it."

"Yes, my Lord," Cain said. But as he turned away, I saw the red marks on his wrist.

"My children," the Almighty said. "Think on what I tell you as you leave for another year."

My eyes narrowed. Would we not feast together this time as we had every other year?

"The one who will atone for your mistakes will be the greatest servant to ever live. Next year, all will be made clear." He turned his eyes toward me; yet there was no joy, only sorrow. "But remember what will happen if you fail to meet me here."

I nodded, for no words would come.

He nodded back, turned, and began to walk back through the flames guarding Eden.

Sarah stared wide-eyed and whispered, "Is that all?"

As Father's form disappeared, Abel nodded. "I believe so."

Chapter 42

We stood dumbfounded for some time after the Almighty left. The sun was high, and the Almighty had rejected Cain's offering after an entire year of him laboring endlessly to please him. Now, the fire that burned inside Cain seemed ready to spill over.

Yet he just kept smiling that tight smile.

To see such an inappropriate expression on the face of someone I knew was ready to break alarmed me. I knew I should speak to him and offer some sort of comfort.

But I was too disappointed to do anything but criticize him. Because all I could see was the face of little Ayah, the baby girl we lost. Now, I realized that I had secretly begun to believe Eve's lie, that if Cain pleased Father, we would gain our daughter once again.

It felt like losing her all over again.

I ached and ached and ached, but did not cry. I wanted to weep, to scream, to do anything. But all I could manage was to keep breathing.

"Abel," Cain said, breaking the quiet.

Abel stared at him. Wary.

"Congratulations," Cain said.

Abel frowned.

Cain's smile widened, but his eyes seemed like spears. "The Almighty will surely choose you."

"I am nothing," Abel said.

"I agree. But my opinion matters not." His smile flattened. "Stay away from Sarah." He held out his hand to her. "Come," he said. "We should return."

"I do not know if I have the strength to make it home," I said.

"Tonight, we marry. Sarah and I will return for this reason."

I blinked at him. I had forgotten that detail, and the pause in my response was as good as admitting it.

The tight smile returned to Cain's face. "Come, Sarah."

Sarah obeyed, and slid her hand into his. His strong fingers engulfed hers, and he pulled her along. She risked one final glance back at Abel, who stood staring after them as if tasting something sour.

. . .

"What do we do now?" I said, long after Cain and Sarah disappeared from view.

Abel scoffed and stared at the twirling flames outside Eden. "How should I know? My brother hates me, and no matter how hard I try, I only deepen his animosity."

"It's not your fault," I said.

Abel turned his dark eyes to me, and I saw in them, for a moment, the flash of his brother's personality. "I would offer my own life to the Almighty, if it would fix him."

"I know," I said. "But your life is every bit as worthy as his."

"Then why didn't the Almighty choose me? If I please him, why are we still suffering? And now, we must return to mother and . . ."

I sighed and pulled the satchel of supplies back over my shoulder. "We are suffering because of Cain's pride. He is jealous of you. Bitter that the Almighty loves you and not him."

"The Almighty *does* love him," Abel said. "I know he does."

"But Cain doesn't see that." I ran my fingers through my beard. "All is not hopeless. We will continue, and pray that his anger will pass. Perhaps, if he heeds the warning of the Almighty, we might return next year and take hold of the promise. Either that"—I threw my arm around his shoulders—"or he may choose you instead."

Abel nodded. "That is not what I want."

"Why?"

"I love my brother."

"He is marrying Sarah. You will be alone. It is better this way. It is fair."

Abel stared at me. "If the Almighty lived according to what was fair, he would have destroyed us long ago."

My heart broadened at the wisdom in my son. I smiled and embraced him. "I am proud of you," I said. "I love you."

"I love you too."

"Come," I said and patted his back. "Let us return home."

He nodded, and we made the long journey home in silence.

Chapter 43

When Abel and I returned, Eve was pacing beside the fire with arms crossed.

We hailed her, and she nodded and ran to us.

"I saw Cain take Sarah to the fields," she said. "I tried to speak with them, but they ignored me. What happened at the sacrifice?"

Neither of us wanted to speak. The silence lengthened until she clapped her hands. "Tell me!" Her chest rose and fell in an uneven rhythm, and she pulled coarse black hair behind dark ears.

"The Almighty rejected Cain's offering," I said.

Her eyes widened. "Completely?"

I nodded. "Abel, please take my bag back to our home and gather water in a basin in the courtyard for later."

He nodded and left, seemingly eager to be gone.

After he disappeared, Eve said, "Then did he accept Abel's offering?"

I nodded.

Relief flooded her face. "So what did he decide?"

"He did not choose."

Anger crackled across her brows. "Why not?"

I sighed and rubbed my tired eyes. "How should I know?"

"You were there, were you not? Just yesterday we held hope for deliverance. Now, Cain and Sarah return too furious to abide my voice. And you tell me our hope is gone, but offer no explanation why."

"Because I don't understand it any more than you do."

"But surely you must know *something*."

"He said that Cain was in danger. That sin was crouching at his door, and that its desire was to consume him, but he must master it."

"What does that mean?"

I threw up my arms. "If you wanted to hear everything for yourself, you should have come."

Her mouth hung as if I just slapped her. "You know I couldn't do that."

I rolled my eyes and turned away. The anxiety that had taken hold in my chest since the sacrifices had grown so much that I thought I might not be able to breathe if it thickened any more.

"Where are you going?" Eve said and followed after me.

"I need rest."

She grabbed my arm. "No, not until you tell me everything."

"Even if I told you everything—and I have no duty to do so —you would feel exactly the same. I left with more questions than answers. I don't know what's going on, but I know that I can't handle anything more right now. I need time to think."

"Is there still hope for Abel?" she said.

"I . . ." I thought about the brilliant Light that had spilled over Abel. Yet he had not cried out. Still, in the wake of that meeting, Abel's only concern had been for his brother's humiliation. "Yes. I think so."

"When then?" Eve said.

"Next year."

"How do you know?"

"He said all would become clear then."

Eve threw her arms in the air and scoffed. "And you didn't think that an important detail? What about Cain?"

"Maybe if he listens to the Almighty's warning. I don't know."

Eve nodded and chewed on her upper lip.

"Give him time," I said. "Give us all time."

"Very well." She let me retreat to the dark comfort of our home.

As the door swung shut behind me and I fell to the bed. The anxiety bled from my chest, and I felt a wash of relief. Closing my eyes, I thanked the Almighty for the day, regardless of how strange or painful it had been. Because I hoped that, given enough time, Cain's anger would dissipate and our anxiety would wane, and we would be able to continue on, stronger than before.

I breathed deep and whispered to the dark, "Tomorrow, all these worries will seem small and distant."

I was wrong.

Chapter 44

Eve woke next to me and pushed herself up on her palms. "What? Are you all right? What's wrong?"

I breathed hard. Wiped my face with a shaking hand. "I just had the worst dream." In it, Cain had called for me, and when he opened his mouth, the serpent had slid out. And then the serpent had opened its mouth, and inside it had been Abel's head, severed and dripping blood to the soil.

"What?" she said. Then seemed to think better of it. "Do I want to hear it?"

I shook my head and stood, steadying myself against the wall.

A high-pitched groan came from the corner of the room, and I held my breath, confused.

"Eve, was that Abel?"

"I don't know." Eve stood with me, and we shuffled forward to see who was in our home. Eve patted the coverings, and there came another groan—female.

"Sarah?" Eve said. "Wake up."

Sarah groaned and yawned. "What time is it?"

"The middle of the night," I said. "What are you doing here?"

She sat up and hugged her knees. "Cain left." Her tone of voice was flat and distant.

"What do you mean?" Eve said. "He abandoned you on your wedding night?"

I took stock of our surroundings. "Where is Abel? He's not here, as he was last night when we went to sleep. Was he with you last night?"

Sarah nodded. "He came to speak with Cain. Cain grew angry. I tried to calm him, but Cain commanded me to be quiet. Abel left for the fields. For a while, Cain stayed with me. He would not abide my speech, so we sat in silence. Then he left. I followed him at a distance and saw him in the fields. Then . . . I came here."

"What was he doing in the fields at night?" I said.

"Abel went to check on his flock. Cain went to find him."

"This was before you went to sleep?" Eve said.

"Yes."

I stood and opened the door to peer at the night sky. "It has been many hours." I retreated inside. "Where is Abel?"

Sarah rubbed her arms as if a chill had overtaken her. "Perhaps you should check our other home." She looked up at me with such weight that I felt she was trying to communicate something to me.

I considered her. Cold fear crept up my legs. What did she fear to share with us?

I hurried out the door, leaving Eve and Sarah alone. I crossed the many paces to the other home, which sat like a giant huddling under a shadowy cloak.

I knocked on the door and heard a male voice say, "Come in."

Relief flooded my veins. I pushed open the wooden door, entered the shadows, and said, "Hello?"

"Hello, son," the voice spoke again, and the relief I'd felt in my veins turned to ice.

Chapter 45

I stood dumbstruck as my Father's Light grew, driving back the shadows in both the home and in my heart. I felt pain in my chest and rubbed the skin of it. He stood, no longer wearing that stained tunic, but rather a brown travel shirt and pants, with sandals bound to his feet.

"You are right to think that something strange must have happened to bring me here from Eden," Father said. "When I entered Eden after the sacrifices, I changed into these clothes and left to follow you home."

I narrowed my eyes. "I did not see you."

"No," he said. "You wouldn't have. I kept my distance."

I tried to think through how he had spent all the hours since. Had he met with my boys in the fields? Is that what Sarah had kept to herself? The thought made excitement rise in my chest. "Have you come to choose Abel?"

He frowned. "No, son."

I blinked. Looked at the calluses on my palms. At the cut I'd received when my hand slipped while attempting to sharpen my axe.

The pain was still there as I pressed the wound. And I

considered the ache in my chest at the presence of his Light. "Then what has happened?"

My Father stared at me, eyes filled with compassion as broad and deep as the lake surrounding the Tree of the Knowledge of Good and Evil. "Sarah knows more than she admitted."

"Is that why she told me to come here?"

The Almighty nodded. "Though she did not know I would be here. Come, let us go to them, and I will reveal the truth."

He led the way back to our home, his body lighting our surroundings like a glowing torch. When we returned to our home and opened the door, Father's Light blasted away the darkness, and Eve and Sarah cried out.

"W-what—" Eve stuttered.

"It hurts," Sarah said. "The light hurts!" She began to cry.

The Almighty's Light dimmed, and he stared at us soberly. "My Light hurts those who tend evil in their hearts. Tell me, Sarah, why did my Light hurt you?"

"I-I-I . . ." Tears fell down her young cheeks. She bit her lip and moaned, then wept into her hands.

Father sighed and sat cross-legged.

"What have you done, Sarah?" Eve said.

"She has witnessed a tragedy," Father said.

In my mind, I saw Cain and Abel in the fields. Thought of Cain's anger, his cold, calculating fury.

My pulse sped.

"When Cain went to the fields, he rose up against his brother and killed him."

The details of the brick, shelves, and furniture blurred and blended into a blank stone slate. "What?" I heard myself say.

"Abel is dead," Father said. And the emotion gripped his throat so hard his next words came out as a whisper. "I met Cain in his home, with Sarah."

Eve whirled to Sarah. "You were there? You knew and didn't tell us?"

Sarah tried to hide herself. "I—"

Our Father raised his hand and said, "I am not finished speaking."

Eve's mouth clamped shut, and her eyes registered fear.

Our Father nodded, but did not stop staring at Eve with all the intensity of the flames outside Eden. It reminded me of the wrath he showed when we ate of the fruit we should not have eaten. "I appeared to Cain and said, 'Where is Abel your brother?' He said, 'I do not know; am I my brother's keeper?'"

"And you just sat there," Eve said to Sarah in a low voice.

Sarah's shoulders shook with shame as she pulled her tunic over her head to avoid looking at us.

"Quiet," Father commanded, and he seemed to grow larger, and his Light stretched until it engulfed the room.

Eve quieted.

"Interrupt me again and you will face my wrath."

She bowed and shook.

"What did you do after he lied to you?" I asked Father.

"I said, 'What have you done? The voice of your brother's blood is crying to me from the ground. And now you are cursed from the ground, which has opened its mouth to receive your brother's blood from your hand. When you work the ground, it shall no longer yield to you its strength. You shall be a fugitive and a wanderer on the earth.'"

I remembered my nightmare then, and how Abel's blood had dripped to the soil I had been formed from. "Dear Almighty God," I whispered.

"Where is Cain?" Eve said. "How did he respond to your words?" And I knew her concern was layered with the hopes and fears of a lifetime.

"He said, 'My punishment is greater than I can bear. Behold, you have driven me today away from the ground, and from your face I shall be hidden. I shall be a fugitive and a wanderer on the earth, and whoever finds me will kill me.' Then I said to him, 'Not so! If anyone kills Cain, vengeance shall be taken on him sevenfold.' And I put a mark on him, lest any who find him should attack him. Finally, he fled from my presence."

The silence engulfed us, broken only by Sarah sniffling.

"Eve," Father said. "Long ago you said that I should come here. You used that as a reason to not meet me outside of Eden. I am here now. Tell me, will you offer penance for the evil you've tended against me?"

"You took my daughter," she said, voice shaking with anger.

"Do you believe your sin disconnected from Ayah's death?"

"Ayah?" Eve said, and her eyes widened as she looked at me.

I nodded. "That is the name I gave her."

Eve's face reddened.

"Ayah will never come back to you," Father said. All his anger was gone, and his voice was as quiet as Eve's. "And neither will Abel. You will lie awake at night, imagining him walking through your door, but he won't."

"Why?" Eve said.

"Because evil brings consequences. It is the way of the world." His eyes seemed to melt with sorrow. "Do you not remember my warning to you in Eden? That you would surely die?"

"Yes, but . . ." Her fingers clenched.

"But it feels wrong," he said. "Because it is."

"Then change it!" she yelled. "Stop it. Stop everything."

"If I did, all the lives I have ordained to come after you will never be. Cain would be left hopeless, for to end everything is to begin the judgment. Cain would be left in endless darkness, alone, without any chance for redemption."

Eve cowered.

"Who are you to question me? I am the one who gave you life. I am the one who put words in your mouth, who gives you the power to question and defy me."

I could see the hatred burning in her eyes. But her fear kept her words at bay, for she knew beyond any doubt that he could crush her with a word.

"My ways are not your ways," he said. "But I promise that all things work together for the good of those who serve me. In the end, the faithful will find life that never ends, free of the evil that stalks your souls. That, too, is a part of the promise I gave you in Eden, and as surely as I live, it will come to be."

"How?" she said. "Cain is without hope, and Abel is dead."

"You will see. But first, I will open your womb."

Eve's frown fell away. "What?"

"You will not bear any sons. Not until you repent. But . . ."

"You are giving us a daughter to replace Ayah?" I said.

"Not replace her," Father said. "No one could replace Ayah. But you will experience new life again. By my word, you will bear all the daughters you could desire. But unless you exchange your bitterness for thankfulness, your generation will come to an end."

"This is a curse disguised as a blessing," Eve said.

"Call it what you may. It is more than you deserve." And though his words were harsh, the spirit he spoke them in was gentle and filled with remorse. For what good father refuses to discipline his children?

Eve opened her mouth to protest, then closed it and nodded. She could not lie so boldly to our Father's face, for to be in his presence was to be made aware of your own evil more acutely than any could bear. And she knew that she was in the wrong, and that every word the Almighty spoke was both good and kind.

And still, she hated him.

The Almighty stood. "It is time I returned. Adam?"

"Yes?" I stood, hoping he would embrace me or offer at least some words of comfort.

"Will you meet me next year outside Eden?"

I nodded as tears came to my eyes. "Yes," I said. "I promise."

He frowned and shook his head. "Don't promise."

And with that, in the space of a blink, he was gone.

Chapter 46

Before Father left, we had not realized how his Light had actually lifted the burden of our emotional darkness. In his absence, we ached so deeply for his return that words crumbled on our tongues. We wept, each one of us, for the secret pains we'd hidden for years.

For the pain of his holiness was altogether different from the ache of the chains that bound our souls.

I wept for Ayah. For Cain. For Abel. For the love I'd tasted from Eve, but now doubted would return.

Because how could she ever recover from such a loss? How could we return to who we were? To the love we lost?

Our family, our hopes and dreams, everything had been shattered in the instant Father told us that Cain had murdered Abel. For Cain had proven himself incapable of mastering the sin that had consumed him, and Eve's womb was cursed to never bear an heir to atone for our mistakes.

Unless she repented.

Yet she was too locked within the prison of her emotions, and I was powerless to fix her.

I remembered the serpent's piercing, silver eyes from before, in Eden.

The serpent. That insidious beast of all beasts.

This was the serpent's work, just as my nightmare had foreboded. First, it stole our joy in Eden. Now, it broke our family, and the hopes we'd held for a future.

I wanted to find it and wrap my hands around its neck. Why had the Almighty not destroyed it after it led us astray in the garden?

My anger roiled and spilled over, attaching itself to anything and everything. I wanted to break every piece of pottery lining our shelves. To face Cain and beat him as he had beat my son.

Cain had been the vessel through which the serpent struck. In my dream, the serpent had slithered out from inside him. And when I awoke, I'd found Abel dead.

My little, dark lamb. A life too brief, and all too fitting of his name.

Abel. *Breath*. Gone like a spirit on the wind, devoured as I'd seen him devoured by Eve in that nightmare all those years ago.

My eyes widened, and I realized that Father had shown me this would happen. But I had been too dull to realize what it meant.

For Eve had refused to return to the Almighty. And I had failed to make her return. If she had come to the Almighty and offered penance, Cain would not have felt the pressure he did. Because we had pushed him to become more than any boy could, and in striving to become what he couldn't, he had been broken.

Now he believed Abel a usurper, and that the only way to make certain Abel didn't take everything was to end him.

I looked at Eve, who wept in the cold corner of the room.

Fury curled my fingers into fists, and I had to look away to tamp it down.

Sarah wiped her face dry, then rose, and exited.

Eve didn't so much as blink.

I stood and faced her. "Eve."

She stared at the wall as if my voice hadn't sounded.

"Eve!"

Her eyes rolled toward me, dimly registering my expression. "It's over," she said.

She was right. All we had planned had crumbled. "But we still have Sarah. We have each other."

She laughed.

"Do not mock me," I said. "I am worthy of your love, and so is Sarah."

"I do not deny that."

"Then why do you laugh?"

She raised her hands in surrender, and her face held no pretense, no mask. There was just Eve, the woman I had known and loved, broken beyond repair. Her voice came as a whisper. "I'm empty, Adam. I have no love left to give."

I pressed my temples with my palms and, instead of arguing any longer, exited to find Sarah.

My daughter. The last of my children.

Chapter 47

As I crossed the space between our homes, Sarah swung open the door and headed east. I stopped and watched from the shadows, expecting she would soon turn back. There was nothing east of her home. Our gardens were west and north, and our pastures were nearby to the south.

When she did not turn back but instead sped up, I quietly ran after her. Luckily, I was barefoot and careful of my footfalls. When I was finally within reach, and knew she could not outrun me, I said, "Sarah!"

She stopped and peered over her shoulder. "Go home, Father."

I slid to a stop several paces away, breathing hard. "What are you doing?"

She stared at me with hands on her hips and adjusted the bag slung over her shoulder. "Go home and stop worrying." She tried to keep walking, but I followed.

"Are you leaving?"

She stopped. Eyes bright, filled with tears. "You weren't supposed to find me."

I shook my head. "I won't let you."

"I'm not your little girl anymore."

"Stop speaking nonsense."

"I am Cain's."

I stuck my fingers in my ears to make certain I hadn't misheard. "Are you mad?"

She turned away. "I didn't expect you to understand."

I grabbed the shoulder of her shirt. "He murdered your brother! Why would you go to him?"

She gritted her teeth and glared at my fist holding her shirt. "There's nothing left for me here."

"You're mad. You need rest. Come, I will bring you home. In the morning, all will be clear."

"Stop!" she said.

"Come home, now!"

She struck my arm with more intensity than I'd ever witnessed from her. "His child grows within me!" Tears grew in her eyes and spilled down her cheeks.

I blinked and stepped back. "What?"

"It's been months, Father." She lifted her shirt and showed me the subtle bulge in her lower abdomen.

My mind spun. I tried to think of how neither of us could have noticed. She had been wearing bulky clothing for days. And I had not witnessed her bathing in months.

But how could this have happened without me knowing? She had slept with Eve and me all this last year. And she was nearly always with Eve.

Unless . . .

That time I found her beside the stream late at night with Cain, long before they were married. Could he have . . .?

I opened my mouth, but no words came.

"I'm tired of living the life you command of me," she said. "This is my decision. I will return to the father of my child, for I will not let my baby grow without its father. Neither will I let Cain die in the wilderness, alone and forgotten."

"How could you let him violate you?"

Sarah's face registered anger. She scoffed and shook her head. "This is why Cain feels the way he does about you."

"What are you talking about?"

"I was offered to Cain a full year ago. You and mother decided for us, remember? When he asked me to prove my love after seeing me with Abel, what could I say? You understand nothing of the pressures you put on them. Nor of the suffering I've endured."

"I did nothing but care for you and try to teach you to obey our Father."

"Liar," she said. "You put the weight of the world on the shoulders of two boys. The weight you yourself failed to shoulder! And you hated Cain for working harder and better than you."

"He failed, and my Father rejected him. He made an embarrassment of me!"

An owl screeched in the distance, likely swooping at a rat in the brush.

Sarah shook her head. "This has nothing to do with you." Her eyes canvased my body, from top to bottom. "Go home, Father. I have nothing for you. And you have nothing for me."

"No, Sarah . . ." I reached for her, but she turned away and walked on. "Sarah!" I called, but she ignored me. I cupped my hands around my mouth and said, "What about mother!"

She looked over her shoulder and raised her hand, then continued walking.

I fell to the ground and struck the dust. Over and again, until pain shot up my arm. I wept, and the dirt stuck to my eyes and cheeks.

"Almighty God," I said. "Have mercy. Have mercy!"

But there was no response.

Because Father was gone. For I had sinned against him. My eldest son was gone and hated me for putting the weight I failed to bear on his shoulders. My youngest son was dead. And our daughter had abandoned us for the one who shattered our family and gave her a child I believed I would never meet.

Fury filled my bones until I felt I would burst into flames and be scorched to ash. I had no focus for my anger other than

Cain. I knew without even asking that Eve would command me to go after Sarah and apologize for everything. To invite both of them to live with us.

I also knew that, like Eve, I was a slave to the tempest that raged inside me.

If I saw Cain, I would not hold back. I would kill him. I would beat him back to the dust from which his brother's blood cried. He had ruined our family, destroyed my life, and stolen my beloved son. He'd destroyed the love of the woman who had been formed to love me.

But if I killed him, I would bear the vengeance of my own Father, sevenfold.

So, instead of following her, I raged to the night sky.

Until my vitality was spent, and I went and found Abel in the field and carried him home. When Eve saw him, she threw herself over his body and wept afresh as I dug a grave outside our home.

I placed his body inside it. Then, just like with Ayah, I pushed the dirt back over him.

Doing so broke something deep inside me. Afterward, we both stood staring. At everything. At nothing.

Then I entered our home, which held the weight of a million memories I could never forget.

Chapter 48

Our grief counted our moments as days. Each hour burdened
with so much aching pain that a week felt an eternity.

Despite this, time wore on, and the pain wore at our features
until the frown lines that marked our cheeks were delved as deep
as the cracks between bricks.

To lose Ayah was horrible enough. To then lose Abel and
experience a schism so deep that we could never see Sarah
again—it seemed for a while a fate worse than death.

But even the deepest of pains cannot last forever. For the sun
rises, and the sun falls, and like the phases of the moon pull at
the tide, the subtle change in seasons pulls minutely at the soul.
Until one finds that weeks later, there appears some unexpected
sparkles of beauty amidst the endless gray. So small that at first
they go unnoticed.

Yet they gather and multiply, and soon there's no denying
that joy, at least in moments, has returned.

But with the capacity for joy comes the desire for more. And
with dreams for more comes the ache of dissatisfaction.

So it came to be that six months after losing Abel, Eve stood
outside our home in the pouring rain with arms outstretched to

the sky. I watched her from inside the home, knowing she needed this moment to herself.

But I wanted to join her. To feel free enough to toss away my clothing and dance naked in the rain. To feel the warm summer deluge and thank our Father for the simple joys he embedded into life.

I stayed, instead, and fiddled with a frayed weaving on a basket that held excess wool for patching clothes and coverings.

Until the door clacked shut behind me, and I turned to see Eve dripping wet. I stood and retrieved a covering for her to dry off with, but she pushed it away and pressed her lips against mine with such passion that I stumbled backward.

We held each other to stay upright, and after laughing, I kissed her back, until I felt her lips shake, and realized the wetness on her cheeks was no longer just rainwater.

She wanted to love me. She had said so more than enough times. And yet the pain had been like a dam in a river. "Until it lessens," she had said, "I can offer you no affection."

I did not question her, but held her, urged her toward the bed, and thanked the Almighty for washing enough of her pain away that she could feel the joy of love, if only for a moment.

. . .

Within weeks, we realized she was pregnant, but she remained cautious. She did not want to lose this child as she had Ayah. And neither did we want to have a child and raise them to be like Cain.

But how could we stop when there was nothing else for us in the world but the joy of raising children? We knew that they would be our hope, even as they had been our sorrow. We believed that the love would be worth the pain of loss.

For even if we had known that to have Cain and Abel would lead to the pain it had, we would not have traded those days with them.

Not for anything in the world.

But Cain was no longer who he had been.

Still, as Eve's belly grew, my anxiety heightened. She'd taken to staring toward the eastern sky in the mornings. She did not speak of Sarah or Cain, for we had long since agreed not to.

But I could tell she was dwelling on the past. I would touch her belly and try to redirect her to the hope for our future child within her womb. But her mind reached backward like a plant reaches for sunlight.

To focus only on the future seemed an impossibility for her.

Still, amidst the worry, there was a greater sense of joy, for with purpose comes satisfaction. And our purpose, in those months, was to bring a new child into the world to salve our loneliness.

We did not speak of our fallen hopes. We did not mention the promise of the Almighty.

Her pregnancy was not like the one with Ayah. Eve had only mild nausea in the early portion of her pregnancy. She had no dizziness and never fainted. All seemed well.

Until the week of my yearly journey to Eden.

. . .

"I wonder if Sarah ever thinks of us," Eve said.

I was digging through the soil with the metal hoe I'd crafted, but stopped and leaned against the shaft. Sweat had soaked the shadow of my hands into the wood, and I rubbed at it as I considered how to respond. "I know you have been thinking of her a lot."

"Don't you?" she said.

"What sort of question is that?"

"An honest one," Eve said. "Will you answer it?"

I lifted the hoe and scratched at the soil some more. "What do you want?"

"I want to talk."

"You want more than that. Otherwise you wouldn't have brought it up."

She raised one brow. "You're wrong. I do just want to talk. We haven't been able to talk about it for all these months. It's suffocating me."

"We agreed long ago it would do us no good."

"I changed my mind."

I stared at her. "You want to find them."

She shrugged. "What if we did?"

"It wouldn't change anything."

"You don't know that." She crossed to me with her basket so that we might throw more weeds into it.

I swept the newly dead growth into a pile. "It would be bad timing."

She sneered and lifted the pile into the basket. "Why? Because you want to leave me again to go see Father?"

I stopped and gave her a glare that said more than she'd allow me to with words.

"I need to know she's all right," Eve said. "She was with child!"

"She will never live here again."

"She might," Eve said.

"The Almighty cursed Cain to wander, and Cain would not let her leave him."

"Men are not always so powerful as you think," Eve said, and her eyes conjured that dangerous gleam I'd come to fear.

I gritted my teeth. "I'm not going to go find her."

Her face reddened, and she threw her basket as far as she could, spilling all the weeds we'd labored to organize. "I can't sleep anymore."

"I heard you snoring last night."

"Did you also hear me wake and weep until sunrise?"

"If you believe they would actually return, why not go find them yourself?"

"Because the only reason they aren't living here right now is you, and you know it."

"How is it my fault?" I tossed my hoe and pointed at her. "You pressured them, same as me!"

"Cain knows how I feel," Eve said. "Sarah confided in me, and in Cain. I was aware of more than you."

"Really? Like what?"

She crossed her arms over her bulging belly and turned. "I don't need to prove myself to you."

"Then neither do I need to pander to your mad wishes."

Her eyes glared sideways. "I'm not mad."

"You seem like it."

"I knew of her pregnancy weeks before you did."

My eyes widened, and my mouth hung open, but when I saw her smug expression, I wiped it from my face. "Then why didn't you tell me?"

"Because you would just have grown angry and accosted Cain about it. You were always too hard on him, and I couldn't risk it. It would have made everything worse."

"As if him murdering Abel wasn't bad enough."

A dark shadow passed over her eyes, but she pushed it away.

"And why did he do that?" I continued, for she had lit a fire in my veins, and I wanted to drive it back into hers. "Because of the pressure you put on him to live up to your dreams, to set you free from the curse you purchased by eating the fruit in Eden."

She flew at me and struck me in the chest with her palm. "You pushed me to do it, then leveraged God to break our family!"

I held her stare.

"I told you before that men are not always so powerful as they think," Eve said.

I narrowed my eyes.

"If you won't go to them, perhaps you're right that I should. After all, maybe they would welcome me."

"Do that and you're a bigger fool than I thought," I said.

"Am I?"

"What if Cain kills you?"

She shrugged. "What if he does?"

"You're mad," I said. "Raving mad."

She smiled. "If I am, then you have no choice but to offer

them the chance to come home. To have a real relationship with us again."

"I'm not living with that murderer," I said and turned away, not wanting to give in to her manipulation.

"He murdered our son because he believed Abel was slowly stealing everything from him. His birthright as firstborn, the love of Sarah—that was why he was so controlling toward her —, the blessing of the Almighty to redeem our world from the curse, and finally . . . your love."

"I loved both my sons, until one of them showed himself a monster."

"He never believed you loved him."

I picked up the hoe again and pointed it east. "That's his problem! Not mine!"

"Is it?"

I began scraping at the soil again, but my fingers felt untrustworthy. "I'm going to meet Father outside Eden, and he will bless us and give us joy to salve the suffering we've endured this year. And you are going to stay here and keep yourself and the baby inside you safe."

A long silence passed. She took a deep breath and turned away. Then paused and said. "If you go to the Almighty instead of our children, you'll come back to an empty home."

She left me in the field to gnaw on her words.

Chapter 49

Days passed, and nothing I did changed Eve's mind.

It wasn't as though I truly expected her to change her mind. She never did. It was just that her mind worked in ways I found strange and sometimes it was hard to tell if she was thinking with clarity or blinded by emotion.

When I woke early two mornings before the day I would need to meet the Almighty, I rose quietly, exited our home without waking Eve, and considered my options. If I delayed any longer, I would be forced to flee to the Almighty and lose both Eve and our unborn child. No matter what happened, I could not live alone in this wilderness. The emptiness would consume me like the gaping throat of the serpent. I had no reason to believe Father would accept me back to live with him. How could I pass through the flames unscathed?

And what hope did we have without Cain fulfilling the prophecy or Eve repenting to Father?

I rubbed my face hard. If I left immediately and found them quick enough, I could still, perhaps, make it back to Eden in time. And maybe, if doing this gave Eve closure, she would finally be able to let go and repent, and once again bear sons to fulfill the prophecy.

I groaned and cursed myself for not thinking of it sooner. Why had I not realized that I could both please her and Father? I had been blinded both by my pride and my fear of facing Cain. I'd worried what my son might do when he saw me. Would he slay me too? Were Sarah and her child even still alive? Or had he killed them and lived alone, foraging through the wilderness?

Either way, I could not let my wife wander pregnant through the wilderness to find a madman and face danger alone.

I entered our home, no longer caring whether I woke her. The door slammed behind me, and Eve shuffled and woke.

"What are you doing?" she said as I rummaged through containers to find the bread we'd made just the day before.

"Readying myself for the journey." I stuffed all the food I could into one of my woven shoulder bags that Eve had made for me, then found clay containers with soft stoppers to fill with water. I did not know how long I would be wandering the wilderness, nor how much access I would have to water. Thirst struck quickly in the dry desert, even in spring.

"I thought you would leave tomorrow?"

I cleared my throat and stared down at her. "I'm doing it," I said. "I'm finding them."

Her eyes widened, and she pushed herself to her feet with some difficulty, for her belly had grown uncomfortably large. "Truly?"

"I might find Sarah and her child dead, and Cain a madman wandering the desert. If I do not return, know that he slayed me as he did Abel and that your only hope is to return to Eden and beg for Father to protect you and the child you are carrying."

She crossed the room and tossed her arms around me, tears springing from her eyes and wetting my tunic. I held her upright so she would not stumble and fall. "Thank you," she said. Then she let go and backed up. "I dreamed that they were alive. Thin, haggard, but alive. I know it's true, as deeply as I know that the baby within me is alive." She placed her hand on her belly. "We must offer Cain and Sarah the chance to return, to find forgiveness and acceptance. If we don't, I will carry too many regrets to my death. I could not live with myself knowing they are suffering and we offered them no help. It doesn't matter what they did. They are our children."

"Keep yourself safe," I said. "And keep your fire burning."

She nodded, then went out and started a fire. I finished packing, tied shoes to my feet, and walked east with the heavy bag over my shoulder as the smoke rose behind me.

. . .

I had often traversed the wilderness in search of firewood, but aside from our yearly journey west to Eden, I'd not spent more than half a day outside the boundaries of our home. And not since first leaving Eden had I spent so much time in the open alone.

The rocky hills and scraggly grasses had grown wild and unpredictable. Little crawling beasts darted out of the brush, and birds of prey floated in slow half circles high above like shadows against the clouds.

I walked all day and only once came across a small pond. An emaciated wolf jogged by and gave me no more than a glance before scuttling out of sight.

I stopped only once to rest and eat. I'd drunk small sips throughout the day, but as I finished a crumb of bread, my thirst overwhelmed me. I opened one of the three containers of water and drank half of its contents in a single draught. When finally I continued walking, the break had served only to make me more aware of the ache in my feet from the stony paths. And my lips were cracked and flaking despite the water I'd consumed.

Once, I saw a gathering of antelope grazing. When they saw me, they bounded away. I kept my bearings by the position of the sun. As night fell, navigation became more difficult. Luckily,

I had studied the stars enough to navigate with reasonable confidence.

But with night came a cold wind that thickened my thoughts and slowed my progress. After the first night watch, it seemed the shadows came alive with nocturnal sounds. The sky swarmed with bats that quietly swooped at the clouds of insects that had harassed me all day.

I would have continued longer, but I could hardly see more than a few paces in front of me. And if our children were sleeping, I could have walked right by them and never noticed.

I searched for any caves or natural shelters in the immediate area and decided to weather the night balanced between the branches of a young tree, so that no beasts would find me or raid my bag of supplies.

I slept fitfully for a while, then woke to a bat perched above me fluttering its wings. I tried to close my eyes and chase the dream still lingering like a shadow at the edge of my awareness, but the cold wind brought a shiver, and the fluttering bat unnerved me.

I lowered myself to the ground and dug out a crust of hard bread. Each bite was a battle. I gave up halfway through and exchanged it for the rest of my first container of water. I stretched and noticed the sky glowing dark blue. A swath of clouds was flying on the eastern wind, and the moon hung just above the rim of hills.

I stood and made my way farther east. I walked until mid-morning before looking up and realizing I did not recognize where I was. I had been so exhausted from a night of sleeplessness that my thoughts had been lulled by the steady onward motion of my feet.

I sighed and spun, canvassing every span of my surroundings. There was nothing, save for the endless rock, desert brush, and sporadic birds of various sizes.

The temptation seized me to turn back. If I returned in haste, I could still make it back to Eden in time.

I shook my head and pushed the desire away. Unless I ran

out of food and water, Eve would not suffer me to return without word. And if I did not find some way to please Eve and calm her fury toward Father, we would never experience the fulfillment of Father's prophecy and the reversal of our evil.

The only choice I had was to hurry on and find Cain and Sarah as quick as I could.

I walked faster now, and from time to time climbed trees atop hills to see farther. But I saw no sign of anything.

How far had they gone? Was I too far south . . . or north?

When the sun began to dip on the second day, I turned west and closed my eyes. "Forgive me," I whispered. And I prayed that the shifting wind would carry my words far enough that Father might catch them and know that I wanted to be there with him.

But instead of his warm embrace, the sun set and I felt the gaze of stars like silver eyes gazing down at me with delight.

Again, I climbed a tree and searched the surroundings for any sign of firelight.

Slowly, my mood sank into despair.

I sat with my legs on either side of a wide branch with my back to the trunk. I dug through my bag, hoping to find something I'd forgotten I'd packed. But there were no new items. Only the dry bread, the containers of water, and an additional set of shoes in case I tore the ones on my feet.

I hung the bag around my neck and positioned it between my legs. I waited until I was so tired I worried I might slip into dreams and fall, for this tree was not one easy to sleep in.

I slid to the ground and decided to keep walking, regardless of the dark. My eyes burned, and I could not rub the ache from them. I stumbled onward, staring at the ground ahead of me until finally, after what seemed an entire week, the sun rose, and I raised my head.

I was down to my last container of water.

I sat on a low, flat stone and stared into the container. What was the point in continuing? I had not eaten in over a day, and I had barely enough water to see me home. The wilderness was so expansive that I could search for weeks and find nothing.

Yet to have thrown away my chance to see Father for nothing was maddening. Besides, if I returned, Eve would only try to force me back out again and again until we found them.

I glanced up. Ahead was a small forest. The wilderness here had more grass and less dust. I was thirsty, and where there was a forest, there had to be water. I would enjoy filling my containers and washing the dust from my face.

I stood, put the stopper in the container, and shoved it back into my bag. The trees ahead were tall and offered thick shade with broad leaves. Had it been the middle of summer, I would have welcomed the change. But having spent each night a little too chilled for comfort made the sudden drop in temperature unpleasant as I walked between the closely set trunks.

The open sounds of the wilderness fell away as I walked deeper, and the many leaves seemed to reflect and magnify my noises. I found myself breathing carefully and stepping lighter without thinking.

Little furry beasts hopped back and forth, too quick and furtive to identify. Birds fluttered from branch to branch, hidden by the shadows and leaves. The chortle of a small stream led me past a patch of thorny bushes.

Dappled light filtered through the canopy and set the water glistening. I dropped to my knees and splashed my face. The water was cold and clear. I poured out the excess from my last container, then filled all three anew and drank one dry before filling it again.

I sat cross-legged and closed my eyes to enjoy a moment of quiet peace.

It seemed I could hear the world growing. The steady sound of time moving forward. I could smell musty piles of leaves with mushrooms pressing them aside. And . . . something else. Something acrid. And dark.

I opened my eyes and sniffed. I knew that smell.

I pushed myself to my feet, slung the pack over my shoulder, and tried to listen past the chortle of the water. I heard nothing and could no longer sense it on the wind.

But I knew what I had smelled.

I tried to find the sky, but the canopy was in the way.

I crossed to a nearby tree that seemed taller and stronger than the others. I tested the lowest limb, then dropped my pack and swung up. I climbed to the top, limb over limb, and as I clung to the tree and felt its trunk bend, I saw the unmistakable line of smoke rising from a small clearing toward the south end of the forest.

I let myself down as quickly as I dared and swept off so fast that I forgot my pack.

I skidded to a stop in the dead leaves and returned to throw it over my shoulder before sprinting on again.

The land dipped and rose at difficult angles, and I slid down an incline as I tried to rush across the rim. I had to grab hold of young trees to keep myself from slipping. My mind spun, and my heart thumped so loudly I hardly even noticed my footfalls anymore, though I knew they were clumsy and hard.

I rushed ahead, and when faced with a wall of bushes taller than me with hard limbs and fragrant flowers, I forced myself through. The branches tore the strap of my bag, and I had to hold it in my fist to continue.

I could see a soft glow ahead. An orange circle of light cast by the fire spewing that gray pillar of smoke. I closed my eyes and thanked Father for leading me to our children. Then I remembered I had abandoned him to achieve this goal and felt a sickening guilt spread through my abdomen. I swallowed hard, steadied my breathing, and slowly entered the clearing.

Even the wind seemed to hold its breath as I walked to the far side of the clearing and reached the broad fire now burnt mostly to ash. Near the fire was a single wooden hut covered with thatch. "Sarah?" I said quietly and peered inside the hut. There were clay pots, bedding made of animal skins, and a small table with wooden seats. But all was hastily built, as if only temporary.

I went back to the fire and looked around the clearing. I saw nothing else that seemed manmade. I heard a soft noise, as of a small beast snuffling, and turned to the edge of the forest close to the hut. I tried to peer within and listen, but it was dark and I saw nothing.

I walked to it and placed my hand on the trunk of a tree right at the edge, then heard the noise again and realized it was coming from above me. I slowly lifted my head and a dark figure leapt out of the branches.

I scrambled back and fell to my seat. The figure rushed toward me, into the light, holding the tip of a wooden spear aimed directly at my chest.

"What do you want with us?" Cain's eyes gleamed above the shaft of the spear.

I stared at him, taking in his withered figure. The strength of his arms was there, but his cheeks were sunken with hunger and his clothing bulky and oversized.

"Speak!" he yelled, and the tip of the spear touched my chest.

I scooted back. "Eve sent me," I said.

The snuffling noise sounded again, and I glanced into the trees and spotted Sarah holding a small bundle atop a wooden platform that had been built into the tree.

Cain yelled and jabbed the spear into my arm hard enough to draw blood. "Look at me."

I looked at him.

"Go back, Sarah," he said.

I stared at him, even as I heard her working her way down from the platform on some sort of ladder.

"I said go back!" he said. "And you . . . ." He drew a bit closer. "Why did you come?"

"Can a father not desire to see his children?"

"Not you," Cain said.

"Surely you can imagine what it is like to lose a child."

Cain gritted his teeth and jabbed at my chest again with the spear, digging in and causing a sharp pain.

I cried out and shuffled back, working myself to my feet.

"Threaten my child again and I will run you through," he said.

"It was not a threat."

Sarah appeared behind him. Her eyes as bright and alive as ever, though her face, too, was thin and weathered. And she looked older, much older, though it had only been a year. The child was bundled and strapped to her chest. "Father," she said.

Cain whipped round and pointed into the tree. "Go back!"

"Don't hurt him," Sarah said.

Cain's face reddened with fury, but she edged toward me as if she thought I were a dream, and Cain did not stop her. She was reaching out, as if to touch me. I offered my hand in return as the baby on her chest cooed, and I looked down and saw the strangest sight as Sarah's fingers brushed mine. The covering fell back from the child, and I saw its eyes. They were a bright, luminescent silver. And its head was not covered in hair, but rather two small pointed horns sprouted from the top of his skull.

Sarah followed my gaze and realized the covering had fallen just as Cain swooped in and pulled it back and stepped between us, separating Sarah's fingers from mine, leaving a distant buzzing sensation where my daughter's fingers had once again found their home in my hand.

My eyes narrowed as I considered Cain, my son, now a man so foreign, bent on separating me from the daughter I had protected all my life.

"You've seen us," he said. "Now go."

"No," I said. "I can't."

"Then you will find your home on the end of this spear," Cain said.

"Stop it, Cain," Sarah said and pulled hard on the arm that held the spear.

"I don't trust him," he said.

"He did not come to harm us."

"You know nothing," Cain said, and for the first time I saw the fear in Cain's eyes.

"Son," I said and spread my hands in surrender. "I did not come to harm you."

I thought of what Eve had said of Cain's distrust for me. How he had never felt truly loved by me. How I had been too hard, and that I was the reason he did not live with us. I had failed the Almighty to come here and realized for the first time the true extent to which I had failed my family. Was I destined to break everything? Tears burned my eyes, but I pushed them away.

"Then why did you come?" Cain said.

"I came on behalf of Eve . . ." I paused. "And myself. To ask if you would consider coming back, to live with us."

Cain's eyes narrowed as Sarah's widened. Sarah looked at Cain.

"Liar," Cain said.

Sarah stepped around Cain. "Why do you want us to return?"

"You are our children," I said. "Do you not feel you would do anything to be with your child?"

It seemed my words touched both of them, but in Cain's eyes flickered a battle between painful longing and distrust. "I don't believe you. You don't want us to live with you. You just want me to return so that you can find the redemption you long for. Sarah told me what the Almighty said. That Eve will never bear another son."

I felt heat rise to my face. "He did not say never," I said.

"I am no fool," Cain said. "I am done with you and your God."

Fear crackled down my spine as his words reminded me of the silver eyes of the serpent, and I considered the little baby bundled to Sarah's chest. Could they be, somehow, harboring a child possessed by the serpent? A brief thought flashed through my mind to take the child and dash it on the ground—but it was a baby! I did not know that it was evil, regardless of the strangeness of its appearance.

Furthermore, it was my daughter's firstborn son. My first grandchild.

No, I could do nothing to that child. Especially when my own children were standing here, waiting for me to explain myself. And I had abandoned my own Father for this exact moment. "Think of what day it is," I said.

Cain's eyes searched the distance, as if calculating hard. His mouth hung open, and his eyes widened. Finally, he nodded and pressed his lips together. "So, you are done with your God as well."

"I came for you." And now the tears grew in my eyes so quickly that I could not tamp them down. I wiped my face. "No matter what you choose, I love you, son."

Cain swallowed, but the action seemed difficult. He took a step back, face pale as he took in my figure. My words seemed to have struck him deeper than any weapon ever could.

I offered him my hand. "Please," I whispered. "Please, son."

He stared at my hand. I could see the longing in his eyes. Could feel the ache in his heart. "We are happy here," he said.

Again, I considered their withered figures. The hasty construction of all they'd built. They had not lived here long. They had been wandering from place to place, chasing wild game, foraging for food because of the curse that had stolen Cain's ability to work the ground.

"You don't appear happy," I said.

"We have survived, and we will continue to. We don't need you."

"Do you not desire to come home? To remain in one place and thrive together?" I said.

Sarah's eyes gleamed with emotion over Cain's shoulder, but Cain lowered his spear and said, "Go."

"Cain," Sarah said.

"If I ever see you or Eve again," Cain said, "I will not hesitate to kill you both."

I stepped back and raised my hands in surrender. "I will go," I said.

But Cain followed until I passed the fire again and the little thatched hut. Sarah stayed back by the tree with the platform in it. Staring after me, waving. I waved back, and Cain prodded me hard with the wooden end of his spear. "Don't look at her."

I did as he commanded and, as I passed within the edge of the forest on the far side, looked back one final time to see Cain watching me. Eve had been right. I longed for Cain's return as much as she did. And here, I had found him, and he had not killed me.

But still, his refusal meant that all hope for him was gone. And if Eve ever tried to return to them, she would be struck down as well.

I hoped this would be enough to salve her heart and win her repentance. If not, we would all die a cursed death, drowning in sin.

Chapter 50

When I finally returned to Eve and the fire she'd kept burning all that time, she threw her arms around me and kissed my neck. "I was so worried for you," she said. "Why did it take you so long?"

I sat beside the fire and told her all that had happened.

"So," she said, staring at the flames. "You were right."

I shrugged. "We both were. I could tell they wanted to live with us. But what happened between us runs too deep."

"And now, the Almighty . . ." She picked at her flaking lips with her slender fingers.

"He said that we will never see him outside Eden again."

"Will you go still, just in case?"

I nodded. "Keep the fire going."

. . .

I found a sacrifice and carried it on that long journey that we'd traversed so many times before. My legs were heavy, and they ached with pain. But when I arrived at the entrance of Eden, I saw nothing. Only a stone wall where the entrance used to be. The twisting flames were gone.

I stood and considered if I might have taken a wrong turn, but no. This was the exact spot. My perfect memory would not let me forget.

And the Almighty was gone.

I was too exhausted to weep. This, after all, was what I had been told to expect. But I had doubted his word, just as I had doubted his promise that we would surely die if we ate the fruit we should not have eaten. Still, I longed to see Father again. To experience the searing intimacy that was our own within that first garden. To love and be loved by him.

I had traded him for earthly things. For shadows and beings made in his image. I had thought it would bring me happiness. Or that somehow, I could have everything at once—my Father, my sin, my wife, my children, my pain, my joy.

But sin acts like cracks in a jar. Everything put inside just spills out across the soil.

So I returned and offered the lamb as a sacrifice within our actual home.

The following year, I made the long trek again only to find that stone wall staring back at me.

Every year I did this, until twenty years passed, then fifty, then a hundred. But you must not misunderstand. No one else joined me on these journeys. Our daughters all stayed back with Eve, for this was a private duty.

In all that time, she refused to let go of her bitterness toward the Almighty. Perhaps because each year, when I made the journey back to Eden, the wounds were driven home once again. But I no longer cared. I had won my wife's love and intimacy, only to find that it was not what I needed.

I needed my Father. And yet, he was all that I could not have.

For I had made my choices. And sin has consequences. Still, I hoped . . . Could I be forgiven? Could I experience the redemption my heart longed for? That I dreamed of at night?

Finally, 130 years after we came to life in Eden, I found Eve kneeling outside our home, weeping to the sky, crying out, "I am sorry. I'm sorry. I was wrong. I was so wrong."

That year, she gave birth to a son. And she named him Seth and wept over him, and said, "God has appointed for me another offspring instead of Abel, for Cain killed him."

After Seth, she bore more sons and daughters. And those sons and daughters bore more children. And you, yourself, Enoch, are the fifth generation from Seth.

But never have we found intimacy with my Father. And never again has he spoken to me in dreams. He has spoken to none of us but you.

Which makes me think . . .

Chapter 51

Adam stared at Enoch with such intensity that Enoch stood and considered leaving. He did not know what Adam would ask but was uncertain he could fulfill the longing he now understood had driven the man all these years.

"Last year, I lost Eve," Adam said. "I am left only with an insatiable longing for my eternal Father, whom I abandoned out of cowardice and fear of losing temporary pleasures." Adam rushed forward and knelt before Enoch, grabbing hold of his wrists and pleading. "Tell me. Is there any hope for me to see him again?"

Enoch considered the first of all men. The father of everyone. "I . . . I don't know. Who am I to say?"

"Tell me you will pray for me," Adam said. "You are Father's chosen prophet. He listens to you and speaks to you in dreams, does he not?"

Enoch nodded. "As he did to you, long ago."

"It has been centuries since last I dreamed. Please, just ask him for me. I will not beg him to undo all my mistakes. I only want to see him—one last time."

Enoch blinked, considering Adam's story and the pain so

visible in his eyes. More than ever, Adam's longing touched Enoch's heart.

The man's wrinkled face shook with emotion. "I shared my story with you. You will grant me this one request, won't you?"

Enoch bowed. "I told you I would. How could I deny you now?"

"Thank you," Adam whispered and let go of Enoch's wrists, sinking back against the wall.

"I will need to leave soon," Enoch said.

Adam nodded. "So long as you tell me Father's response before you leave, you may go anywhere."

"Thank you for trusting your story with me," Enoch said.

"Thank you for listening." Adam looked at Enoch and smiled. Peace settled his face for the first time since entering that ring of firelight and beginning his story.

And with that, Enoch left Adam's small home and returned to his own.

Then, beside his bed, he folded his hands and prayed, "Almighty God. You see all. You know all. You understood what Adam would request of me, even before me bringing it to you in prayer. Please, answer him through me. Will you forgive him? Will you meet with him one final time?"

Enoch waited in the silence. When there was no response, he laid himself down, wearied by the many hours of heavy listening. And, as his eyes closed, he fell into a dream he would never forget.

. . .

Enoch stood in a vast, flat expanse covered with tiny rocks. The sun was gone, and stars shone in a strange arrangement overhead. A man rose before him, naked, with his back to Enoch; his skin was dark. Another man joined him in a white tunic stained with red splotches. They walked away together, hand in hand. Until the dark man laid down to sleep and his body stilled and crumbled, then blew away like dust on the wind.

But the shadow of him remained like a thing of substance on the ground. The form of the body that used to be there.

The man in the white tunic lifted the shadow. As he did so, the shadow brightened and the darkness slowly was replaced with Light. The man in the white tunic wiped the man's face, as if pushing away tears. Then they embraced, and all was replaced with Light.

The two of them turned to Enoch, and the man in the white tunic said, "Let the old man go west. There he will find me. I will provide a sacrifice. But you must not join him, for it is time you went east."

. . .

Enoch woke. It was day, and the Almighty had answered his prayer.

It was time for him to delve into dangerous lands and face the children of the serpent. For he had also dreamed of that child with horns, the one Adam failed to destroy. It still walked the earth, an abomination in human skin. And it was the very reason for the coming destruction of the world through water.

Enoch would face it, not in person, but in spirit. And he and his progeny would stand against it. Until the world was drowned, and all the men of dust who beat their chests to the rhythm of another Music were washed away.

But first . . .

He returned to Adam's home and knocked on the door. When there was no answer, he opened and entered. Adam was asleep, leaning in that same westward position.

Enoch knelt and nudged Adam's shoulder.

Adam breathed in and opened his eyes. As his thoughts registered, fear tightened his face and he grabbed Enoch's shoulder. "Please," he said. "Tell me. Don't keep me waiting."

Enoch nodded. "He said, 'Let the old man go west. There

he will find me.' But I cannot join you. For he has demanded that I go east and face the evil all our mistakes have birthed."

Adam rubbed his bloodshot eyes. "What about a sacrifice? Does he demand one?"

"He will provide one." Enoch helped him up, and Adam threw his arms around Enoch.

"Thank you," Adam whispered in Enoch's ear. "For freeing me from this weight. For speaking to the Almighty on my behalf."

They let go, and Enoch smiled. "I owe everything to you."

Adam nodded. "Even your pain."

Enoch nodded. "Even my joy."

"Stay safe," Adam said.

"I will be in the hands of the Almighty. Where else is safer?" Then he added with a painful smile. "Or more dangerous?"

Adam nodded and shook Enoch's hand. "I am glad we spent this time together."

"So am I," Enoch said. "I will never forget it."

Then Enoch and Adam both exited his home, and Adam began walking west. He didn't look back even once as he disappeared into the distant light of the day.

Then Enoch turned and walked into the dark land far to the east. The land where the children of the serpent reigned. And he envied Adam, first of all men, and wished he too could walk, just once, with his Maker.

Maybe, in the end, what Adam said would come true, and Enoch would not have to face death to walk with his God.

But first, he would face the darkest evils of the world.

Epilogue

As Adam walked west, he thought the sky looked even more beautiful than when he first walked the paths of Eden. To have shared his struggle in full detail with another had brought back the old emotions, and now he felt himself released, as if the thoughts had held him strangled and sharing them drained their power.

Birds flew and chirped in the morning sun. The wind traced its fingers through the leaves of the bushes and the small trees dotting the hillsides. But the way felt longer than he remembered.

It is because I am not as young as I used to be.

His legs burned as he attempted to reach the top of another hill and more thoughts came.

What will Father say to me?

Will he welcome me as he used to?

Or has too much time passed?

Surely he knows how I tried to return to him.

But that is not enough, is it? To do well after evil is not enough to atone.

So what is? Did I not sacrifice? Does he not have my heart? Do I not now know that he is the greatest love I ever had? And yet he has not returned in all these years.

By the time Adam reached the stone wall where the entrance to Eden used to be, his wrinkled face was wet with tears. He fell to his knees and crawled to place his hands on it. Then he pressed his forehead to the stone.

"Father," he called. "Are you in there? Please."

He heard footsteps, and his breath seized. He spun and searched the surroundings, but he saw no one. Only empty, wild lands, insects on grass, and little bushes swaying in the wind.

"Turn around," a voice said.

He spun back and found that the stone wall was gone. In its place blazed a great, terrible fire.

Adam cried out, tossed his hands over his eyes, and pressed his forehead to the ground. "Have mercy," he whispered.

Footsteps neared. A warm hand settled on his shoulder.

Adam's breaths came rapid and shallow.

The warm hand slid further and two arms encircled him. "I have missed you," Father said.

Adam's body shook with emotion. For it was all he had wanted—to know that Father still cared for him.

Father lifted him into a full embrace. He held Adam's old, frail body until the waves of emotion released him, and he was able to step back and take his Father in.

He gasped. "You look just like you always did."

Father nodded, but his face was sober.

A thought took hold of Adam. Where was the sacrifice? He did not see any animal. And how come the entrance to Eden had returned?

His eyes widened. Was Adam himself to be the sacrifice? Or maybe he was already dead. Or dreaming?

Father shook his head, face lined with pain. "No, my son. This is not a dream, and you are not dead. Neither are you the sacrifice. The entrance to Eden is only open for today. And you will not enter," Father said. "You must live many years yet."

"Then what will the sacrifice be, for this time I am spending with you?" Adam said, breathless.

Father opened his hands and offered them to Adam, who looked down and noticed deep, dark scars.

"Me," Father said.

Confusion narrowed Adam's eyes. "But what of the promise?"

"I will fulfill it."

"It won't be Seth?"

Father smiled. "All you need know is that I have forgiven you. And taken away your guilt. I love you. Now and forever."

Tears came again, and Adam threw his arms around his Father—the Almighty Creator of the universe. "It is all I ever wanted!"

And Father's voice lifted in a great Music that seemed to fill the sky with laughter.

The very same song Adam remembered him singing at the beginning of all things. He realized then that the Father's will had not been broken by his evil, yet was still coming to be.

"What beauty," Adam said. "What love." And all his fear fell like dust.

Study of Genesis 1-4

There is a difference between remaining Scripturally faithful, and remaining faithful to cultural interpretations of Scripture. A book like this is bound to offend many people's ideas of Genesis because there are as many different interpretations of Genesis as there are denominations in the world. The Jews interpreted Genesis wildly different from Western Evangelicals, or Catholics, or Baptists.

I used to be very dogmatic with my interpretations of Genesis. Then I discovered that quite a few of my ideas about Genesis were not based on the text itself (such as the idea that Noah was mocked for his belief in an impending flood, which is found nowhere in the Bible). After thinking about this for some time, I realized that when my interpretations were not based on the claims of Scripture itself, they were as likely to be wrong as anyone else's imaginative guesses.

This simultaneously pushed me to base my ideas more closely on Scripture, and also to give more grace to those who have plausible guesses on what Scripture remains silent on.

For example, Scripture never says that Adam spoke to the serpent, but if he was present, it seems like a plausible possibility. Still, because Scripture does not say that the serpent spoke to Adam, the serpent refuses to speak to Adam in this book.

In this study of Genesis, I endeavor to explain my reasons for interpreting the text the way I do, as well as to support some of the creative decisions I made while writing this book.

If you have biblical reasons for disagreeing with any of the interpretations I share in this section, feel free to email me through my website contact form with the verses in question. My goal is to let Scripture inform my writing, not the other way around.

I enjoy receiving specific, helpful feedback that allows me to make these books better. Already, several readers have helped me improve these books. I am very thankful for that. And because I'm self-published, I can make changes and have them published within 24 hours! However, I've also grown tired of people claiming I violated a "Scripture" that does not exist. So, it is helpful to look up the verses before writing a review or message.

Overview of Genesis 1–4

This section is meant to be read alongside the actual Scripture, so grab your Bible, and let's jump in. Genesis 1–4 contains the origin of life and the story of Adam, Eve, and their children.

Chapter 1 is the creation account detailed in 6 days, along with God's explanation to Adam and Eve of the general order of the world. Chapter 2 describes the first Sabbath, then repeats parts of the creation story to dive deeper into the creation of Adam and Eve. Chapter 3 explains the fall of humanity, subsequent curse, and expulsion from Eden. Chapter 4 gives us the repercussions of the fall through Adam's family and distant descendants.

Textual analysis

In Genesis 1:1, the universe is chaotic and filled with darkness.

Out of this chaos and darkness, God brings all light, beauty, goodness, and life into being. This shows that everything good that we know and care for originates in and is sustained by him.

Here are how the days of creation break down:

1. Light is made, and day and night are ordered.
2. Water and sky are organized.
3. Land and vegetation are produced and ordered.
4. Sun, moon, and stars are ordered.
5. Creatures in the water and the sky are created.
6. Land creatures, bugs, and mankind are created.

When each set of living organisms is created, the text indicates that they are formed according to their kinds. Dogs were made to resemble dogs. Oak trees were made to resemble oak trees. But humans are different. Humans were made to resemble God.

Often I've thought of Jesus as being made in the human image, because the Bible tells us that he *became* a human. But Genesis tells us that God made us in *his* image. He was pre-existent. This is confirmed by Jesus himself when he says in John 8:58, "before Abraham was, I am." And in John 1:3, we are told that, "All things were made through him, and without him was not any thing made that was made." And in Genesis 1:26 God says, "Let *us* make man in *our* image . . ."

I'm not convinced we know all of what this means. But it is clear we were made to resemble him in our physical, emotional, and spiritual existence, as well as in our original moral purity.

Indeed, in Eden, we see God is physically present in the Garden. Because Jesus is the only incarnation, the most obvious conclusion is that Jesus was that physical representation present in the Garden, due to his pre-existence and eternal nature. While this may seem strange, it is the common, historical interpretation.

I know, it hurts my brain too.

But the perfect humanity and perfect divinity of Christ is referred to in theology as the hypostatic union, and it was discussed as a cornerstone of Christian theology all the way back at the Council of Ephesus in the 5th century.

This is why I tried to show God as not only the Almighty Creator and Judge, but also as a present, personal Father, the way that Jesus would have been in real life.

Some people have taken issue with God appearing so human in this book.

However, Jesus *is* human. And divine. Again, this is a cornerstone of Christian theology.

In Genesis 1:28, God blesses humanity and says, "Be fruitful and increase in number; fill the earth and subdue it. Rule over the fish of the sea and the birds of the air and over every living creature that moves on the ground."

He gives to mankind and all the animals every fruit-bearing tree with seed in it, and every seed-bearing plant on the earth, for food.

I found this interesting for multiple reasons.

Adam and Eve would pick fruit from the branch, thus severing it from its source of life. They would then take a bite. When swallowed, that bite would be broken down and turned into energy, and the waste would be expelled to give back nutrients to the soil. This is the way we know the biological world works, and nothing spoken at the fall seems to have changed that.

This makes many people uncomfortable because it has been widely taught that nothing could have died before Adam and Eve sinned. However, the Hebrew term for death in Genesis is never applied to plants, only to animals and men who have the breath of life. Classically, in Hebrew, plants were not considered "alive," and because they were eaten (and digested - which is a decay process) before the Fall, it is clear that plants decaying is not an issue.

See this article by Answers in Genesis for more info: https://answersingenesis.org/biology/plants/do-leaves-die/

So, what exactly was this pre-fall state like?

Many teach that there was no evil in creation before humans

sinned. However, to believe this, we must ignore that the serpent (one of God's creations) lied to Adam and Eve *before* they sinned. In addition, the forbidden tree was called the Tree of the Knowledge of Good and Evil (not "the Tree of Good and Evil").

Adam and Eve, prior to consuming the forbidden fruit, had not yet experienced the dichotomy in themselves. They had never before embraced evil and, therefore, did not deserve death, because we know that the wages of sin is death (Romans 6:23).

They were clearly immortal, and the Bible links sin inseparably to the origin of human death. This was what Pelagius and Augustine argued about, and what the Council of Carthage in the year 418 saw as central to the Gospel. This argument was *not* over plants, but people.

This early Genesis account is about the corruption of humanity and how humanity's corruption had negative repercussions on all of creation. We are told exactly what those negative repercussions are, so we should be careful claiming that they somehow go beyond what God stated.

I was surprised to learn that the Bible never uses the term "perfect" to describe creation. Instead, at the end of each day, the Bible says that God declared it "good." What does this mean, exactly?

Here is what we know. The world was good. Mankind was morally pure. Evil was present in the serpent (and therefore in the Garden) before Adam and Eve sinned. And Adam and Eve understood death, to some extent, because it was used by God as a warning to keep them from sinning (Genesis 2:17).

In the beginning of chapter 2, we see God blessing the 7th day—on which he chose to rest—making it "holy." This word "holy" means "to make perfect" or "to purify and set apart." There are layers to the meaning here, and it connects with the rest of Scripture in unique ways.

For example: Scripture states that by Christ's sufferings, he was "made perfect" (Hebrews 2:10, 5:8–9). We know he was morally flawless to begin with, so the term "perfect" here seems to refer to some sort of "fulfillment."

God's vision for perfection seems to be greater than mere moral perfection. There is a "wholeness" that is filled up in dynamic relationship, in real life lived out. The Sabbath rest appears to be part of this process. But this leaves me with unanswered questions.

Namely, I can't parse out with confidence (from the Biblical text itself), exactly what the pre-fall state was like. I run into the need to make assumptions and offer imaginative guesses to attempt to fill in the gaps in our knowledge.

Yet everything seems to harken back to that theme of God's will for a progressive "making perfect" of the world—even a morally pure world. This would mean that life in Eden was dynamic, rich, and filled with growth in many ways.

After the mention of the Sabbath, we return to an abridged creation account in chapter 2, to reorient us as we dive deeper into Adam and Eve's lives.

We seem to be back on day 3 of creation in Genesis 2:4. Then, in Genesis 2:7, we are suddenly on day 6. We know this is an abrupt shift because verse 8 says God had planted (past tense) a Garden in the east, in Eden, yet in verse 5–6, no plants of the field had yet sprung up. So, there seems to be a passage of time between 4–6 and 7–8 of likely only a couple days.

A misunderstanding of this shift in chronology is part of what gave rise to the belief that it never rained before the Flood.

I disbelieve this theory. First, because it is not supported by Scripture. Second, because it defies the laws of physics, which God spoke into existence in the first 6 days of creation. Third, because nothing at the fall addresses any change to the basic laws of physics.

Just in case you think I'm a quack, I am not the only one who now disbelieves that it never rained before the Flood. The theologically conservative ministry Answers in Genesis also advises against teaching it here: https://answersingenesis.org/

creationism/arguments-to-avoid/was-there-no-rain-before-the-flood/

Moving ahead through the text, we are told that in this Garden are both the Tree of Life and the Tree of the Knowledge of Good and Evil. Then, in case we doubt that this is a physical reality, we are given details about the rivers that watered it, and the types of precious stones and metals that could be found in that land.

This seems to hint at the potential of Adam and Eve unearthing precious metals and gemstones while in Eden. That's why I thought it would be fun to have Adam and Eve finding precious gems while still in the Garden.

We are then told that God put the man in Eden to work the Garden and take care of it. God told him to eat from any tree except the Tree of the Knowledge of Good and Evil, because if he ate of it, he would surely die.

After this, God states that it's not good for man to be alone. Again, I think this goes back to that theme of a progressive "making perfect" of the world. It would not be a *sin* for man to be alone. Rather, there is a fullness that God intends that is bound up with the lives of men and women together.

Then, in the next verse, Adam is shown animals. He names them, but no suitable helper is found. In response, God anesthetizes Adam for the world's first surgery and makes a woman out of his rib. Adam wakes up and sings a beautiful poem in 2:23, "This is now bone of my bones and flesh of my flesh; she shall be called woman, for she was taken out of man."

It may seem odd that Eve is not named in this section, and some have even built a strange mythology out of it. I believe what's going on here is the poetry is driving the narrative.

Adam's name in Hebrew means, "man." And the poem he speaks is showing how Eve came "out of man." This is the reason, the Bible explains, for a man to leave his parents to become one with his wife.

The structure and poetry is built up for this final claim, which explains the origins and beauty of the marriage covenant.

It is a fulfillment of the divine order that a man and woman be joined together, because woman was taken out of man to begin with. It also shows that the will of God is fulfilled in part by this covenantal relationship.

The final verse in Genesis chapter 2 states that the man and woman were both naked and felt no shame. At this point, we end up back where we were (chronologically speaking) at the beginning of chapter 2.

Even in historical narrative in Scripture, the narration does not always happen in "chronological" fashion. This continues to happen throughout Genesis, like in the Babel story.

This is because these ancient verses are more than just narrative. They are also Hebraic poetry.

For this reason, many have called the early part of Genesis a "true myth." What they mean is that it's a work of poetry that communicates the epic account of the origin of the world in the same way that national myths attempt to do—only this account also happens to be historically true.

I like this title, "true myth," because it shows us that this section is much more than just dry narration. It's beautiful. It's poetically formed, with layered meaning intended by God himself.

God does not want us to turn off our brains when we engage with his Word. Neither does he want us to turn off our imaginations or our appreciation for his beauty.

In Genesis 3:1, we are introduced to the serpent. When it says he was crafty, that seems to be a positive description of his intelligence. But immediately, we are assaulted by his challenge of whether God spoke the truth.

It is unclear if the serpent was fallen before this moment, or if we are watching the serpent's fall play out just ahead of humanity's fall. Either way, the serpent and the woman enter into this volley of words that muddies the waters until Eve is so confused that she doesn't even notice the serpent's lies. She is lulled by them into tasting the forbidden fruit.

In Genesis 3:6, after she eats, the Bible tells us she gave some to Adam, and he ate. Thus begins the horrible downward spiral that runs through the rest of Genesis. You may have noticed that I structured the plot of this book around a similar downward spiral.

Some have mentioned that they struggle to accept the idea that Adam could be held responsible, in part, for Eve's mistakes. Yet the Bible clearly shows that because of Adam's sin, we are all cursed. God clearly put the weight of the entire human race on his shoulders. I wrote this book, in part, to explore what this could have meant.

The way Scripture speaks of Adam's culpability, and the way the Genesis account is written, seems to imply that Adam was present with Eve when she tasted the fruit.

Yet when God questions them, Eve thrusts the blame on the serpent, not Adam.

If Scripture holds Adam ultimately accountable for the fall of humanity, that seems to imply he was involved, to some extent, in Eve's decision. Either by refusing to stop her, or perhaps by some other means. I wrote this book in a way that I thought showed how Adam could be held responsible, yet which matched the sparse details given in the Genesis narrative.

The New Testament claims that Eve was deceived and ate the fruit, but Adam was not deceived (1 Timothy 2:14). I am personally convinced that this statement is about the male gender's increased responsibility and culpability, rather than being a statement about the general susceptibility of women to false ideas. How many times has my wife been right when I was fooled? Way too many times. Sadly, this verse has been used to proliferate sexism under the guise of Christianity.

I reject this view and believe there is much biblical precedent that maintains a complementarian view of gender, which affirms the goodness and worth of both genders equally, yet which assigns different roles to each.

Regardless, Scripture seems to be stating that Adam was fully aware of the evil he was committing, and this is an implied reason for why Scripture tells us that the sin nature is passed down from father to child, not from mother to child.

This is the origin of "patriarchy." It is also what makes the virgin birth of Jesus so important. Jesus did not inherit the sinful nature because he was not conceived by an earthly father. His father was God himself, and so he was born without the sin nature, like Adam. This is why Jesus is referred to as the "last Adam" (1 Corinthians 15:45).

Adam and Eve then hide themselves in the Garden because they're afraid that God will see their evil. They hear God's physical presence in the Garden as he walked in the "cool of the day" (3:8). God calls them out, and they explain what happened. Then he gives his poetic curse of the serpent, Eve, and all of humanity.

In the curse of the serpent, we are given the prophetic promise of the Savior to come, which Adam and Eve—and the Jewish people—clung to.

The curse to the woman does not seem to introduce pain for the first time. It says, instead, that her pain in childbirth would be "increased." This, taken at face value, implies that pain existed before the fall, which would be in line with what we've discussed so far.

It is also interesting to realize that birth is not all candies and roses. It has been cursed by God.

The rocky relationship between man and woman, and the vulnerable position of women, is detailed in verse 16. This is part of what gave rise to the relational struggles Adam and Eve went through in this book; the same issues we face on a daily basis, although hopefully not to the same extent (yikes).

Adam's curse also makes survival more difficult and work-centered. The grace of the pure, restful love they experienced with God in Eden has been burdened by evil and becomes "painful toil" (3:17).

Finally, we are then told that Adam names his wife "Eve" because she would become the mother of all the living (3:20). It is unclear if this is another jump in time, or if this is chrono-logical.

Regardless, the chronological account is taken back up in 3:21, where God makes coverings for them, and then expels them from the Garden so that they would not live forever in such a state.

Death, in this instance, is a bizarre sort of gift, because to live forever in a state of sinfulness would be a horror. It is also the fulfillment of God's own promise that they would die, even while he gives them the mercy to continue living and to hope-fully be reconciled to him someday.

Here I want to offer a note on how I interpreted the pres-ence of the Tree of Life in Genesis.

In Revelation 22, we hear about the Tree of Life in the future paradise we will live in, which I view as a sort of return to the Eden state. Revelation 22:2 states that the Tree of Life bears fruit every month. So, I envisioned that in Eden, God might have brought the fruit to them at regular intervals.

That is why I have them eating it in Eden. I envisioned that the effects of the fruit wore off after they experienced sin. This is just one interpretation, and I realize others may see it differently.

Because this book is fiction, I had to make many imaginative inferences from the text. Keep in mind that this book is not a theo-logical treatise. I tried to craft it with accuracy, so far as I could, but there is too much ambiguity to be rigid about many of the details.

Finally, at the end of chapter 3, we're given the crazy account of the cherubim that was placed at the entrance to the Garden of Eden with a flaming sword flashing back and forth to guard the way to the Tree of Life.

After they leave, there's no going back.

Chapter 4 begins by detailing Cain and Abel's births. It is interesting to note that the text only states Adam lying with his wife—and her conceiving—once. Yet it states that two children are born.

Some scholars believe this implies that the boys were born twins, because all throughout chapter 4, this theme of "so and so lay with his wife, and she conceived and bore so and so," is kept to a consistent 1-to-1 ratio.

In addition, if Cain and Abel were born twins, as Jacob and Esau were, that would make further sense of Cain's jealousy over Abel.

Regardless, in Genesis 4:3, we suddenly see Cain and Abel (presumably as adults) sacrificing to the Lord and speaking with him in person.

This is interesting because we are not told of any sort of reconciliation between humanity and God. In addition, it would seem they are not living in perfect union, because Cain is so far gone already.

We are left to speculate about what happened after they were expelled from Eden. I envisioned that this would be an annual sacrifice, to mirror the future temple sacrifice in the Holy of Holies.

This is a logical connection because the temple was constructed with tons of imagery from the Garden of Eden, according to God's instruction, as a sort of mini-symbolic Eden within Israel. A place where God could dwell, as he dwelt in the Garden with Adam and Eve.

Finally, Cain murders his brother, and God curses him to wander. Cain complains, and God shows his immense love and compassion by protecting Cain from harm.

Yet if Cain's lineage is a sign of his future relationship toward God, we may assume he never repented. Because after he settles in the land of "Nod"—which means "wandering," thereby fulfilling God's prophecy—we are told that Cain's family starts building cities and having children.

Cain has a child and calls him "Enoch," which means "new beginning." Later, there is another "new beginning" in Seth's line, who is the Enoch in this novel and who was the first prophet of God. Scripture says that Seth's Enoch walked with God and never died, because God took him (Genesis 5:24).

Cain's "new beginning" rolls down into Lamech, a polygamist murderer who was proud of his violence (Genesis 4:19, 23–24). Then it rolls even further, into the sinful behavior that sent the Flood.

Seth's "new beginning" rolls down into a different Lamech, who is the father of Noah, through whom the world is saved from total violent destruction by water.

And this is where we are left, and where the next book in the series picks up. However, I'd like to make one final note. In chapter 6 of Genesis, we are told of strange beings called Nephilim. There are many interpretations of this section of Scripture. I do not know which one is true.

Traditionally, angels were assumed to be able to take physical form. All throughout Scripture, such as in Sodom and Gomorrah, angels walk about like men. The men of Sodom try to rape these angels, who are shown eating a meal Lot makes for them.

Later the Bible states that these same men of Sodom went after "strange flesh" (Jude 6–7), seemingly a reference to the angels. This seems to be a bizarre reversal of the story of the Nephilim in Genesis 6, because in Genesis 19, the human men of Sodom try to forcibly take angels for sexual pleasure. Yet in Genesis 6, fallen angels appear to forcibly take human women for sexual reasons and to bear strange children through them.

In *Flood: The Story of Noah and the Family Who Raised Him*, I tried to interpret this in a plausible yet unique way. This renders the book with a fantasy feel, though it remains moored in Scripture. I encourage you to try to embrace it as what it is: a fantasy.

Also, be aware that *Flood* is the darkest and most intense novel in this series. If you are disturbed by violence or don't want to read a dark book (even with a hopeful ending), feel free to skip *Flood* and go straight to *Babel*.

The reason for this darkness is the Bible's own claims about the pervasive evil of the people in that time period. "The Lord saw that the wickedness of man was great in the earth, and that every intention of the thoughts of his heart was only evil continually. And the Lord regretted that he had made man on the earth, and it grieved him to his heart" (Genesis 6:5–6).

I hope that these books stimulate thought and help you to fall deeper in love with Scripture. I also hope these books help you see the text of the Bible from a fresh perspective. As always, your source of truth is the Bible.

I write these books not to add anything to the Bible, but to entertain, uplift, encourage, provoke thought, challenge (both myself and others), and to give myself an additional reason to dive deeper into the heart of Jesus.

They're not always comfortable reads. Then again, neither is the Bible.

One final note: I write a weekly devotional at my website, brennanmcpherson.com. If you sign up (https:// brennanmcpherson.com/newsletter/) to get the devotional sent to your inbox every Saturday morning at 6:00 a.m., you'll receive two free e-books. I hope you'll consider joining and that you will contribute your thoughts in the comment section of the blogs.

Blessings and thanks for your support. I'm praying for you. I hope you will also pray for me.

Also by Brennan McPherson

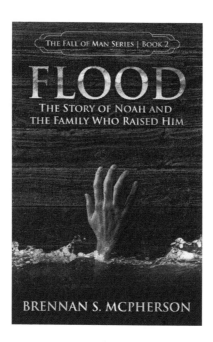

Get your copy today at _floodnovel.com_

Read _Flood_ today to see God's mercy unveiled in a visionary retelling of the story of the worldwide Flood . . .

Beginning before Noah is born and continuing on until the world is washed clean, _Flood_ is a stunning story about family and forgiveness in a world filled with pain.

"A soul-searching, heart-rending, deeply satisfying story." -- Mesu Andrews, ECPA Book of the Year award winning author of _Love Amid Ashes_

Acknowledgments

There are a lot of people who feed into the birth of each book, even for us indy authors who "do it all alone." Thank you, dear reader. Your patronage allows me to continue doing this. Thank you, Anna—my wife, my love, my best friend. Thank you, Willow, for being such a sweet, encouraging daughter. Thank you, Jesus, for taking my sin, my fears, and my hopelessness. Thank you to my critique group, my Master Mind group, all my author friends, and everyone who gave me early feedback and encouragement. You know who you are, and my only regret is that there are too many of you to call out by name! Because I'm not really, "doing it all alone." I'm standing on your shoulders! I love you all for your humility and kindness.

Printed in Great Britain
by Amazon

44557947R00190